DOWN A DARK ROAD

H.W. "BUZZ" BERNARD

SEVERN RIVER
PUBLISHING

Severn River Publishing
www.SevernRiverBooks.com

ISBN: 978-1-64875-358-9 (Paperback)

ALSO BY H.W. "BUZZ" BERNARD

To find out more about H.W. "Buzz" Bernard and his books, visit

severnriverbooks.com/authors/hw-buzz-bernard

To the family of James Burdett Thayer,

the men of the US Army's 71st Infantry Division in 1945,

and my wife, Barbara

"We live in the flicker—may it last as long as the old earth keeps rolling! But darkness was here yesterday."

Joseph Conrad, *Heart of Darkness*

1

The home of James Burdett Thayer
Beaverton, Oregon
August 1992

"I don't want to go," Jim said. He handed a letter to his wife, Pat, his soulmate of thirty-eight years. He knew she wouldn't understand his reluctance to travel to where the letter requested, because he'd never talked about the reasons, but he didn't like keeping things concealed from her.

Pat gazed at the letterhead, read the text, and gave the letter back to Jim. "Why not? It sounds as if it would be an honor . . . besides being a wonderful trip."

"Yes," Jim said quietly. "It's just that I never wanted to return to that country." He paused and gazed into his wife's hazel eyes, eyes that had always reflected her willingness to listen to him, support him, love him. "There are events in life," he continued, keeping his voice low, "that are sometimes best left unspoken about, forgotten, buried . . ." His voice trailed off. His thoughts, despite his efforts to the contrary, wandered back to the final days of World War II in Europe.

Pat smiled. "I won't pretend to understand, Jim—perhaps someday you'll be able to tell me—but you don't refuse a request from the Secretary of Defense, do you?"

He looked again at the letter's salutation: Colonel James B. Thayer (ret.), US Army Reserve; Oregon Civilian Aide to United States Secretary of the Army. And at the signature: Richard B. Cheney, US Secretary of Defense.

"No," Jim answered his wife, "you don't."

The letter presented a straightforward request. It asked Jim to represent the Secretary of Defense at a ceremony in Vienna organized by the Austrian government to pay homage to the millions of Jews who died in the Nazi death camps during the war. It also requested that Jim represent the Secretary on a tour of Jewish cemeteries and ghettos for the survivors of the camps that had been organized by the United States Holocaust Memorial Council.

"I've always sensed," Pat said, "that you were surpassing memories, at least a few, of certain things that happened at the end of the war. I hope someday you'll be able to talk about them, to unburden yourself from whatever you went through over there, to release—oh, I don't know—any demons you might have imprisoned in dungeons into the light of day . . . and let them wither."

"Someday," he said, "in my own time, I will. Maybe."

"In your own time," she repeated in a whisper. She wrapped her arms around him and leaned her head into his chest.

Flughofen Wien
Vienna, Austria
November 1992

JIM STOOD ALONE—AMID a swarm of travelers—in the arrivals area of the Vienna International Airport. A sign in large white letters above a sprawling arrivals/departures electronic display said *Willkommen*. He appreciated the sentiment, even though he'd had no desire to ever set foot in Austria again.

In the four-plus decades since he'd last been in the country, he had tried to forget what had happened here during the final days of the greatest war in history on the European continent. He'd witnessed things, done things, experienced things that men should never have to. Especially young men—he'd been barely twenty-three when he found himself entangled in a web of savagery that even today seemed unimaginable.

He had, successfully he thought, interred the memories of those things he'd witnessed, those things he'd done . . . had to do. But now they swarmed back to him in an unbidden rush. A soft hammering, an incipient pain, pulsated in his head. Memories attempting to escape. Memories he had purposely suppressed and never discussed . . . not even with Pat, and certainly not with any of his five children.

He turned away from the electronic display, searching for the person who was to pick him up, but whom he'd never met, only heard of—Simon Wiesenthal, the famed "Nazi Hunter." Despite his escort's ominous title, Jim had nothing to do with Nazi hunting, at least nothing in a direct sense. He knew, or at least was reasonably certain, why the Holocaust Council had requested his presence here. But even though he understood the motive behind the request, it made it no less difficult for him to accept. Not when he had banished it—forever, he had hoped—from his memory bank.

"Jim Thayer?" a voice said.

Jim turned. A man stood to his left. Not Wiesenthal, but a balding gentleman, neatly dressed with an avuncular appearance and wearing spectacles with rectangular lenses.

The man repeated, "Jim Thayer? I don't mean to intrude." He remained at a respectable distance.

Jim thought he detected a trace of a Texas twang in the man's voice, a brittle edge to the traditional Southern lilt. He heard something else, too, an intonation he couldn't quite identify. At least the man seemed no threat.

"Yes," Jim responded, "I am Jim Thayer. And you are?"

The man stepped forward, extending his hand. "Wolf Finkelman. I thought I recognized you when we came through customs."

They shook hands, Finkelman using a two-handed grip, one that suggested something beyond a friendly, traditional greeting.

"You recognized me?" Jim said, puzzled. "We've never met."

"Your photograph is in the program for the commemoration ceremony tomorrow."

"It is? I'm afraid I wasn't aware of that. I haven't seen one."

Finkelman fixed Jim in a gaze that seemed to reach deep into Jim's soul, exuding warmth and profound gratitude, perhaps coated with a bit of awe.

"I want you to know something," Finkelman said, his voice low and husky, "I wouldn't be standing here today if you hadn't come when you did forty-seven years ago. I was fourteen years old then and I would have been dead within twenty-four hours had it not been for you."

He released his grasp of Jim's hand. A tear glided down his cheek behind his rectangular-rimmed glasses.

GERMANY

2

Bayreuth, Germany
April 14, 1945

Second Lieutenant Jim Thayer, 14th Infantry Regiment, 71st Infantry Division, US Army, sat at a table in a semi-roofless Kaffeehaus in war-torn Bayreuth, Germany. He sipped a cup of Ersatzkaffee, false coffee that tasted like ink. He'd been told it was made from roasted chicory roots, but could also include malt, barley, rye, or acorns. Jim thought he detected notes of Turkish tobacco and lightweight motor oil, too. He missed real coffee. He missed a lot of things, most of all attending school at the University of Oregon in the southern end of the verdant Willamette Valley. He missed helping on his grandparents' farm farther north in the state in the rich, fertile Yamhill Valley where tree fruits, walnuts, and berries thrived. And he missed gleefully leaping over thunderous Pacific breakers ending their lives on the chilly beaches of Oregon. Yes, he missed a lot of things.

Jim and his reconnaissance platoon had earned a breather, a few days off from their relentless dash through France and Germany. The fighting in and around Bayreuth had dwindled and Jim's unit had been ordered to stand down after completing its mission—searching for mines on the edge of the city prior to the army launching a furious ground assault. Ink-and-oil coffee aside, Jim welcomed the downtime.

The battle for Bayreuth—located roughly halfway between Berlin and Munich—had been brief but decisive. The 71st Division, on its push toward Bavaria, had taken advantage of the pummeling of the city by previous aerial bombardments and artillery attacks, and quickly dispatched its defenders. The German Wehrmacht was clearly on the run. Defeated.

Much of Bayreuth—a town that dates back to the twelfth century—had been reduced to rubble. On the fifth through the eleventh of the month, about a third of the city, mainly public buildings and industrial works, had been flattened by relentless air strikes. Over a thousand people had been killed.

Jim stared at his Ersatzkaffee—more than half a cup remained—and pushed it away from him. He decided he'd punished himself enough.

"Hey, Jim," a voice said.

Jim looked up. His company commander, a captain, stood over to him.

"Come on," the captain said, "I got a Jeep. Let's go do the town."

"What?" Jim didn't mean his response to sound incredulous, but knew it did.

"I got a Jeep. We can go visit Wagner's house."

Jim knew the captain meant Richard Wagner, the famous German composer known primarily for his operas—*Der Ring des Nibelungen*, *Die Walküre*, *Tristan und Isolde*, to name a few. The captain—a Harvard grad, an attorney, and an accomplished pianist—absolutely adored Wagner and his music. Ironically, so did Adolf Hitler, or so Jim had heard.

Jim stood. "Sir, I don't think that's a good idea. There's still sporadic shooting in the streets. It's dangerous out there."

"Ah, phooey, Jim. It's almost over. This is the opportunity of a lifetime. Come on. Think of it. How many people can say they visited the home of one of the most famous composers in history?"

"You don't even know if the house is still standing."

The captain moved closer to Jim. "It has to be. We wouldn't destroy the home of Richard Wagner, would we?"

Jim caught a whiff of alcohol on the officer's breath. A ripple of instant disgust swept over him. "With all due respect, captain, did you forget our gentlemen's agreement?"

A week prior, Jim had had to arrest two of his riflemen for drunkenness in Speyer, Germany, just west of the Rhine River. Jim and the captain agreed that such behavior was intolerable. The men would need to be court-martialed. He and Jim further agreed that as officers, the two of them must set positive examples. They made a pact that neither would consume any more alcohol. Period.

"Jim, Jim. It's okay. I just had a little celebratory sip or two of champagne. Whaddaya say. A trip to Wagner's lair?"

"I think I must decline, sir. This is still a combat zone. If you don't mind, I'll remain here with my unit. And if I may speak freely, captain, I think you should, too."

"You worry too much, lieutenant. I'll be back before dark." He slapped the weather-beaten table with the palm of his hand. "Chance of a lifetime."

With that, the captain sped off in search of Richard Wagner's home. Or whatever might be left of it.

Late in the day, approaching ten, Jim poked his head into the hotel lobby that served as the company's makeshift headquarters.

"The captain around?" he asked.

"Haven't seen him since midday," a corporal responded.

Jim hiked up to the second floor and rapped on the captain's door. No response. He tried the door handle. Unlocked. He carefully cracked open the door and peeked in. No captain. Jim sighed and returned to his billet. There was nothing he could, or would, do in the dark. But come morning, if the company commander had not returned, Jim knew he would have to go in search of him. So much for downtime.

Shortly after sunrise, Jim went back to the temporary headquarters and again inquired after the captain. No one had seen him. Once more, Jim climbed the stairs to the commander's room to make sure he hadn't snuck in unnoticed overnight and collapsed in his bed. He had not.

Jim hurried back to where his platoon had spent the night, in the rubble of a post office, and rousted out his platoon sergeant, Sergeant First Class Hank Bowerman.

Jim liked Bowerman, a career NCO, even though the guy tended to be rough around the edges in both demeanor and language. Squat and squinty-eyed with a shock of unruly auburn hair, Bowerman took care of the boys in the outfit—and that's all they were, really, boys—most without the experience the sergeant possessed. He'd come out of Bristol, Connecticut, where he'd grown up hunting deer, turkeys, and squirrels in the nearby Litchfield Hills. He was at home with a gun and in the woods.

Another plus about the sarge was that he spoke a little German. He'd grown up in a bilingual family. His grandfather was German, an immigrant who had crafted clocks in Bristol, and changed the family name from Bauman to Bowerman . . . to better fit into American culture. Bowerman's father was a cabinetmaker. But Henry—or Hank, as he preferred to be known—had no desire to work with his hands. The outdoors had become his calling. Hiking, shooting, camping, living off the land. The army provided a natural fit for those inclinations.

At twenty-six, several years Jim's senior, he was the "old man" of the platoon and Jim often deferred to his judgment in combat situations. So far that had proved wise. They'd taken no casualties, and Jim intended to keep it that way. Especially since the end of the war had to be only days away.

"Come on," Jim said to his sleep-groggy sergeant, "we got a mission. The captain's gone missing. No one's seen him since yesterday. Get the Jeep. We need to find him."

Bowerman stood, farted loudly, and pulled on his gear. "Any idea where he went?"

"Yes. But I don't know if he made it. The city was still a hot zone when he took off. For all I know he could have been wounded or killed or even taken prisoner. We have to find out."

"Yes, sir. I stowed the Jeep in a garage about a block from here. Be back in five."

The two men began their quest, winding through the narrow streets of Bayreuth. The detritus of battle—shattered glass, chunks of concrete, twisted metal—littered their route. Bomb craters pockmarked boulevards and sidewalks, and smoke from burning buildings drifted through the city. At least the fighting had ceased, and army MPs patrolled the streets and stood watch at major intersections.

Bowerman drove and Jim navigated. Not that he had anything to navigate by. They stopped and asked an MP if he knew where Richard Wagner's home was. All they got in response was a shrug and a "Sorry, sir." They tried again at the next big intersection and got a similar reply.

Bowerman suggested asking a local, if they could find one. In short order, they did—an emaciated elderly woman sweeping glass off the sidewalk in front of what likely was her home. It still stood, but displayed shattered windows from street level to its third floor.

She appeared alarmed as the two soldiers approached, but Bowerman calmed her down quickly, explaining in German they only wanted directions to the Richard Wagner house.

She nodded in response, then gesticulated incessantly as she babbled on for almost a minute, seeming to point generally toward the south. At least that's the way it appeared to Jim.

"Vielen Dank," Bowerman said when she had finished.

Jim fished a Hershey bar out of his field jacket and handed it to her. She dissolved into tears and kept repeating, "Segne dich, segne dich."

"She's saying Bless you, bless you," Bowerman explained.

Jim nodded at the lady and smiled.

"Did she know where Wagner's place is?" he asked his sergeant.

"She was talkin' pretty fast and I didn't get all of it, but I think we have to head southeast until we find a park called Hofgarten. The guy's home should be adjacent to that, on the east side, it sounded like."

Jim and Bowerman set off again in the Jeep, picking their way through the debris-strewn streets and lanes until they found the park. It had not fared well. Broken trees and shell craters gave silent testimony to the fighting that had gone on there.

"There's a sign over there," Bowerman said, and pointed toward the edge of the park.

They drove to the sign. The post it was mounted on leaned at a forty-five-degree angle and the sign itself, wood, had been charred, probably by an exploding artillery shell.

Jim saw a reference to Wagner Haus on the sign. "Must be in that direction," he said, and gestured toward a cemetery just beyond the boundaries of the park. On the far side of the cemetery sat a battle-scarred stone house, large and stately, but wounded.

. . .

"THAT'S GOT TO BE IT," Jim said. "Let's see if we can find our way to the front of it."

Bowerman steered the Jeep through passages partially blocked by downed oak trees and, here and there, the bodies of dead German soldiers. Eventually, the two Americans reached a long, narrow lane, lined with shell-shattered trees that led to the front entrance of the home. The house, though still intact, had taken a brutal beating. Broken glass and huge chunks of stone littered the ground all around its perimeter, legacies of repeated bombings. The facade of the once lovely structure appeared as though a vengeful giant had taken a sledgehammer to it.

Bowerman pulled up to the front steps, but the entrance to the home was blocked by fallen timbers and piles of stones.

"Turn off the engine," Jim said.

The sergeant did and they sat in the Jeep and listened. And they heard Wagner. At least someone playing his music on a piano. The two soldiers stared at each other. Bowerman rolled his eyes.

"When, sometime later in life, you remember the bizarreness of war," Jim said, "remember this day. Let's drive around to the side of the house and see if there's an entrance there."

They found a doorway with the door blown away. Adjacent to it sat an empty US Army Jeep.

"Wait here," Jim said. "I'll go in."

He mounted a set of steps just inside the doorway that led up to the main floor of the house. In a dimly illuminated corner of a what he presumed to be a parlor, the captain sat at a huge Steinway, its top strewn with empty champagne bottles. With his head tipped back and his eyes closed, he ran his fingers deftly over the keys of the piano. Jim had no idea what piece the captain might be playing, but the notes echoed off the bare walls of the bombed-out home in melodious resonance.

Jim walked to the captain's side. "Sir," he said softly, "it's time to get back to headquarters."

The captain opened his eyes and looked at Jim, but kept playing. "Jim, it's wonderful to see you. Have a seat. Enjoy the concert."

"Captain, I think—"

"No, no. No talking. Listen. You're hearing Wagner in his own home. Imagine. How many people are ever afforded that privilege?"

Jim didn't view it as the captain did, a privilege, but as dereliction of duty. He worked to tamp down his incipient anger.

"Captain, stop." He laid his hand on his company commander's shoulder. "We were worried about you. We're going back to the hotel. And I mean now. Please."

"You don't understand, Jim. This—" he stopped playing, lifted his hands from the keyboard, and made a sweeping gesture around the room "—is the most glorious day of my life."

"Time's up, sir. For you, the day is over. We're still fighting a war. You can come back here after everything settles down, after the Germans surrender." Jim placed a hand under the captain's armpit and gently hoisted him off the piano bench. "Sergeant Bowerman's waiting for us in a Jeep outside. He'll take you back to headquarters. I'll follow in the Jeep you brought."

448TH BOMBARDMENT (HEAVY) GROUP

8TH AIR FORCE

3

448th Bombardment (Heavy) Group
Seething, England
April 25, 1945

United States Army Air Forces Captain Maurice Nesmith, Mo, stepped from his prefabricated Nissen hut in the wee-hour blackness of an English morning. He had never gotten used to the humid dankness that clung to the British Isles like a damp, woolen blanket. It felt so unlike the semiarid freshness of California's San Fernando Valley, where he'd grown up on a citrus farm. That was another thing he missed in Merry Ol' England—oranges, grapefruits, limes. But scuttlebutt had it the war in Europe would soon be finis and many units would be winging their way home. But as of today, with the war still on, his bombardment group had a mission to fly.

As Mo waited for his ride to the mess hall in the blackout conditions of the inky darkness, he could hear the snort, roar, and growl of B-24 engines being revved up and tested at full blast by the midnight-shift mechanics, the unsung heroes of America's air power, the "paddlefeet." He felt his face, clammy in the moist air, but smooth and clean-shaven. The oxygen mask he would don at high altitude would fit snuggly.

The truck arrived and bore him and other bleary-eyed crew members off to the mess hall. There his nose was assaulted by the usual breakfast barrage of stale grease, burnt coffee, and acrid cigarette smoke. At least today, as part of the group of airmen preparing for a combat mission, he would be served real eggs instead of the powdered yuck. Add to that English butter, marmalade, and hard toast, and he knew the meal would rate as semi-palatable.

As Mo sat at a long table savoring delicious forkfuls of genuine eggs, his newly assigned copilot, First Lieutenant "Stumpy" McGuire, plopped down beside him. Stumpy, so nicknamed for his height-challenged stature, hailed from Wichita, Kansas. Mo had flown with him a couple of times, but didn't know him well. He knew enough, however, to be aware Stumpy could drive a B-24—a big bomber that could be a handful to fly—as well as anyone, so had no qualms about doing business with him.

"Morning, Mo," Stumpy said. "Picked up any rumors about our target for today?"

Mo shook his head. "Nothing. You?" He eyed his cupful of coffee, but decided he didn't want to destroy the taste of the eggs, so held off on sipping it.

"Nobody's talking," Stumpy responded. Targets were identified for the bombardiers and lead crews at pre-briefings, but they were supposed to remain mum about them until the main briefing after breakfast.

"We'll find out soon enough," Mo said.

"You know, the rumors going around are that this will be the last mission for the 448th."

"Last or not, people will still be trying to kill us."

"You know, I sure love it that you can put a happy face on everything," Stumpy mumbled, and dove into on his eggs.

Mo thought about the missions he'd flown since arriving at Seething almost a year ago. He'd reached the maximum authorized number of thirty-five, but with aerial combat ready to cease, he'd decided one final run couldn't hurt. He realized he'd grown battle weary, but at least had remained short of being burned out, otherwise called "flak happy." *Yes, one final mission, I can do that.*

On his 448th résumé so far were raids against airfields, transportation facilities, and V-weapon sites—V for Vengeance, Hitler's Buzz Bombs—

prior to D-Day; bombing runs on enemy positions in France in support of Allied operations at Caen and the breakthrough at St. Lo; supply drops to combat units near Nijmegen in the Netherlands during Operation Market Garden; raids on transportation and communications centers in the Ardennes during the Battle of the Bulge; and airdrops to troops near Wesel, Germany, to aid in the airborne assault across the Rhine.

Today's raid might not be as challenging as some he'd flown, but neither would it be a milk run. His B-24, christened *Rub-a-Dub-Dub*, would be stuffed with five-hundred-pound bombs and headed for someplace deep in Germany or Czechoslovakia or Austria. *One final mission.*

Mo polished off his coffee, grimaced at the taste, stood, and slapped Stumpy on the back. "Well, partner, let's go find out what exotic travel itinerary the army air forces has planned for us today."

In the briefing room, Mo and Stumpy seated themselves on one of the wooden benches and waited for the festivities to begin. A black curtain at the front of the room hid a ceiling-to-floor map of western Europe . . . and the 448th's route and target for the day. A third officer, *Rub-a-Dub-Dub*'s bombardier, First Lieutenant Buddy Skaggs from Kennesaw, Georgia, sat down next to Mo.

"Well?" Mo said.

"Y'all are gonna love it. Scenic tour of Europe's most beautiful mountains."

"Bavaria?"

Buddy offered only a wide-eyed wiggle of his eyebrows, caterpillars dancing, in response.

"Thanks, Groucho," Mo grumbled.

Right behind Buddy came Second Lieutenant Wilson "Willy" Provost, the navigator, a smart kid from New Hampshire who'd dropped out of Dartmouth to join the army right after the Japs did their thing at Pearl Harbor.

Mo made a quick count of the officers present for the briefing—enlisted crew members were being briefed separately—and guessed there'd be about three dozen airplanes enjoying today's "scenic tour."

The chaplain, or padre as he was often called, Lieutenant Colonel Thomas Arbuckle, entered the room, moved to the front of it, and offered a quick prayer to launch the briefing. A sergeant called the crews to attention. Colonel Charles Westover, the 448th commander, strode to a position in front of the black curtain and said, "Seats."

The aircrews seated themselves.

"Gentlemen," Westover said, "some good news to start the day. Great news, actually. Today will mark the last of strategic bombing raids by the Eighth Air Force in the European Theater."

A cheer arose from the assembled men. Handshakes. Backslaps. Arms raised in the air. But they quieted quickly. They all knew they had one more raid to execute. One last mission before their number-one dream would become reality. Home.

Colonel Westover made a few additional remarks, then turned the briefing over to Major Quentin Rounds, a freckle-faced, lanky aviator who'd flown his thirty-five missions—including a crash landing at Seething he and his crew had walked away from—and stayed on with the 448th in a staff position.

"Good morning, men," he said, and slid back the curtain covering the map. "Today's round-trip ticket, courtesy of Uncle Sam, will offer you a splendid view of the Austrian Alps as you journey to the beautiful city of Salzburg and back."

"Hopefully back," someone in the assembly piped up. The comment was supplemented by a chorus of assorted groans and moans.

"I know, I know," Major Rounds retorted. "It could have been easier, but at least you'll have a herd of Mustangs riding shotgun, so that should keep the Luftwaffe off your butts." The Mustangs, P-51s, were America's premier fighter aircraft—fast, deadly, and long-range.

"How much oomph has the Luftwaffe got left?" someone asked.

"Not much. Most of their equipment has been destroyed or captured. And most of the pilots they have left have virtually no combat experience. They're scraping the bottom of the barrel."

"What about those things called jets?" Mo asked.

Rounds cleared his throat. "The Me 262s? Yeah, they've got a few of those, emphasis on 'few,' but they have only a limited combat range, so their threat is minimal."

"But not zero?"

"No, not zero."

"And if we encounter one, what's our best tactic?"

"Pray," someone shot back.

The quip drew a few chuckles.

"Like 'God is my copilot?'" someone else chimed in.

"I dunno," Mo responded, "not sure He's passed his check ride yet. I think I'll stick with Stumpy."

"All right, all right, guys," Rounds snapped, "let's get back on track here. Your target is a railroad marshaling yard. The bombardiers and navigators have been briefed on the route, IP, and bomb-release point. We'll fly in four boxes of ten at staggered altitudes. Your route will take you a little south of Munich, so you should avoid the ack-ack there, but the antiaircraft defenses are still robust around Salzburg. You'll be coming in from the west there. Egress initially will be to the east, a little deeper into Austria. But you'll turn quickly back to the west-northwest and head for home over Germany via Nuremberg and Frankfurt. Both are in Allied hands now."

The next half hour of the briefing dwelled on the details of the raid—specific targets within the marshaling yard, estimated enemy resistance, codes of the day, and aircraft positions within the bombing formations. The briefing concluded with the weather rundown—only scattered cumulus and altocumulus were expected over the target—and finally the time hack.

The time hack allowed all crews to set their wristwatches to the same time. The watches could be stopped, set to a common time, then restarted on a signal from one of the navigators.

"Coming up on oh-four-fifteen in thirty seconds," the nav said. Mo waited, fingers on the restart button. "Ten seconds," the nav called out. Then, "Five, four, three, two, one, hack!" Mo pushed the button.

The officers trooped out of the briefing room, made one last pass through the locker room to make sure they had all their critical gear, then waited for a six-by-six—a six-wheeled truck—to ferry them to the flight line.

In the distance, Mo could hear the chugging chorus of the "putt-putts," gasoline-fueled portable generators used to provide electricity to the airplanes as ground crews prepared them for the day's bombing mission. He hoped it would be the last time he'd ever hear them.

The truck arrived, the crew clambered in, and the six-by-six lumbered off. The men remained silent, each lost in his own thoughts, dealing with his own fears, or perhaps just trying to blank everything out, as they jounced toward the bombers.

The aircraft squatted like aluminum and steel mastodons on the tarmac, beasts waiting to be brought to life. Big and ugly. Despite that, Mo had come to love *Rub-a-Dub-Dub*. She certainly lacked the aerodynamic sleekness of her cousin, the B-17, the Flying Fortress. But she had proved tough and reliable, taking more than her share of cannon rounds from Messerschmitts and ground fire, but managing to stay aloft. Even with one of her four twelve-hundred horsepower Pratt & Whitneys shot to hell, she could still fly as fast on three engines as a B-17 could on all four.

The B-24 had been nicknamed the Liberator, but with the plane's boxy, big-bellied fuselage and its Mickey Mouse–eared twin vertical stabilizers, crews had other names for it. The *Flying Boxcar*, the *Pregnant Cow*, and *Ford's Folly* (for those built by the Ford Motor Company). For Mo and his crew, however, B-24 tail number 036275 was just *Rub-a-Dub*, for short.

The truck reached the bombers and the men spilled out. They went to work donning the last of their flight gear. Except for the flight deck, the plane was unheated, and at altitude, especially near the open waist gunner windows, temperatures would tumble to Siberian winter levels. Most of the crew tugged on winter jackets and trousers, and leather helmets lined with sheepskin.

Some wriggled into electrically heated "bunny suits," but the gear sometimes delivered a bit too much warmth to certain body areas—behind the knees and crotch. Since a lot of the guys weren't real keen on roasted nuts, they didn't bother with the bunny suits. Mo didn't need the heavy-duty warmth, but made sure he had his gloves and shearling-lined flight jacket.

He and Stumpy performed the walk-around of the aircraft, examining the tires and making cursory checks for gasoline or hydraulic leaks.

"Everything looks good, Stump," Mo said. "Mount up. I'll be along in a minute or two. I want to give everyone an attaboy and thank you before we start our commute." Stumpy nodded and tugged himself up into the aircraft through the open bomb bay doors.

A thin layer of mist drifted across the airfield. It brought to Mo's mind Sherlock Holmes and English moors and the books by Sir Arthur Conan Doyle that he had read in high school. Above the mist lay a stratus overcast, opaque and wooly. A thin silver streak on the eastern horizon offered the first hint of dawn.

Rub-a-Dub-Dub's crew began clambering into the aircraft. Buddy, the bombardier, and Willy, the nav, wriggled up through the nosewheel well into their positions—Buddy in the lower nose, Willy behind and just above him.

"You guys are the best," Mo yelled. "Let's get it done, our final curtain call."

The remainder of the crew—the flight engineer/top turret gunner, the radio operator, the two waist gunners, the ball turret gunner, and the tail gunner—entered the B-24 via the bomb bay. From there they would move to their assigned positions along a narrow, corrugated steel catwalk. Mo slapped each man on the butt and gave them words of gratitude as they hoisted themselves into the big bomber.

Mo entered last. He sidled forward on the catwalk, then up a tall step onto the flight engineer's deck, followed by a shorter step up into the cockpit. Stumpy sat in the copilot's seat with the preflight checklist already open in his lap.

"Whattaya think, captain," Stumpy said, "piece a cake?"

"Last day on the job. What could go wrong?"

They both smiled. They both knew plenty could.

"All right," Mo said, "let's do the check."

"Roger that," Stumpy responded. "Flight controls?"

"Free and correct."

"Flap handle?"

"Neutral."

"Fuel boost pumps?"

"Off."

And so on. They completed the entire checklist in a minute and a half.

Now they waited for the final signal that would indicate the mission was a go. The putt-putt continued to chug, feeding power to the sleeping aircraft.

"Okay, there it is," Mo said, "we're on." He pointed out the windscreen at the sky where a green flare illuminated the base of the stratus in eerie emerald-gray tones.

The ground crew disconnected the mobile power unit and the morning fell strangely silent, but only for a moment before forty Liberators began to crank their Pratt & Whitneys. *Rub-a-Dub-Dub*'s ground crew chief gave a thumbs up. Mo and Stumpy ran through the start procedures for engine number three, the one nearest Stumpy, and the big radial-piston motor coughed and sputtered and spit black smoke into the morning bleakness as it came to life. The awakening of the aluminum-and-steel monster had begun.

The start-up of the other three engines followed in sequence. *Rub-a-Dub-Dub* shook and jiggled and rattled as it awoke from its slumber. The smells of one hundred–octane fuel, hydraulic fluid, motor oil, and exhaust fumes filled the vibrating B-24.

"I think she's eager to go to war," Mo said through the interphone to Stumpy.

Stumpy nodded. "Maybe anxious to get it over with."

"Get us there and back, old girl, just one more time," Mo said, and patted the center console of the Lib, as though patting the head of a faithful hunting hound.

Again they waited, but this time in a roaring, rattling, shaking, fully awakened beast. They waited for the caravan man at the side of the runway to flash a green light from an Aldis lamp, the signal to begin taxiing. The caravan man remained in touch with the tower and a Jeep at the end of the runway—for visibility reports—before flashing the "move it out" signal.

Mo and Stumpy ran through the final checks and engine run-ups, then guided *Rub-a-Dub-Dub* onto the taxiway. Entering a parade of Liberators, she waddled along, creaking and groaning and growling.

Mo and Stumpy watched as the bomber ahead of them, *Nazi Nemesis*, lifted off from the runway, struggled into the air, and disappeared into the gray flannel blanket overlaying the English countryside.

Mo moved *Rub-a-Dub-Dub* into takeoff position and held the brakes with the toes of his boots. He made one final quick scan of the instruments.

"Looks good," he said. "Ready?"

"Ready," Stumpy responded.

Mo released the brakes and shoved the throttles forward. Stumpy placed his hand beneath Mo's on the throttles to make sure they didn't slip when Mo took his hand away to operate the control wheel. A thunderous roar reverberated through the aircraft and *Rub-a-Dub-Dub* lumbered down the runway, gradually gaining speed. At one hundred knots her wheels lifted from English soil.

"We're on our way to Austria," Mo announced over the interphone.

"Wish we were on our way back," Buddy responded from where he knelt in the bombardier's position in the nose.

The B-24 punched through the stratus deck into bright sunshine and Mo and Stumpy began their search for the Judas Goat.

4

448th Bombardment (Heavy) Group
Bombing mission to Salzburg, Austria
April 25, 1945

Rub-a-Dub-Dub climbed above the stratus deck into a clear sky painted with only wisps of cirrus.

"See it?" Mo asked Stumpy.

"There's a bird up ahead at our two o'clock. Could be it. Looks like it has some Libs in-trail."

Mo squinted through the windscreen, into the rising sun. "That's it. Our Judas Goat." He banked the B-24 to the starboard and continued a slow climb.

Rub-a-Dub-Dub closed in on the Judas Goat, a garishly painted war-weary Liberator stripped of armament, used as an assembly ship for large bomber formations. The 448th employed an elderly bomber decked out in a distinctive yellow and black checkerboard scheme. Other Judas Goats Mo had seen were painted with eye-catching stripes, polka dots, and even zigzags.

"Probably don't need one today with the great visibility we've got," Stumpy said. But of course, in crappy weather—instrument weather—the assembly ships proved vital. Sometimes the bombers on a raid, occasionally from different bases, would have to climb through twenty thousand feet of heavy cloudiness to find the Judas Goat on top, in clear conditions, where the bombers could gather. Once the raid had been assembled, the assembly ship would break off and head for home.

"Ya know," Mo said, "I heard a story about a Judas Goat called *Spotted Ass Ape* that once flew all the way to Germany on a raid."

"No bombs though?"

"Didn't even carry gunners."

"Brave but stupid."

"You ever hear of *Wham Bam*?" Mo asked.

Stumpy shook his head.

"Assembly ship for the 453rd Bomb Group piloted by Major Jimmy Stewart."

Stumpy turned, looked wide-eyed at Mo. "The movie star?"

"Yep. He flew along with a raid all the way into France before he turned back. Told his crew, 'If anyone breathes a word, I'll kill ya.'"

"I guess that's how film idols get their combat experience."

"Nah, Stewart's flown his share of real raids. I know he's been awarded an Air Medal and a Distinguished Flying Cross."

The Judas Goat pilot flew a racetrack pattern over the southern reaches of the North Sea as the 448th ships settled in behind him. Only three birds had been forced to abort immediately after takeoff, one because of engine failure, the other two due to hydraulic leaks. So the raiders would head toward Austria at virtually full strength.

The Mustangs appeared far above them as the assembly ship waggled its wings and sent the bombers on their way. Their flight path would take them first over the Low Countries, then across western and southern Germany into Austria.

Rub-a-Dub-Dub settled into its position in the lead combat box on the right outboard side of the formation. The box flew at twenty-two thousand feet with the other boxes staggered down to nineteen thousand.

"Nice day for flying," Stumpy said.

"Yeah, nobody's trying to kill us," Mo responded. "Yet."

With their oxygen masks in place now, they breathed clean, cool air.

The mechanical and petroleum odors that had permeated the ship disappeared, but the roar of the massive engines continued to reverberate through the Liberator as it jiggled its way toward Salzburg.

With the Wehrmacht all but defeated and the Allies occupying most of Germany, the Luftwaffe did not rise to meet the B-24s. Mo knew it would be a different story once they reached Bavaria and western Austria, however. Whatever dregs the German air force had left would challenge them, taking off from the few bases, very few, that remained intact around Munich. The bomber formation, the P-51s still riding shotgun above them, blew in and out of cirrus while below the combat boxes, patches of altocumulus hung over the Bavarian countryside.

South of Munich, Mo contacted Willy on the interphone. "How far to the IP?" IP—the initial point, the landmark where the bombing run would be initiated.

"Twenty-four minutes, sir."

"Okay, guys," Mo said to the crew over the interphone, "we'll be in Injun country shortly. Heads up."

Mo called Buddy. "Ready to leave the Thousand Year Reich something to remember us by?"

"Roger that. My pleasure, sir."

The combat boxes reached the IP and the bomb bay doors of the aircraft yawned open. From now until the completion of the attack, all planes would key off the lead aircraft of the formation. In the lead plane, the bombardier, peering through his Norden bombsight at the target, would tweak the plane's heading to correct its drift—its lateral movement caused by the wind aloft—and feed them into an automatic pilot. In effect, the bombardier would take over steering the bird. The job of the pilot—all the pilots in the formation, Mo included—would be to hold the bomber at a constant speed and altitude throughout the bomb run.

In *Rub-a-Dub-Dub*, Buddy would sight through his bombsight for range only, not deflection. The lead bombardier would take care of that. Then, when the lead plane dumped its load, *Rub-a-Dub-Dub*, along with all the other bombers in the formation, would trigger theirs.

To Mo, this always seemed the most perilous part of a mission—flying straight and level at an unvarying speed over enemy territory. You became a sitting duck in a shooting gallery, but not one that employed toy rifles. The Krauts who hunted American bombers blasted away with high-explosive shells up to three-and-a-half inches in diameter. A well-placed projectile could bring down a twenty-ton Liberator or decapitate a two-hundred-pound human.

Yet, straight and level. The slightest deviation from the data fed into the autopilot could result in a massive error regarding where the bombs hit. You could obliterate a schoolhouse instead of a rail yard. Blow up a church instead of a munitions factory. Destroy a home instead of a command post.

Mo and Stumpy held the Liberator steady as in tunneled in and out of clouds. The engines maintained their purring growl, all business. Only a minor jiggle or two interrupted an otherwise smooth attack run.

"There they go," Stumpy said. Sixteen five-hundred pounders tumbled out of the lead bird in a well-spaced sequence and began their parabolic dive toward earth, subject to the physical parameters that had been fed into the Norden bombsight: type of bomb, fall rate, altitude, airspeed, crosswind.

"Bombs away," Buddy said into the interphone. *Rub-a-Dub-Dub* jumped skyward as eight thousand pounds of weight left her in a matter of seconds.

Mo found it curious, or perhaps instructive, that the mere second or two delay in seeing the bombs released from the Lib leading the way, to the time the other bombardiers managed to toggle their loads, required that the lead bird aim just short of the desired impact point. That would allow most of the bombs from the group to hit closer to the target.

"Let's get the hell out of here," Mo said, and banked the bomber to the port.

But the Austrian and German defenders of Salzburg had found them. The first ack-ack shell exploded directly in front of Run-a-Dub-Dub. Despite that, she barreled straight through the roiling black smoke and pieces of shrapnel without suffering any damage.

"HEY, GUYS," Buddy screamed into the interphone from the bombardier's spot in the nose, "I'm trying to sleep down here."

"My apologies," Mo answered.

"Just don't let it happen again."

"Well, shit," Stumpy said, "I guess the heinies didn't like our going away gift."

"So let's get going away then," Mo said, and shoved the throttles forward.

More flak exploded around them, filling the sky with black balls of death. But it seemed too little too late as the 448th Liberators drove hard east, thundering away from Salzburg. Mo turned in his seat to look back toward the marshaling yard. Fire and smoke billowed skyward.

"Looks like we made a good run," he announced to the crew. "Let's go home."

A couple of cheers came in response, several quick clicks over the interphone, too, an informal sign of acknowledgment.

But the celebration proved premature.

A pair of German fighters, Messerschmitt Bf-109s, plunged out of the sky and dove at the fleeing bombers.

But the attack appeared clumsy and tentative. As Major Rounds at the briefing had said, the Luftwaffe was likely scraping the bottom of the barrel for pilots, jamming young aviators with little experience into cockpits. The P-51s that had been escorting the 448th fell on the Messerschmitts like hawks on doves. Within thirty seconds both German fighters were trailing smoke and fire and spiraling toward the Austrian earth in a death dive. One pilot managed to get out. A parachute blossomed as his Messerschmitt plowed into the ground and erupted in a sphere of fire. The other pilot, perhaps already dead at the stick, rode his aircraft all the way down.

"Poor kids," Mo muttered.

"Poor kids, my ass," Stumpy snapped. "They were gonna kill us."

"Lambs to the slaughter."

"Yeah, right. Well, war doesn't make any distinction between lambs and lions."

"I'm glad it's almost over."

"Everyone is."

The next attack seemed to come out of nowhere. Cannon fire tore into *Rub-a-Dub-Dub*'s starboard wing, ripping it from tip to root. Something, some kind of aircraft, flashed in front of the B-24 like a high-speed bullet.

"Good fucking grief," Stumpy screamed. "What in the hell was that?"

Mo whipped his head to the left and glanced upward just in time to see a small, streamlined aircraft painted in green camouflage rocketing upward at a speed he believed impossible. Two Mustangs gave chase but got left in a trail of exhaust.

"I think, Stump, we just got smoked by a German jet."

"Jesus Christ. It makes our P-51s look like Model-Ts trying to compete with Indianapolis 500 race cars."

Mo swiveled his head to the right to stare at the starboard wing. So did Stumpy,

"Oh, Christ," Stumpy yelled. "We got more than smoked, captain. We're on fire."

Flames shot from engines three and four.

"Looks like we got a ruptured fuel line, too," Mo said, struggling to control a quiver in his voice. "Kill the fuel flow. Feather the props."

"No good. Wing's on fire."

"Gotta leave then."

"Yes, sir."

Mo rang the alarm bell three times in quick succession, notifying the crew to prepare to abandon ship. Then he went on the interphone. "Sorry, guys. Little delay in our homecoming. Two engines out, wing on fire. I can fly *Rub-a-Dub* on two engines but not on one wing. We're gonna have to jump. I'll give the alarm one last, long ring when we're down to ten and it's time to bail. Godspeed." He hoped to God the bomber would remain flying until they reached ten thousand feet.

With no time for anger, disappointment, or fright, Mo focused on keeping the plane aloft, getting his men out, saving himself. That's all that mattered now.

He and Stumpy struggled to keep the B-24 on a straight course, cranking in a lot of rudder to compensate for the loss of thrust on the starboard side. Flames and smoke streamed from the burning wing, leaving a ragged obsidian trail in their wake as *Rub-a-Dub-Dub* continued to sink toward the green Austrian landscape.

"Ten thousand," Stumpy said.

Mo hit the alarm bell, one long ring, Go.

"Get to the bomb bay, Stump, and out," he said. "I'll be right behind you."

Mo watched for the 'chutes. They came. At least something good in a shitty situation. Buddy and Wally tumbled out the nosewheel door. The flight engineer/top turret gunner, radio operator, and Stumpy exited through the forward end of the bomb bay. The ball turret gunner and both waist gunners fell from the rear end of the bay. Finally, the tail gunner jumped from the rear emergency exit.

"Nine good 'chutes," Mo whispered to no one. "My turn." *Rub-a-Dub-Dub* continued its descent, now down to five thousand feet and sinking rapidly as the aerodynamic characteristics of the burning wing were eaten away by the fierce flames. Mo knew he didn't have much time left before the wing separated from the fuselage and the plane became a lead sled.

He reached for the autopilot switch.

"Oh, dear Jesus." Dead ahead and in the bomber's death trajectory, a small Austrian village appeared. Mo had no desire to levy additional death and damage on civilians, friendly or not, especially with the German Wehrmacht on the run and the war winding down. So he fought the controls for another few seconds, struggling to keep the burning bomber aloft and allow it to clear the little town.

He wondered if he were a fool. *No good deed goes unpunished.* And he wondered if God had a say in that.

The extra few ticks of the clock allowed him to witness something else, too. A Mustang jockey had apparently managed to punch a couple of fifty-caliber rounds into the engine of one of the German jets. A camouflaged-painted Me 262, one of its under-wing turbojets trailing smoke, blew past *Rub-a-Dub* as if it were parked. Mo watched as the Luftwaffe pilot scrambled from the cockpit, sprawled onto the wing, then plummeted earthward, trailing a ribbon-like streamer. In an instant, the streamer blossomed into a parachute canopy and halted the aviator's plunge. Mo could see the German would land not far from where he himself would likely hit the ground . . . if he were able to get out.

Mo held the control wheel of the B-24 in a death grip, battling to keep the bird aloft. But his arms could finally do no more. They quivered in painful exhaustion. The village flashed beneath him.

"Bye *Rub-a-Dub*," he mouthed. "You been a great lady. Sorry." He released the control wheel, flipped on the autopilot, wriggled out of his seat, and raced down the steel steps onto the bomb bay catwalk. Wind swirled and howled through the interior of the dying Liberator like a chorus of crazed banshees. Dense smoke and the acrid odor of burning oil, fuel, and steel filled the air.

Without hesitating, Mo faced forward, and—as instructed—dove head-first off the catwalk into the void.

Realizing he was likely a thousand feet or less above the ground, he yanked the ripcord on his parachute immediately. The canopy opened, jerking him upright. He crossed his ankles to protect the "crown jewels" and simultaneously knifed through the canopy of a fir forest. He yelped as spiny needles slashed his face and hands. His descent ended about ten feet off the ground. There he hung suspended in his 'chute, its canopy entangled in the boughs of what he guessed was an old-growth tree.

As he dangled over the Austrian earth, a sound threaded through the trees, a voice calling, "American, American, where are you?" Good English but with a guttural German edge.

Jesus, Joseph, and Mary, he thought, *the damned Luftwaffe bastard who just bailed out wants to finish the fight*. Mo remained silent, hanging in his 'chute, blood trickling down his cheeks and the back of his hands. He felt for the .45 in his shoulder holster. Still there.

I'm not going to die hanging in a tree. That Nazi sonofabitch can kill me in the air, but not here, not now, not this way. Not with the end of the war just around the corner.

He waited until the voice of the stalking German faded into the distance, then cut the risers on his parachute and slid through the lower branches of the fir onto the duff-covered forest floor. He realized the extra seconds he'd remained in *Rub-a-Dub-Dub*—to allow it to clear the little Austrian village—before bailing out had put him miles from where the rest of his crew had landed.

But with the damned Nazi on his tail, Mo knew he had no time to track down his buddies. His number-one priorities: evading his pursuer and staying alive.

UPPER AUSTRIA

5

Near Obern am Inn
Western Austria
May 3, 1945

Lieutenant Jim Thayer's platoon, moving in single file over the top of a dam spanning the Inn River, stepped onto Austrian soil as one of the first American combat units to enter the country. The dam had been secured the previous night by the 66th Infantry Regiment attacking directly across the top of the structure while simultaneously using storm boats to ford the river and flank the dam's defenders.

Under fire, the assault teams had deactivated demolition charges that had been placed on the dam by the German Wehrmacht. Now Jim led his sixteen-man team into Austria—or at least what had been Austria prior to the German Anschluss of 1938—over the iron-railed crown of the dam, coils of barbed wire on their right forcing the infantrymen into a narrow column.

Once on the Austrian side, Sergeant Bowerman moved forward to walk beside Jim. "Well, here we are in Austria, Loot. How many rivers have we crossed in the last ten days?"

Jim tipped his helmet back on his head and titled his face toward the warmth of the spring sun. A barn swallow darted overhead in pursuit of a morning delicacy. "Hadn't really thought about it," he answered. "Let's see, in Germany, we crossed the Naan, the Danube, the Isar, and now this one."

"The Inn," Bowerman said.

"You know, we've been gobbling up twenty-five or thirty miles a day," Jim said. "Hard to believe."

"The damn Krauts are finished and the bastards know it," Bowerman growled. "They're a hell of a lot more interested in departin' than defendin' now."

They reached a small meadow outside the village that stood on the banks of the Inn near the dam. "Let's hold up here," Jim said, "and wait for the engineers to get our half-tracks and Jeep to us." Even with the barbed wire removed, the passage over the top of the dam would measure no more than eight or nine feet in width and would require careful navigation. The engineers preferred to handle driving any vehicles over the structure themselves to avoid any "unfortunate circumstances."

Jim removed a map from a pocket in his field jacket, knelt, and unfolded the chart over the spring grass and tiny wildflowers that had just begun their rebirth following the harsh Upper Austrian winter. He flattened the map with the palm of his hand and beckoned Bowerman to join him.

"Sarge," he said, "the war's almost over. I want our guys to get home. Safely. In one piece. But we still have a job to do. Let's make sure we do it carefully."

"I gather we're bein' used as bait again," Bowerman said sardonically.

Jim grunted. "Recon platoon, you mean," he corrected.

"Right. Move forward 'til we get shot at, then report to battalion where the damn Krauts are."

"Our orders are different today. We're to block any Wehrmacht elements trying to get the heck out of Germany into the Alps. Rumor has it the Nazis are going to try to make their last stand in the Tyrol."

"Where's that?"

On the map, Jim moved his finger to the southwest. "Here, about a hundred kilometers from where we are. In far western Austria adjacent to Switzerland. Nothing there but mountains. Big ones. The Nazis are supposed to have stored up tons of ammo and food and built impregnable fortresses there. Their Alamo."

"Ya think Hitler will try to reach the Tyrol?"

"Sure, if he hasn't already. I hear the Red Army took Berlin yesterday. If der Führer is still there, he's screwed."

"Let's hope."

Jim nodded his agreement. "Anyhow, as soon as our vehicles get here, we'll head toward this crossroads." Jim pointed at a spot on the map.

"'Bout fifteen klicks from where we are now, I'd guess. Looks like it's just outside this little town called Hörbach." Bowerman tapped the map with his finger.

"Yeah, I figure we'll go as far as the crossroads today and see what we can see." Jim refolded the map and stood. Every muscle in his body throbbed. But with the end of hostilities in sight, the aches and pains of combat no longer bothered him. "Let's move out, sarge, and see if we can at least beat the Russians to the crossroads."

"Any idea where the Reds are?"

"Not sure. They occupied Vienna a couple of weeks ago, so they can't be far from here. We're headed east, they're headed west. We're maybe a day or two apart. Who knows, we might even get a chance to shake hands with them."

Bowerman grunted and spit, but didn't respond.

No sooner had Jim and Bowerman finished their chat than the platoon's Jeep and two half-tracks arrived. Each of the three carried a mounted Browning fifty-caliber machine gun. With their one hundred-ten-round belts, they provided Jim's small unit an impressive amount of firepower.

Bowerman stood and signaled for the platoon to resume its eastward trek toward the crossroads. The unit separated into two columns, one on either side of the dirt road they were on. The vehicles, now driven by Jim's own infantrymen, brought up the rear.

The redolence of spring filled the air. Soft aromas arose from patches of freshly tilled earth resting rich and black in the sun, from oak and beech resuming life, from wildflowers—yellow, blue, purple—bursting forth with eternal hope. Overhead, in a sky speckled with flat-based cumulus, birds dipped and dove and soared, twittering and chirping, oblivious to the flow of armies—men bent on ending, not renewing, life, not venerating it, not embracing it—that fanned out beneath them.

To Jim, the day seemed cloaked in irony. Around him and his men he sensed not only a comforting, welcoming peacefulness, but simultaneously an aura of grave danger and agonizing suffering. It unnerved him. More than ever, he wanted this war, at least the fighting in Europe, to be over. *It's odd*, he thought, but with the end of combat so near, he felt an even greater concern for his men. No one wants to be the last to die on a battlefield. That would leave too many shoulda beens, coulda beens, and maybes.

He turned to Bowerman, who marched beside him. "So, after this is over, sarge, home to Connecticut?"

"Naw, not me, Loot. I'm an army lifer. Maybe thirty days leave. Then off to kill Jap bastards on the other side of the world. In for a dime, in for a dollar. You?"

"Back to Oregon."

"Ya grew up on a farm, right?"

"Yes. Raised by my maternal grandparents in the northwest part of the state. In a county called Yamhill."

Bowerman chuckled. "You grew yams?"

"Alfalfa, hops, and corn."

"Miss it? Ya goin' back to farmin'?"

"Nope. I'll return to college. I dropped out of the University of Oregon . . . so I could do this, tour Europe."

"All expenses paid."

Jim snorted. "I dunno. I think *we* pay all the expenses."

"Ain't that the friggin' truth, Loot? Tell me, what were ya studyin' at the university?"

"Journalism. But I don't think that's for me. I'll probably try something different . . . if and when I get back. But I don't know what."

"Got a gal?"

Jim laughed softly. "Not really. Not just one, anyhow. I dated a lot. A few real lookers, too. Maybe even a few who might miss me. But I never found a lady I wanted to settle down with. How about you?"

"Once I joined the army, I guess I never really had time to pursue

romance. But maybe I'll try to find a nice—strike that—naughty gal in Gay
Pa-ree before I head back to the states. I—"

Bowerman halted abruptly and signaled with his hand for the platoon
to stop. He leaned close to Jim. "Whaddaya think about that stand of woods
up ahead of us, sir? Good place for Krauts to be hidin'."

Jim surveyed a wooded area that lay maybe five hundred meters distant,
flanking the road. A soft breeze whispered over the land. He signaled for
the engines of the vehicles to be shut off. Except for the twittering of birds
and the occasional over-the-horizon whump of artillery, no other sounds
reached his ears.

"My guess would be there aren't any Germans there," Jim said. "As you
mentioned earlier, they're probably a lot more keen on heading for the hills
than they are in setting up ambushes. Still, guesses can kill you. Let's go
around the woods. We can move through that field there," he gestured at an
abandoned, unfurrowed plot of land to their right, "and circle around the
trees to the south. We should be able to reach another road we can follow
north to the crossroads."

The sergeant nodded. He scanned the field. "Mines? Booby traps?"

"Doubt it," Jim responded. "Again, I think the Jerries have lost interest.
But let's keep an eye out. Ready?"

Bowerman gave a hand signal and the infantrymen stepped off into the
field, single file, weapons at the ready, Jim leading, vehicles at the rear. The
soil squished beneath the men's boots, the legacy of recent rains. Jim moved
carefully, surveying the ground in front of them for signs of danger.

"Just like the old days, huh, Boss?" Bowerman whispered from
behind him.

By "old days," he meant when the platoon had first arrived in-theater.
As part of the 71st Division, it had landed in Le Havre, France, in February.
Initially, it had been tasked with clearing land mines along the Maginot
Line, the defensive line—concrete fortifications, tank traps, heavy weapons
emplacements—the French had constructed along their border with
Germany in the 1930s to deter aggression. It hadn't worked. The Germans,
when they invaded, merely ignored the obstacles and swept into France
north of the line through the Low Countries.

Jim's platoon had gone to work as assigned, but found many of the mines past their prime and less than effective, though still dangerous. Despite all the things that could have gone awry, Jim guided his men safely through their task.

"I don't know which is worse, sarge," Jim said. "Being on the pointy end of a spear as a recon patrol, or poking at things in the dirt that can turn you into hamburger."

Bowerman moved forward to walk beside Jim. "There ain't no good assignments in war, Loot."

"Nope, you're right. No good memories, either."

"Funny ones sometimes, though, huh?"

"Funny?"

"Not ha-ha funny. I mean like weird. Bizarre."

Jim looked over at Bowerman, his face haggard and unshaven, reflecting the almost nonstop movement and battles of the last few days. Jim decided that he, himself, probably looked no better. But it annoyed him that people sometimes said it was difficult to tell whether he, Jim, was unshaven, or just didn't have anything to shave.

"Bizarre?" Jim asked.

"I was thinkin' about Bayreuth."

"Oh, that. Wagner's house? The captain?"

"Yeah, what ever happened to him?" Bowerman asked, as they continued to plod through the muddy Austrian field.

"Well, I couldn't arrest a superior officer," Jim said, "but the captain managed to, as Shakespeare said, hoist himself on his own petard. Remember the two enlisted guys I arrested in Speyer?"

"They were court-martialed, right?"

"Yep, a couple of days after our little Wagnerian adventure. The captain, because he had a law degree, was assigned as the military judge for the trial. Only he didn't show up for the proceedings."

"I'll bet the battalion commander was pissed."

"Livid. The court-martial was rescheduled. But again—"

"Let me guess. The captain was a no-show."

"I was told, in no uncertain terms, to go find him and get 'his ass' to the court. I found him in his room, drunk. He told me there was no way he could run a court-martial. I said I didn't care. My orders were to get him there. He said he understood and, to his credit, gave it the old college try, but not before telling me he needed just 'one more drink.' That wasn't my problem, so I let him have it."

"I helped him to the courtroom—a vacant garage, as I recall—and he somehow managed to get the proceedings started. He began by swearing in the court's members. But he dropped the form he was reading from, bent over to pick it up, lost his balance, and sprawled on the floor in a splotch of dried-up oil and grease."

"End of the proceedings?"

"End of his career. He was relieved of command. I guess he's probably back in the States now, waiting to be drummed out of the service."

"And here we are, sloggin' through mud and shit, still fightin' Krauts, and tryin' not to get our butts shot off." Bowerman grunted and spit into the fallow field.

They pressed on with no further conversation. Only the growl of the platoon's vehicles, the occasional clink of a canteen, or the noisy squish of boots in the mud joined the barely audible warble of songbirds and the lazy buzzing of bees.

After about fifteen minutes, Bowerman hissed a warning. "Hold it, Loot. Movement." He inclined his head toward the woods.

"Down," Jim commanded.

The platoon members dropped into prone firing positions. The machine gunners in the vehicles swung their weapons in the direction of the trees. Jim did, too, bringing his M1 Carbine to bear on the woods. As an officer, he also carried a Colt .45 handgun, but left that for close-quarters combat.

They waited for several minutes until the movement abruptly manifested itself. A handsome red stag emerged from deep in the trees and scanned the field, moving his heavily antlered head slowly from side to side.

"Wow," Bowerman whispered, "ten points at least."

"No Germans in there," Jim said.

The riflemen stood and moved on, now less concerned with noise control. The young soldiers bantered back and forth with each other. A few smoked.

They reached the road that would lead them north to the crossroads. It turned out to be paved but potholed and cracked. Still, it appeared easily passable and probably inviting to any enemy formations wanting to escape into the Alps.

Jim halted the platoon again and spoke to his men. "Okay, let's move carefully now. I want riflemen on each side of the road as we go north. I'll lead the left file, Sergeant Bowerman, the right. I want one half-track in front, one in the rear, Jeep in the center. Don't bunch up. Stay alert." They headed toward the crossroads.

They passed through a small farm village studded with a handful of Bavarian-style homes, the kind that made Jim think of gingerbread houses. Nobody greeted them, no one threatened them. A few of the homes flew white flags made from bedsheets or linens. Faces peeked at the soldiers from behind lace curtains.

"We're probably the first Americans they've seen," Bowerman said.

A dog scurried across the road in front of them, gave a desultory bark, and disappeared behind a building that appeared to be a Gasthaus.

The patrol continued up the road for another twenty minutes before reaching the intersection with the dirt road they'd been on previously.

"Okay, guys, let's take a break, grab a bite to eat," Jim said.

Bowerman walked to where the lieutenant stood. "Pretty quiet here."

"Don't bank on it continuing," Jim said. "We are, for all intents and purposes, in enemy territory."

As the riflemen prepared to dig into their K-rations, Bowerman called out, "Hold it, hold it. Listen." He placed a forefinger over his lips, a signal for silence.

The thrum of motors, fairly large ones, floated through the air, mixing with the chitter and squeaks of chipmunks and squirrels.

Jim looked at Bowerman. "Panzers?"

6

Somewhere between Salzburg and Linz
Western Austria
May 3, 1945

Mo, Captain Nesmith, stepped from the small, dilapidated forest house where he had sheltered for the last two nights. He gazed out at a dew-coated meadow that lay below him. He didn't know exactly where he was, only that it was somewhere in western Austria northeast of Salzburg.

Now, he had a decision to make. He could hunker down in place and wait for the Americans—who, he guessed, had to have reached Austria by now—to find him, but at the same time risk being discovered by German ground forces or the Luftwaffe maniac who'd been trailing him since the day they'd both bailed out. Mo after losing *Rub-a-Dub-Dub* as it exited its bombing run over Salzburg, the German after getting his jet blasted out of the sky by an American Mustang.

Or, Mo's other option was that he could make a dash toward the northwest and try to reach the advancing US Army. He hadn't seen the Luftwaffe prick for several days, so maybe the guy had grown weary of the chase.

The last time he'd spotted the bastard had been maybe three days ago. Mo had been crossing an open field when the German appeared on a ridge about two kilometers to his east. The Kraut had waved his arms over his head and yelled Stop or Wait or something. But Mo had sprinted away and then maintained a double-time pace for the remainder of the day.

He'd stumbled onto the rundown house he now occupied the following day. He guessed the place was some sort of summer residence that had fallen into disuse. It had no source of heat, no glass in the windows, and no insulation, but was sturdily constructed and must have been a comfortable place to hang out in during the warmer months.

There were signs of vegetable and flower gardens that had likely once thrived, but now had been deserted and left unattended for several years. Wildflowers, weeds, and saplings had taken over. Whoever had spent time here had kept bees, too. Several long-abandoned hives testified to that.

He hated to leave the place. Its walls provided shelter from the winds, its tile roof kept him dry, and he'd even found some food . . . sort of. He'd uncovered a sack of potatoes stored in a wooden chest buried in the ground, and came across a couple of jars of homemade strawberry jam on a shelf in the house. The potatoes and jam provided welcome supplements to the meager sustenance in his survival kit: four sticks of Wrigley's chewing gum, two chocolate ration packages, and a handful of caramels.

Oddly, he longed for the meals, as ersatz as they might have been, at his home base in Seething. The aircrews there bitched endlessly about the powdered eggs, bland biscuits, and brick-like pork chops that appeared on their plates day after day, but Mo would have proclaimed such offerings now as delicacies fit for a king.

At any rate, despite the pseudo comforts of home that existed in the little Austrian forest house, Mo knew he'd be pressing his luck by remaining. Sooner or later his Luftwaffe nemesis would stumble upon it, or a band of SS troops fleeing for the Tyrol would find it. If he'd bailed out when the rest of his crew had instead of remaining in the cockpit and guiding the dying *Rub-a-Dub-Dub* past the village, he might be with friends now. But he wasn't. He was on his own and knew damn well he'd better get moving. Hopefully, into the hands of American infantry or armor.

He watched the meadow awhile longer, saw no movement nor anything threatening, so decided to shove off. He made sure his Colt .45—his only weapon—remained snug in his shoulder holster, that his survival kit was secure, and his canteen full, then zipped up his leather flight jacket and moved downhill toward the meadow.

The sharp bark of a fox brought him to a standstill. He listened attentively for several minutes, heard nothing in response that suggested it might have been a signal used by the Nazis, then resumed his trek.

"Probably seen too many Cowboy-and-Indian movies," he muttered.

He hiked into the meadow along an old footpath now overgrown with weeds and grass. He knew he would leave a trail through the dewy grass that would be easy to follow. But so be it. He couldn't remain in one spot any longer and expect not to be discovered. Besides, he banked on Americans being nearby. They'd been ready to cross the Danube more than a week ago, on the day of his raid, so surely they'd reached the Inn River separating Germany from Austria by now.

The footpath led to a little-used dirt road that stretched to and from wooded land bordering the meadow. He pulled a compass from his survival kit, got his bearings, then chose to turn right, the direction he thought most likely to lead toward US forces.

He walked for an hour or more, accompanied only by the twitter of birds, the occasional scream of a hawk, and the hum of one or two early-to-work honeybees. The journey seemed almost pleasant—the coolness of a spring morning embracing him, the scent of wildflowers and evergreens permeating the air, flat cumulus beginning to blossom overhead. Cumulus Pancakus, a weather-guesser friend used to call them, giving them a pseudo technical name. Poking fun at their lack of vertical development.

Yes, the day seemed almost pleasant. Yet Mo knew danger lurked at every bend in the road, in the dimness of every shadow in the sun-dappled woods, in the breath of every puff of wind that might camouflage the sound of a predator. He felt again for his .45.

He continued on until midday, encountering no one on the road. Slowing his pace, he fumbled in his survival pack for something to nibble on—a piece of chocolate, a caramel. He found the chocolate, stopped, broke off a chunk, and popped it into his mouth.

· · ·

PERHAPS THE GROWING warmth of the day, maybe the bucolic surroundings, had made him just a bit less alert than earlier. He heard the footstep in the dirt behind him just a second too late. But he heard it and reached for his pistol.

"Nein," came a harsh command.

Mo stopped his movement.

"Hände auf den Kopf." Another harsh command.

Mo had no idea what he was being told to do. *Shit*, he thought, *shit, shit, shit*. He knew he'd screwed up, become too relaxed, and maybe just had his "last supper." He didn't know if he'd been intercepted by the Luftwaffe pilot, a ground combat unit, or an Austrian civilian. It probably didn't matter. At this stage of the war, he doubted anyone was interested in taking prisoners. Too much bother if you're trying to save your own hide. Easier—maybe even more fulfilling—to just exact revenge.

"Hände auf den Kopf." The order shouted in his ear.

He remained motionless. The muzzle of a gun pressed into his neck. Someone grabbed his arms from behind and yanked them upward, placing his hands on top of his head. He heard more footsteps, and voices speaking in German, behind him.

A Kraut soldier, wearing camouflage battle dress and the iconic coal scuttle helmet, stepped in front of him—several paces away—and leveled a rifle at him. Mo stared not at the weapon, nor at his captor's face, but at the collar insignia on the German's tunic, and swallowed hard. Twin lightning bolts. He'd been taken prisoner by the Waffen SS.

Among US pilots, it had become common knowledge that if you got shot down in enemy territory and captured, hope it would be by the Germany Army, the Heer, or the Luftwaffe, not the Gestapo and certainly not the SS.

Mo squeezed his eyes shut and prayed that his death would be swift. If he had anything going for him, it would be that these guys were in a hurry to reach the Alps and wouldn't screw around torturing him.

Mo opened his eyes as a second soldier, this one wearing an officer's billed field cap, moved from behind to face him. He pulled a pistol, a Luger Mo presumed, from a holster on his hip and placed the barrel under Mo's chin. Using the gun, he tilted Mo's face upward.

Mo stared into an unshaven, unwashed, and uncaring countenance that stared back at him with dark eyes, and perhaps an even darker soul.

Somehow, the SS officer managed a grin. "American," he said, "Dein Krieg ist vorbei." He withdrew the pistol and stepped behind Mo again. "Auf deinen Knien," he shouted.

Mo didn't react, having no idea what the German had said. He stood still with his hands on his head.

The shouted command came again, this time with the barrel of the Luger pressing down on his shoulder. Mo didn't move. The officer removed the barrel of the pistol and shouted something else. A pair of hands grabbed Mo's shoulders and slammed him into a kneeling position.

Mo heard the sound of a round being chambered in the Luger. He felt the muzzle push into the back of his head.

"Yea, though I walk through the valley of the shadow of death," he began in a whisper.

7

The hamlet of Parzham
Western Austria
May 3, 1945

In a tiny village twenty miles southwest of Linz, Austria, Frieda Mayr and Hauptsturmführer Karl Jagensdorf sat in comfortable silence—the kind that develops with being together for an extended period—at a small wooden table in the Hauptsturmführer's cottage enjoying breakfast. Dust motes floated in lazy dips and spins through a shaft of sunlight that had speared through an east-facing window and announced the commencement of a bright spring day.

The Hauptsturmführer broke the silence. He held a bite of Semmelknödel, a Bavarian bread dumpling, aloft on his fork. "So gut, so gut," he said, smiling. "Ich bin so glücklich, dich gefunden zu haben." I'm so fortunate to have found you.

Frieda beamed in response to Karl's approbation of her. A decade younger than the tall, handsome German officer, she, too, felt fortunate—no, *knew* she was fortunate to be the object of his undivided attention. He'd expressed an instant interest in her shortly after the Anschluss of Austria was assimilated into the "Greater German Reich."

In the summer of 1938, Karl had arrived in the town of Wels, where Frieda worked in her older brother's bakery. Long hours and sweaty labor. She almost forgot to breathe when, after visiting the store several times, the soft-spoken, erudite officer had asked her if she'd like to attend the cinema with him on a Saturday afternoon. It seemed like a dream, a fairy tale come true.

The two quickly became an item around town—the angular-featured, aristocratic soldier and the lithe blonde Fräulein from the bakery. She knew she'd ignited envy, maybe even jealousy, in more than a few of Wels's young women. She was also aware there were some of her fellow countrymen who detested the presence of the German Wehrmacht in Austria, or at least what used to be Austria.

Her brother, Bernhard, was one who despised the German "colonization" of Austria. And when she had announced she was leaving Wels and the bakery to move in with Karl in the town of Parzham, ten kilometers to the southwest, Bernhard had felt compelled to give her a stern lecture.

"My dear little sister," he'd said, placing his hands gently on either side of her face and tilting her head so he could stare directly into her eyes, "you cannot trust these people. Please, please, remember they are invaders, not welcomed guests."

"Oh, Bernhard," she'd responded, "you are so out of touch with things, so biased. Remember, a plebiscite was held. Austrians voted overwhelmingly to welcome becoming part of the German Reich."

He'd snorted a derisive laugh and said, "Yes, a referendum cloaked in intimidation. Voting was monitored. There was no privacy. If you voted 'no' you faced losing your job, being harassed, sometimes beaten." He paused. "Sometimes worse."

Frieda had laughed. "You worry too much, brother. You are so much like our papa was. I'm a grown woman. I know what I'm doing. Please, quit treating me like a toddler."

"No, you are not a toddler. But you are barely out of your teens. You have much to learn. Life is not a linear journey into a glorious sunset, my dear. It is a twisting, turning road filled with surprises and switchbacks. Yes, at times it can appear bright and welcoming. But there are dark stretches in which danger and disappointment lurk. You cannot go through life wearing blinders, pretending all is well."

"Ach, you are such a pessimist, brother. Karl represents the best of Germany. He is a true gentleman."

"No," Bernhard had snapped. "I'm warning you, he is not. I've read about these people, heard about them, the Nazis and the SS. Please, please, listen to me, little sister. These are wolves in sheep's clothing. I beg you, stay here in Wels. Be friends with Hauptsturmführer Jagensdorf if you must. But I implore you, do not invest your life with him."

She'd giggled and said, "Oh, my, my dear Bernhard. You should have been a playwright and not a baker. You could have written wonderful Shakespearean tragedies."

Despite her brother's admonitions, she'd left with Karl and never regretted it. Karl always treated her with nothing but respect and kindness. And even those who had, on occasion, made their dislike for the Germans and the Anschluss manifest, he handled with aplomb and due regard.

She remembered one instance in particular. She and Karl had been strolling through Parzham on a soft summer evening—bats wheeling and darting through the dusk, the pleasant odors of bratwurst and beer hanging in the air—on their way to a minor festival of some sort. She'd donned her favorite dirndl, and Karl wore—freshly pressed—his green-gray service uniform, an officer's visor cap, and polished-to-a-shine, calf-high jackboots.

A middle-aged man, weaving slightly—too much "celebration" perhaps —approached them. "Swine," he hissed at Karl as he neared him, his voice tinged in venom. "Invader. Butcher." He stopped and spat at Karl's feet. Beneath a dim streetlamp, the spittle glistened like shattered glass on one of Karl's gleaming boots.

Shocked, Frieda grasped Karl's arm in a stunned reflex. Karl halted, glanced down at his boots, then looked up at the man. Frieda saw a cold, blue fury ignite in Karl's eyes, yet his voice remained calm and well modulated, and his manner controlled, as he spoke to the man.

"Sir," he said, "have I offended you?"

"Your presence offends me," the man snapped, his words slightly slurred. "It offends all of us."

"Perhaps you misunderstand my presence then, the German presence."

"No, thieves and murders, I do not misunderstand."

"I see, Herr—? Would you be so kind. I am Hauptsturmführer Karl Jagensdorf, Waffen SS."

"My name is not important," he growled.

"Oh, but, sir, it is. If we are to have a civilized conversation about the German Reich, we must know one another's name."

The man laughed. "Civilized? There is nothing civilized about pigs." He reached out to a nearby stone wall to steady his stance.

"Perhaps, sir, you could tone down your rhetoric in the presence of the young lady," Karl said, more of a command than a suggestion. He inclined his head toward Frieda.

The man grunted in response, then pushed himself away from the wall and prepared to continue on his way.

Karl placed his hand on the man's shoulder. "Please, sir, your name. I will contact you and we will discuss, well . . . politics . . . when you are more, shall we say, clearheaded."

"Heinrich Koller," the man mumbled, then stumbled off into the gathering darkness.

"I hope you did not find that too upsetting, my dear," Karl said to Frieda after the man had withdrawn beyond earshot.

"No. I thought you handled Herr Koller quite well."

"Thank you. He and I will discuss our differences soon and settle them like men." Karl paused, then continued. "He will not bother us again."

His words came out firm and confident.

Now, several years after that incident, Frieda responded to the compliment Karl had offered over breakfast. "You are too kind, Liebling. It is I who am lucky. Lucky to have caught your eye . . . your love. You are such a kind man. I know with the war going on, many people, maybe most, do not enjoy what you have been able to provide for us." She gestured at the table where they sat and at the bounty of food it held: cold cuts of ham—Schinken—smoked bacon, slices of sausage, boiled eggs, a fresh pot of coffee, a bowl heaped with muesli.

Karl brushed his fingers through his wavy, blond hair and nodded. "The Wehrmacht sacrifices much," he said, "so it is only right we enjoy minor rewards. We must share them, of course, especially with those we love and endeavor to care for. For me, that is you. Now, let us finish breakfast. I'm afraid—and I'm sorry for not telling you this earlier—I have a long journey ahead of me today."

Frieda widened her eyes in surprise. "You're leaving?"

He reached across the table and rested his hand on top of hers. "Not permanently. You know I would never leave you, my Häschen." Little bunny. "I will return quickly."

"But I worry about you. You know, with the war going so badly—"

"Nein, nein, nein. Where did you hear that?" There seemed a sudden harsh edge to his words.

Outside, a horse-drawn cart filled with sacks of potatoes rattled down a cobblestone street.

"You know, people talk. They say the Russians are coming, that the German Army is on the run in the east, that the Red Army is nearing Berlin and Vienna. That the Americans and Brits are sweeping in from the west. That they've crossed the Danube. That they're coming here." Her voice quivered.

Karl stood, moved his chair next to Frieda, and sat. "You mustn't believe everything you hear, my dear. Actually, *anything* you hear. They are lies, propaganda spread by our enemies to sow doubt in the minds of the people of the German Reich."

"But I've heard from friends who had relatives in Vienna. Relatives who fled because the Red Army has entered the eastern suburbs. Because fighting has erupted in the streets."

Karl shook his head. "Nein. Lies. The enemy has agents who spread falsehoods."

She fixed her gaze on Karl's blue eyes as he continued to speak in comforting tones.

"It's true our military has suffered some minor setbacks, but what many see as defeats and retreats are merely strategic repositionings of our forces." He looked around the room as if searching for an eavesdropper, then lowered his voice to a conspiratorial whisper. "I shouldn't tell you this, but the reason I must leave temporarily is that I've been requested to attend a planning conference in Innsbruck. A great counteroffensive will soon be launched and my insights and suggestions have been requested. I know this much, that within a matter of weeks the Russians will be thrown back to the Urals and the Allies pushed back to the sea." He swiped his hand again over his flaxen hair and smiled. "All will be well. You needn't worry."

"Yes, I believe you. You've always been truthful with me. But . . ."

"But what?" he said softly.

"You aren't in a combat unit. Why must you go to Innsbruck? You have important work here. Who will handle your duties? Who will help the people you've been helping?"

Karl had told her he commanded a "DP Movement Center," helping displaced persons—people uprooted by the war, people who had lost their homes, who had their lives turned upside down—find new homes and new jobs and regain their lives in areas of the German Reich less affected by the fighting.

She loved the work he performed, assisting other people, but understood it could be challenging. He'd explained to her once the reason he always arrived home wearing a fresh uniform and smelling of manly cologne was that the refugees he dealt with were often caked in dust or mud from their journeys, and perhaps hadn't bathed for a month or more. "You wouldn't want to snuggle up next to a pig, would you?" he'd said. "That's not the image a good SS soldier wishes to portray."

Now, in answer to her question about who would help the DPs while he was gone, he said, "I have a well-trained staff, my dear. They will handle my duties while I'm absent. And I won't be away for long, only a day or two."

"Still, I worry."

"About the DPs?"

"No, about us. The talk of what's happening with the war, it's, well, disturbing. Despite what you told me, and I believe you, there's an element of concern that creeps into my head, and my heart, every time I hear the rumors. You know, when you hear the same stories day after day it begins to affect you."

Karl stood and beckoned her to stand. She did, and he wrapped his arms around her and gazed into her eyes.

"You know, I would never let anything happen to you, my Häschen. I would never allow you to fall into the grasp of the barbarians, the butchers, who seek to bring down the Reich. I will have one of my officers come by later today, and tomorrow if necessary, to check on you. And I promise you, I will return. And I promise you, we will drive our enemies from the Fatherland."

Frieda leaned against him. "I know you will," she said, her voice low and husky. Trusting. "I just want all of this to be over. The fighting. The dying. The misery."

"And it will be. And not far in the future. You will see. After the German Reich has completed its conquests and all of this unpleasantness is history, we will travel to my hometown in Bavaria and settle into a joyous life. Ah yes, Landshut is a wonderful place where we will enjoy sprawling forests and farms, exquisite cathedrals and churches, and the company of exceptional people."

"Yes," Frieda muttered into his tunic, "we will be happy there, I know."

"Isn't that what life is about, Häschen, happiness? Freedom from the vermin and lowlifes that make us miserable, that drag the German Reich down, that prevent us from claiming our rightful Liebestraum?" With eyes radiating nothing but warmth, he held her in his gaze.

"It is," she murmured. "I know we must be in the company of such people. People who bring brightness and hope to the world." She smiled and hugged him tighter.

"Landshut, you know, bears a legacy of such people. There was, centuries ago, Louis I, Duke of Bavaria. Then, in the nineteenth century, Johann Michael Sailer, Bishop of Regensburg. And now, a shining light of the German Reich, Heinrich Himmler."

"I've heard you speak of him," Frieda said softly. "The leader of the SS."

Karl embraced her tightly. "Rest easy, my dearest. All will be well."

8

A crossroads near Hörbach, Austria
May 3, 1945

"No," Sergeant Bowerman said, responding to Jim's question. "Not panzers. It don't sound like heavy vehicles, or anything tracked. Tigers weigh almost seventy tons. We'd sure as shit know if one of those suckers was comin'."

"Trucks then?"

"Probably."

"Well, not ours, that's for sure. We don't have any other units over the Inn yet."

"My guess is, Loot, troop carriers. Probably Krauts tryin' to get the hell out of Dodge into the . . . what did ya call it?"

"The Tyrol."

"Yeah, the mountains."

Jim listened carefully to the distant but nearing growls of the approaching engines, trying to discern how many trucks were headed in their direction. "Doesn't sound like a convoy," he said.

"Maybe two or three vehicles," Bowerman responded.

"We can handle that." Jim motioned for his platoon to gather around him. He saw in the expressions of his men a mix of eagerness for combat and anxiety over being able to get home safely, now that the end of the war was in sight.

"We've got some Germans headed in our direction," he said. "Sounds like a handful of trucks, troop carriers, we're guessing. We're going to arrange a little surprise for them. Sergeant Bowerman, I want you to position the men in the trees along the left side of the road just north of the intersection." He gestured toward the direction from which the enemy was approaching. A small ridge, a hump in the landscape, ran along the right side of the road. That made for a perfect ambush setup since any Krauts who tried to escape would face an uphill dash.

"Put the Jeep and half-tracks on the south side of the crossroads," Jim went on, "where they can take care of anybody who might try to break through.

"Sergeant, I want you to take Corporal Reynolds with you. As soon as all the vehicles are in the kill zone, have him greet the lead vehicle with a grenade launch. It doesn't have to be a perfect shot, just enough to serve to get the bad guys' attention and halt their movement."

"Yes, sir," Bowerman said crisply. "Okay, guys. Move out. Take cover. Mark your targets carefully when the shootin' starts. No spray paintin'. And don't get trigger-happy. Wait 'til Reynolds fires his Welcome Wagon pineapple."

The men moved into the forest and underbrush quickly and with practiced skill. They'd done this before. Sergeant Bowerman and Corporal Reynolds positioned themselves just north of the intersection on the west side of the road. Bowerman picked a spot where the grenade launch would easily cripple or halt the lead vehicle.

The half-tracks and Jeep rolled into their assigned positions. The half-tracks found well-camouflaged spots far enough off the road they wouldn't be noticed until the shooting began.

Jim flopped down behind an old deadfall near Bowerman and Reynolds. He rested the barrel of his carbine on the log behind which he took shelter.

A pair of crows, objecting noisily to the beings that had invaded their grounds, circled overhead in a sky filled with marshmallow clouds. The thrum of the motorized cadre rolling along the narrow road toward the Americans grew louder.

Jim worked to control his breathing as he lay hidden in the grass and weeds and wildflowers that had taken root adjacent to the fallen tree. After a few moments he was able to inhale and exhale in a steady, regulated rhythm. But his heart failed to follow suit. Its hammering felt unrestrained, its beats pulsating through his body like the reverberations of a bass drum in a Sousa marching band. He wondered if the crows could hear it.

He flipped off the safety on his carbine. He would pick individual targets and squeeze off carefully aimed rounds when the shooting started. *Don't rush*, he told himself.

The first of the vehicles—an open Kübelwagen, the Wehrmacht's equivalent of the Jeep—hove into view. A spare tire adorned the hood of the vehicle, but it carried no mounted weapons. A German officer wearing sunglasses sat in the front passenger seat. Two others rode in the rear. They obviously weren't concerned about an ambush.

Following the Kübelwagen came two medium-sized trucks, troop carriers as Bowerman had suspected. Their canvas covers had been stripped away from the cargo areas, probably in deference to the fair weather, thus revealing that each vehicle carried at least a dozen riflemen, maybe more.

Jim did the math quickly and knew his platoon was outnumbered by at least two to one. But it still held the advantage. The Germans had no idea of its presence. No inkling that they were about to become the centerpiece of a deadly turkey shoot.

Jim drew a slow, deep breath. Held it. He saw Bowerman tap Reynolds on the shoulder. The corporal, a grenade launcher fitted over his rifle, squeezed the trigger. The grenade flew into the front left wheel of the Kübelwagen and exploded on impact. The blast brought the vehicle to an abrupt halt, pitching its occupants forward, though the driver continued to grip the steering wheel in stunned confusion.

Jim targeted the officer riding in the front seat and squeezed the trigger of his weapon just as the German's head smashed into the windscreen. The windscreen exploded in a spray of glass. The officer slumped forward, then remained motionless. The driver, still dazed, made no attempt to exit the crippled machine. His life came to a quick and brutal end as a volley from Bowerman's Thompson blew away half his skull.

The soldiers in the rear seat of the Kübelwagen attempted to scramble from the now-smoking vehicle, but had no sooner stood and attempted to unsling their weapons than Jim's riflemen went to work on them, dropping them in place.

The trucks following the Kübelwagen stopped. At least a dozen infantry troops spilled out of the back of each. Almost continuous rifle and machine-gun fire from Jim's platoon filled the air. Many of the Germans sprawled on the ground as they leaped from the trucks. The few who weren't cut down immediately attempted to take cover using the vehicles as shields.

Jim knew immediately this reflected their inexperience. He guessed they were mainly very young recruits. A veteran outfit would have turned into the attack with their weapons blazing.

The fire from Jim's platoon's .50-cals proved murderous. Few of the Germans managed to return fire, and when they did it proved embarrassingly ineffective.

The Kübelwagen burst into flame. Thick, black smoke fanned out over the tiny battleground like a moving death shroud. The gunfire reached an earsplitting crescendo. Then, as suddenly as it had begun, it ceased. Neither Jim nor Bowerman gave the order. There were just no more targets left. The entire episode couldn't have lasted more than three or four minutes. For the Germans, Jim thought, it must have seemed forever. It had been a one-sided battle.

Jim's ears rang in sound-deadening echoes of the ambush. The men in the platoon held their positions, no one moving, no one speaking, everyone watching for any movement from the Germans.

There was none.

Gradually, normal hearing returned to Jim. Holding his carbine in a firing position, he stood. Smoke from the burning vehicle continued to cloak the road. The vaporous smog of gunfire mingled with it.

Jim walked from his hiding place down to the road. Sergeant Bowerman stepped from his position to join Jim. Both held their weapons at the ready as they moved toward the bullet-riddled bodies of the Germans and their vehicles.

No sound, except for the crackle and pop of the blazing Kübelwagen, reached their ears. They moved around the now fully engulfed vehicle, giving it and its dead occupants a wide berth. Bowerman knelt by the body of the first German rifleman he reached and examined him.

"Just a kid," he said.

"Probably had no more than a few weeks' training," Jim responded. "The Jerries are desperate. They're pitching school kids and old men into battle with virtually no preparation."

"Jesus, sir. How can they do that?"

Jim didn't answer, not quite ready to accept the enormity of what he and his men had done in the span of mere minutes.

They continued moving among the dead soldiers. The smells of battle filled Jim's senses—the stench of burning gasoline and rubber, the coppery odor of blood, the reek of severe wounds that had splattered entrails and brain matter and feces on Austrian soil.

Bowerman had other words for it. "Good lord, Loot, it smells like shit and bloody guts." He lifted his forearm to cover his nose.

An agonizing moan came from just off the road. Jim whirled, brought his Colt up to a firing position. He stepped toward the edge of the road. In the weeds lay a young soldier, probably no older than Jim. He stared at Jim with blank eyes and extended a bloody hand toward him.

"Vater, Vater," he said in a choking, wheezing whisper. "Hilf mir. Bitte."

The kid had a gaping chest wound. Seconds from death. Jim turned, looked at Bowerman.

Bowerman shook his head. "Nothin' we can do for him. Even a medic couldn't save him."

Jim backed away from the dying soldier. The German again moaned, a sound that cut deep into Jim's soul.

"Morphine?" Jim asked Bowerman.

"Wouldn't do no good. Leave him, sir. Get the men up. I'll tend to him."

Jim, filled with mixed emotions, turned and walked away. Victory buoyed his spirits. Killing churned his stomach, twisted his soul. The only redeeming aspect of what they had just done, if there was one—and that was questionable—is that these weren't *his* soldiers laying on the ground, and that wasn't one of *his* riflemen dying in a ditch with his lungs shot out.

He yelled for his men to form up on the road.

Then from behind him came the sound of a shot. The moaning stopped.

Bowerman walked past Jim without looking at him.

The platoon, many of the men smoking, some grinning, some looking pleased, a few appearing stunned, took up positions along the road.

Bowerman moved back to Jim after a few minutes. "Well, ya know what, Loot? Ya know what we done?"

Jim waited.

"We just took out three full squads of Kraut infantry. Over thirty of Hitler's warriors. And we didn't lose nobody. Couple a minor dings. Not even Purple Heart worthy."

Jim didn't respond.

"Sir, ya hear me?"

"Yes, sergeant."

"Ya don't seem happy."

Overhead, the crows, now joined by others, wheeled above the smoke. Waiting.

"Look, tell the men they did great. Superb job. They did as they were trained. I'm proud of them."

"But yer troubled, Loot. The wounded Kraut?"

Jim nodded. "You *killed* him? You know I can't approve—"

"I don't care whether ya can or can't," Bowerman snapped. "I ended the agony of that kid's last few moments on this miserable, war-torn earth. You tell me—war crime or mercy killin'?"

Jim didn't have an answer. Knew he never would. "It's just that as an officer I can't condone your action."

"Well, what the hell would you have done, sir? Let his excruciating pain go on so he gets to draw a few more tortuous breaths? I hope to God if I'm ever in his position, ya can jam yer .45 against my head and pull the trigger." Bowerman stared hard at Jim.

Jim shook his head slowly, more in uncertainty than negativity. He knew he needed to let it go. "Let's get going, sarge. Our orders are to keep moving, find as many Germans as we can."

"Yes, sir." Bowerman whistled for attention, used his arm to motion the platoon forward. "Let's move out," he hollered.

Mounted in the vehicles, they departed the crossroads. They pushed southeastward under a cloud-flecked, azure sky, leaving behind them the obsidian smoke blotting the sun, dark pools of blood seeping into Austrian soil, and images of young men—their bodies and souls shattered—staring blankly into eternity.

Bowerman rode beside Jim in the rear of the Jeep. "Ya okay, Loot?"

"Fine. I guess I just struggle with killing people. It bothers me. Like that soldier back there who extended his hand to me, dying, asking me for water. I know he was the enemy. That all things being equal, he would have blown *my* brains out given the chance."

"Sir," Bowerman said softly. "He wasn't askin' for water."

Jim stared at his sergeant.

"He thought ya was his father," Bowerman went on "Vater in German is father."

Jim tilted his head back and gazed unseeing at the sky. His chest tightened with emotion. "Good grief, sarge, he could have been a kid from my high school, or a guy who worked on the farm with me, or somebody I went fishing with. You know, you'd think after a couple of thousand years humans would have figured out a better way to settle their differences, their grievances, other than by killing each other."

"Yes, sir, but we ain't. So if we're gonna fight, we might as well be the best at it. And back there, we were. Like it or not, yer a good leader, Loot."

"I guess I don't like it. But your words ring true—if we're going to fight, we might as well be the best at it—and I'll make sure we continue to be. I want these guys to get home. Alive. Here's the thing, whether you're on the right side or the wrong side, war is a waste. I just don't want it to be my men getting wasted."

"Yes, sir. Thank ya, sir."

"And sergeant?"

"Sir?"

"We won't talk about this anymore. No more of my personal philosophy. We've still got a job to do."

Bowerman nodded and flashed a fleeting grin at Jim.

They continued on, jouncing alternately through thick forests and undulating pastures that bordered the narrow dirt track.

After another half hour, Jim told the private driving the Jeep to stop. The half-tracks following Jim ground to a halt, too. "Let's take a break," Jim said to Bowerman. Bowerman hollered at the men to take a whiz, grab a smoke, whatever, but stay alert.

With the engines of the vehicles silenced, and the rattle of the half-tracks absent, the sounds of spring, of renewed life, of hope, sifted back into prominence: the hum of insects, the easy songs of birds, the soft whispers of wind in the boughs of trees.

Jim took out his map again and beckoned Bowerman to examine it with him. "Looks like we're about here, sarge." He rested his finger on the map.

"Yes, sir." The sergeant studied the map for a moment. "And look here. It appears like we're just about to this little village. It should be just down the road from where we are. Might be a good place for Krauts to hole up."

"Hörbach," Jim said, reading the town's name on the map.

"Whaddaya think, sir, maybe a careful approach?"

Jim stood and gazed back in the direction of the intersection where they'd ambushed the Germans. A stratus of black smoke sat on the horizon.

"Yeah. Considering what we just annihilated, in a matter of minutes, was a unit of mostly kids, we probably shouldn't get cocky. There still may be some veteran combat units prowling around that are willing to fight."

"I think yer right, Loot. I'll let the men know."

Still, Jim wondered if they might not be pushing their luck by pressing on. It was getting late in the afternoon now. Maybe, he thought, they should just call it a day and bed down for the night. On the other hand, he knew acting conservatively never won wars.

The platoon moved out toward Hörbach. They hadn't gone far when Jim, now riding in the front passenger seat of the Jeep, spotted a stooped individual moving slowly up the road ahead of them. Jim signaled the Jeep's driver to again stop. Then he dismounted.

"Come with me," he said to Bowerman in the rear seat. They walked toward the figure who had a burlap sack slung over his or her left shoulder.

"Halt," Bowerman called out.

The person—a wizened elderly man with watery eyes and gnarled hands—stopped and turned to face the two Americans.

"Hände hoch," Bowerman snapped.

The old man dropped the sack and raised his hands.

"Was ist in dem Sack?" Bowerman asked. He and Jim halted, keeping their distance from the man.

"Bucheckern," the man said, then continued speaking in German. When he'd finished, Bowerman translated for Jim.

"His German isn't the German I'm used to, sir. It's different. He has an accent, uses some words I'm not familiar with. Austrian German, I guess. But I think he's sayin' he was in the woods gatherin' beechnuts and lookin' for early season berries."

"Beechnuts?" Jim asked.

"He says they make cookin' oil from it. He says soldiers have taken most of the good food in the region. So the people who live here kinda eat whatever they can find—potatoes, berries—if there are any—rabbits and squirrels, stuff like that."

"Have him empty the sack out on the ground."

Bowerman relayed the order to the man and he complied, dumping out a small pile of beechnuts.

"Okay, tell him he can put them back into the sack. And ask him if there are soldiers in the town up ahead of us."

The man scooped up the nuts and refilled his bag, talking all the while in response to the question. After he'd finished speaking, Bowerman turned to Jim.

"Well, we may be about to step into some deep doo-doo, Loot."

Jim detected just a flicker of concern in the sergeant's eyes, something he'd rarely seen before.

Bowerman continued speaking. "The old codger says there's a bunch of Germans in the town, includin' a major. A field grade officer, sir. That could mean we're about to poke a stick into a hornet's nest. Might be what's left of a battalion hunkered down up ahead of us."

"Well, faint heart never won fair lady."

"Shakespeare?"

"No, I don't think so. Just an old saying."

"Might not be a fair lady waitin' for us, sir."

"Only one way to find out."

"Back to the ol' recon platoon schtick, huh?"

Jim nodded.

Bowerman motioned the platoon forward.

9

Somewhere between Salzburg and Linz
Western Austria
May 3, 1945

The sound of a gunshot exploded in Mo's ears as he knelt on the Austrian road, an SS officer's pistol jammed against the back of his head.

I thought you weren't supposed to hear the one that killed you.

The shot, however, hadn't killed him. Mo remained in a kneeling position, his head intact, himself alive. Obviously, the blast had not come from the weapon pressed against him.

Abruptly, the pressure of the gun barrel on his head disappeared. From behind him came loud, raised voices, men arguing. Vociferously. It continued for what seemed two or three minutes, then ceased.

"Aufstehen," a voice barked. Mo could tell the word was directed at him, but had no idea what it meant. He elected not to move.

"Aufstehen!" Again the command.

Mo remained still, fearing if he moved it would be his last.

A soldier, different from the previous ones, stepped in front of him. He leveled a small pistol at Mo, motioned for him to stand. The soldier wore a one-piece tan jumpsuit with snaps and zippers and a blue-gray wool jacket

—no external buttons—that bore the iconic eagle insignia of the Luftwaffe.

Mo stood, but his spirits sank. He realized he hadn't been rescued. He apparently had been turned over to the SOB who'd been hounding him for the past week. He stared into the German pilot's rugged, unshaven face and —beneath bushy, black eyebrows—eyes that radiated hatred. On the collar of his flight jacket he wore the insignia of an officer, but Mo didn't know German ranks.

The Luftwaffe officer snapped a command at Mo, but Mo had no idea what it meant. He didn't react. For his lack of response, the German smashed his pistol into the side of Mo's jaw. The blow stung, but didn't shatter any bone. Stars orbited in Mo's blacked-out vision.

The Luftwaffe pilot pantomimed for Mo to raise his hands and he quickly complied. The German relieved him of his .45.

His new captor and the SS officer traded heated words again, but then Mo heard the troops behind him leaving. The Luftwaffe officer kept his gun aimed at Mo, but said nothing as he held his gaze on what Mo assumed to be the departing SS cadre.

The Luftwaffe pilot motioned with his pistol for Mo to turn around. He did. Then the German shoved him in the back and said, "Gehen."

Mo assumed that meant go or march, so, hands remaining in the air, he stepped off in the opposite direction the SS men had gone. The German followed, prodding him in the back with his pistol.

They'd walked for about ten minutes when the Luftwaffe officer said, "Okay, you can put your hands down." In English.

"What?" Mo wasn't sure he'd heard correctly.

"You don't speak English?" the German chided.

"You do?"

"And German, of course."

Mo lowered his arms and stopped walking.

"Keep moving," the German said. "Just in case one of those SS bastards is following us."

Mo resumed his pace. *SS bastards?*

The Luftwaffe officer moved up beside him, pistol holstered. He spoke to Mo, keeping his voice low. "Captain, I'm not your enemy. Anymore. But you're still in enemy territory and you're still my prisoner. So, if we encounter another SS group, get your hands on top of your head as fast as you can. Verstehen Sie?"

"Veer staying zee?"

"Verstehen Sie. Do you understand?"

"I don't understand a damn thing. What's happening. Who you are. What you're going to do with me. Why you speak such good English."

Confusion buzzed through Mo's thoughts like a swarm of angry bees. His jaw throbbed, his ears rang, disorientation overwhelmed him. He knew he'd come within a whisper of being executed moments ago, but then his "rescuer" clocked him in the head with a pistol and marched him off only to suggest he didn't care for the SS any more than Mo did. And that he wasn't Mo's enemy.

"Let us find a place off the road where we can sit and chat for a bit," the German said. "Oh, and I am sorry about whacking you so hard, but I had to put on a good show for our SS audience."

Mo rubbed his jaw. "Yeah, it was an excellent show."

They walked for another few moments, then spotted a path that led away from the road into a mixed beech and pine forest. "Here," the German said.

They moved into the woods and found a small, shadowed clearing layered in pine needles and flecked with tiny purple and yellow wildflowers. The Luftwaffe officer seated himself on the ground and Mo found an old stump. They sat facing each other.

"So, you are wondering what the hell is going on, no?" the German said.

"Yes."

"Then let me start by introducing myself. I am Major Jürgen Voigt, Jagdverband 44, German Luftwaffe."

"Yakterband?"

Major Voigt smiled. "Jagdverband. It is a special flight unit, 'fighter band' might be a better translation. We fly . . . well, flew . . . the Messerschmitt Me-262."

"Yes. The jet fighter. You guys shot down my airplane."

"And you, mine."

The two men stared at each other in silence.

Voigt broke the hush. "Then I guess we are even."

"Not really," Mo snapped. "There were nine other guys in my bomber."

"Point taken. But I do not consider myself the winner."

"Won the battle, lost the war."

"That appears to be the case. So. I wonder if you would be so kind as to introduce yourself?"

Mo, understanding he was, after all, the Luftwaffe officer's prisoner, remained reluctant to trust him. He studied the man. Medium height, black hair, ruggedly handsome. Any hatred, whether real or manufactured, seemed to have disappeared from his deep blue eyes. But perhaps Mo had misread that earlier. Now his eyes seemed to suggest inquisitiveness, not animosity. But still, they weren't buddies. "Name, rank, and serial number is all you get."

"As you wish. But I know your rank—your captain's bars are on your jacket—and your serial number is of no interest to me."

"My name is Maurice Nesmith. I go by Mo."

Voigt nodded. He slipped his hand inside his jacket and snatched out his handgun.

"Sore loser after all, huh?" Mo said, wondering if he could cover the distance between himself and the German before the German got off enough shots to stop him. It appeared to be a small-caliber pistol.

Voigt seemed to read Mo's thoughts. "Not for you, captain." He lifted his chin, apparently indicating something behind Mo.

Mo turned to look. A rabbit and three little ones stood at the edge of the clearing, eyeing the two men from behind a clump of tall grass.

"I am hungry," Voigt said. "I have not eaten a decent meal in over a week." He slipped the weapon back into his holster. "But I am tired of killing things. Besides, if I fired a shot, it might attract attraction we do not want."

Mo drew a long, slow breath, willing his muscles—that had tensed for a desperate, last-ditch charge—to relax. "Tell me, major, I'm still puzzled. Why the hell have you been chasing me all over western Austria?"

"Fair question . . . Mo. But I am afraid the reason is now a dead issue. I forget how Americans say it. Captured by events, or—"

"Overtaken by events?"

"Yes, that is it. Overtaken. You see, I wanted to get a message to American forces, but I think it is too late now."

"Too late for what?"

"The war, as you noted, is lost for Germany. The SS animals roaming the countryside around here may not agree with that, but we in Jagdverband 44 do. Our commanding officer, Generalmajor Adolf Galland, does not, or did not, want our jets and pilots falling into the hands of the Soviets. As soon as the Americans stopped bombing, it was his plan to get JV-44, as a unit, to the Allies. You see, Galland thinks the West and the Reds will soon be fighting each other, and he wants our squadron to fight on your side."

"Well, I'm pretty sure our bombing missions have ceased," Mo said. "So just how was your general planning on getting your squadron to the Allies?"

"That is where I was hoping you might have helped."

"Me? How?"

Voight cleared his throat. "Admittedly, you were a target of opportunity. I had not planned on getting shot down—nor had you—but if you had allowed me catch up to you once we were on the ground, I was thinking together we might have been able to get word to the Americans. But you kept running like a scared rabbit."

"I thought you were intending to end the battle we'd started in the sky."

"No. Once you were shot down, our fight was over. You see, many of us in the Luftwaffe are—despite what you may believe—not members of the Party, or Nazis as you call them. We have our own code of honor and we fight by that."

Mo nodded, though he remained skeptical of Voigt's tale. It seemed a bit far-fetched to take in hook, line, and sinker. "Okay, let's say I buy into your story. What was the message you wanted to deliver?"

"Simply that we wanted to fly our planes into Salzburg, or maybe Innsbruck, and place them, and us, in the care of the Americans. And—here is the important thing—we did not want the Americans shooting us down as we tried to do that. You know, thinking we were attacking them when all we wanted to do was defect."

"But you believe that's already happened now? That the jets have been turned over to the Allies?"

"It has to have happened. On April 25, when you and I met in the skies over Austria, the Americans were already fighting their way into Munich, and JV-44's base was just a few kilometers east of Munich. The base could not have survived more than a day or two after that."

"So now what?"

"I do not want to be taken by the Russians. And if the SS discovers I fed them a line of bull crap to save an American's life, the Germans would not hesitate to shoot me. So. I wish to surrender to the Americans."

"All the arguing I heard back there with the SS troops, what was that about? What the hell did you tell them?"

Voigt flashed a sardonic grin. "Not the truth."

"Well?"

"I told them I had orders from Hermann Göring himself—"

"Göring, the Luftwaffe boss?"

"Yes. Orders to capture an American bomber pilot because he would have knowledge of new tactics German intelligence had heard of that were going to be employed by the US Army Air Forces. I held up a set of orders for the SS officer to see."

"Such orders existed?"

Voigt smiled and shook his head. "No, of course not. I held up some old promotion papers I had, banking on the fact the SS jerk would be too upset to bother looking at them."

"You were lucky he didn't."

"So were you, Captain Nesmith. But worse, I was counting on those guys not knowing that Göring had been arrested by the SS on April 24 in Bavaria."

"Jesus. You really did climb out on a limb." Mo paused. "The SS really arrested Göring?" If so, Mo realized Nazi Germany really had come apart at the seams.

"Only because we, JV-44, wouldn't. Herr Hitler, cowering in his bunker in Berlin, was afraid Göring would try to represent Germany and surrender to the Americans. Hitler had his armaments minister, Albert Speer, call General Galland and tell him to take Göring into custody. Galland refused.

He wanted nothing to do with that. That is why the SS grabbed the Reichs-marschall."

"Wow." Mo could think of nothing else to say, stunned at what he'd heard so far.

"So, my American partner, I suggest we get moving. We do not need to wait for the SS or the Soviets to find us. What direction do you suggest?"

"I don't know for sure where we are, but let's head northwest. The Americans have to have crossed the Inn River by now and the river should be to our northwest."

"Agreed."

The two men rose and prepared to move on.

"One thing," Voigt said. "If we encounter Americans, I am *your* prisoner. I do not want to get shot on the last day or two of the war." He handed Mo his Colt .45.

Mo noticed a slight tremor in the German's hand, but didn't comment on it. He took the pistol. "And if we run into your SS pals again?"

"Then we are both on the same side."

"By the way, what is that little popgun you're carrying? It certainly isn't a Luger."

"A Luger is too bulky to carry in the cockpit of a fighter. My little popgun, as you call it, is an Astra 300. It is Spanish, .32-caliber. It gets the job done."

They set off in the direction of the sinking late afternoon sun. Their boots crunched softly on the hard-packed gravel and dirt track over which they strode. In the middle distance, a layer of thinning black smoke clung to the horizon.

"The residue of more death, I suppose," Mo said.

"As if we have not already had enough," Voigt responded.

"I've been wondering," Mo said as they continued to walk. "Your English, it's very good. There's still a rough German edge to it, but you're fluent. And it's what we call American English, not British. How did you learn it?"

Voight chuckled. "By being immersed in it. When I was a teenager, I spent a couple of years in America working on my uncle's farm in the state of Minnesota near a town called New Ulm. He grew corn and oats and raised hogs. I learned your language. And I learned how to work hard and follow directions."

"I'll bet that helped make you a good soldier."

"Yes, but I did not want to be the kind of soldier that carried a rifle, slogged through mud, and woke up with frost on his nose."

"I guess that worked out for you."

"Thanks to some barnstormers that passed through New Ulm once. That was so exciting. I knew from the instant I saw their biplanes swooping, looping, and spinning through the air, I wanted to fly."

Voigt laughed to himself and went on. "There was one young lady—I even remember her name, Vivian—who was a wing walker. I thought, so much courage. And wondered if I could ever be like her. It is a good thing women like Vivian don't fly fighters or bombers. I would have hated to face someone like her in combat."

The two men trudged by a patch of clover where dozens of honeybees buzzed in lazy action, taking advantage of the fading warmth of the day.

Then Mo heard something else, another type of buzzing that grew rapidly louder "Best we get off the road, major." The men sprinted into a sheltering stand of trees.

The buzzing morphed into a bellowing roar. Two bulky fighters, skimming just above the ground, screamed overhead, seemingly catching no glimpse of the two uniformed men crouched in the forest.

"Ours," Mo said, once the fighters had disappeared over the horizon. "P-47s, what we call Thunderbolts."

"Ah, yes, Thunderbolts and Lightnings rule the skies now," Voigt said, resignation threading his words.

"I'd guess they're running armed reconnaissance for our forces. So the ground pounders can't be that far away. You ready to go find some Americans?"

Voigt nodded and stood but said nothing. Mo realized it must be difficult for a man to accept defeat in combat, even knowing that additional resistance would be foolhardy, pointless, and probably deadly.

They moved along the narrow road for another hour as the sun dropped lower and lower in the sky before eventually sinking below the western horizon into its nocturnal dwelling. The heavens put on a kaleidoscopic display—for those who cared—shifting from the reds and oranges of sunset, to the purples and violets of dusk, and finally into the black void of night.

"I can't see anything anymore," Mo whispered.

"We must stop," Voigt said, resignation marking his words. His stomach growled. Loudly.

"That'll give us away to the enemy," Mo hissed in an attempt to lighten the moment.

"I'm starving," Voigt shot back. "I should have shot the damn bunny."

"Halt!" a voice from the darkness yelled. "Who goes there?"

10

Just west of Hörbach, Austria
May 3, 1945

Jim studied the old man with the sack of beechnuts and asked Bowerman, "You trust him?"

"I don't trust nobody, sir. But I been thinkin', why would he lie? If he wanted to lead us into a trap, he'd tell us there weren't no Krauts in the town."

"Yeah, but how much is a bunch? Isn't that the term he used, 'a bunch'?"

"Those were my words, Loot. The old guy said many."

"See if you can get him to be more specific."

The sergeant and the aged Austrian plunged into another conversation in German. The elderly man shrugged and shook his head several times.

After they'd finished, Bowerman spoke to Jim.

"The best he can come up with is 'scores.' I don't think he really knows."

"So, maybe twenty, maybe a hundred."

"Whatever. We're outnumbered."

"Yeah. But we were outnumbered at the crossroads back there, too." Jim checked his wristwatch. "It's getting late in the afternoon. Whatever's in the village up ahead, I don't want to deal with it after dark. We need to check it out now."

"Yes, sir."

"Another thing, sarge, let's assume the old guy is telling us the truth. If there are Germans in the town, that suggests to me they've pretty much packed it in, given up. They aren't trying to beat feet into the Alps, they aren't out setting up ambushes, and as far as we know, there's certainly nothing worth defending in the village . . . what's it called?"

"Hörbach, sir."

"Well then, what say we go take a look at Hörbach. From what I've heard, the Nazis are surrendering left and right. Regiment got a message yesterday that said Army Group C, about a million men in Italy and western Austria, raised the white flag a few days ago. And I've heard rumors, pretty solid ones, that all the bad guys in Berlin—almost a half million—called it quits yesterday."

"Yeah, but I'll bet that didn't include SS assholes. Some of those bastards have vowed to fight to the death."

"I know. So let's hope there aren't any SS in the town. Leave the Jeep and tracks here. We'll go forward on foot. Keep the old guy with us."

"Ya got it, Loot." Bowerman formed the platoon into two columns, one on either side of the road. "Be ready for anything, guys," he warned.

They pushed toward Hörbach, Jim leading one column, Bowerman the other. Jim's heart rate edged upward with each step he took. He knew the end of the war had to be only days—if not hours—away. But the truth was, they were still at war, no matter how near an armistice or even a total surrender they might be. He just didn't want to lead his men into a futile battle as the clock on the greatest European conflict in history ran out.

Jim halted the platoon as it reached the edge of the village. The cobblestone street through the center of town seemed quiet. Neat little homes and shops with tile roofs, tiny balconies, and well-tended flower boxes lined the street. Lazy spirals of smoke drifted from a few chimneys. Hörbach appeared to have escaped the ravages of war.

The platoon held its position for several minutes. The only sounds were the twitter of birds and the occasional yap of a bored dog.

"Whaddaya think, Loot?" Bowerman said.

"What I think, sarge, is I don't like this. Little too peaceful."

"Same feelin' I got."

"Tell you what. Ask the old man if he'd be willing to go into town and ask the Germans if they'd be interested in surrendering. That the Americans have them surrounded."

"Worth a try, Loot." Bowerman spoke to the elderly gentleman who listened intently, but looked a bit apprehensive. After some further back-and-forth, the old man rose, nodded to Jim, and walked into the village.

JIM WATCHED through a set of field glasses as the nut-gatherer disappeared into a small church in the center of Hörbach. For several minutes, nothing happened. The semblance of a bucolic spring day in an Austrian village continued.

Finally, the door to the church opened and two men in uniform stepped out, one waving a white flag. Jim judged their distance to be about three hundred meters from where he stood. He waved them forward and continued to watch them with his field glasses.

"Careful, Loot," Bowerman said. "Don't trust these bastards."

"Got it," Jim said. The two Germans moved toward Jim and Bowerman at a steady pace. One appeared to be an NCO, the other, an officer.

"Oh, good God," Jim said.

"What?" Bowerman squinted at the approaching soldiers.

"SS," Jim said, a catch in his throat. His heart rate ratcheted up even further.

"No shit, Loot?"

"Sure looks like it to me."

"Talk about deep doo-doo." Bowerman turned and issued an order to several of the platoon's riflemen to keep their weapons trained on the Germans.

The two enemy soldiers approached within ten meters of Jim before Bowerman commanded them to halt.

The German NCO wore a camouflage field uniform and a green-gray field hat. The officer wore a camo field jacket slung over a black uniform—the uniform of Waffen-SS Panzer units. An iron cross hung beneath his throat. He glared at the two Americans. Jim caught something in the German's stare that made him truly uneasy—something primitive, militant, maybe even desperate. An old scar slashed diagonally across the SS officer's left cheek seemed to draw his mouth into a permanent sneer. As he halted, he appeared ready to render a traditional military salute, but then stopped, continuing to hold Jim in an icy stare.

"Ich bin Sturmbannführer Gerhardt Schäfer," he snapped, drawing himself to rigid attention, "Bataillonskommandeur, 3.SS-Panzerdivision, Totenkopf." His voice resonated with command authority.

Bowerman translated. "He says he's Sturmbannführer—that means assault unit leader, equivalent to a major, I think—Gerhardt Schäfer, battalion commander in the Third SS Panzer Division, 'Death Head.'"

"Wonderful," Jim mumbled, "an SS field grade officer."

He looked the German officer in the eye. "Second Lieutenant James Thayer," he said, "platoon leader, 14th Infantry Regiment, 71st Infantry Division." He resisted the temptation to salute a senior officer, and instead drew his sidearm.

"Zweiter Leutnant?" Schäfer said, his words coated with disdain.

"He don't much care for the fact yer a Second Looey, sir," Bowerman said.

"Well, I can't help it. Maybe he'd like to give me a battlefield promotion."

"I'd better not translate that, sir."

"Okay. Let's try this. If he's a Panzer commander, ask him where his armor is."

Bowerman spoke in German to the SS officer, who in turn growled a lengthy reply, all the while holding Jim in a death stare.

After he'd finished, Bowerman translated for Jim. "As near as I can figure out, Loot, his division was pretty much wiped out durin' a fightin' retreat from Hungary. Most of what was left of the outfit, which wasn't much, I gather, ended up in Czechoslovakia, but part of his battalion made it here."

"Ask him how many men he has left."

Bowerman asked, but Schäfer, his voice edged in anger—or maybe frustration, Jim couldn't tell which—refused to answer.

"What's he want then?" Jim said.

Bowerman spoke to Schäfer again. The German replied, his voice rising in volume, his words coming out clipped and sharp. Jim, though he knew he held the upper hand, couldn't help but feel a tinge of intimidation in the presence of the irate senior officer, enemy or not. He also knew he couldn't display any uneasiness in front of his men.

Bowerman turned to Jim. "The major says he wants to surrender, but only to an officer of equal or higher rank."

"Jesus, Joseph, and Mary," Jim muttered. "Tell him I'm the only officer around."

Bowerman did, but Jim could tell Schäfer didn't accept that. He shook his head and shouted, "Nein, nein."

"Sorry, buddy, but I'm it," Jim shot back at him. The guy reminded him of a bully he'd known in high school.

Schäfer launched into a tirade, his anger now manifest, spittle flying from his mouth, his face turning a mottled shade of crimson. The NCO accompanying him took a step back, the white flag he'd displayed earlier clutched to his chest.

After the SS officer had completed his rant, Bowerman spoke to Jim. "I think the guy's a nutcase, sir. He says he refuses to surrender to a junior officer. I dunno if it's some half-assed code of honor these SS SOBs have, or if the major just doesn't have all his sails up, but he says the only way he throws in the towel is if he kills you first, then himself."

"Well, I'm not *that* keen on his surrender."

"No, shit, Loot. What are we gonna do?"

"Keep him talking."

Jim, without taking his eyes off Major Schäfer, told his radioman, Private Erickson, to contact regimental headquarters. "Ask that a field-grade officer be dispatched to Hörbach on the double," he said. "Tell them we've got a hairy situation here, that we need at least a major for an SS battalion commander to surrender to. Come to think about it, tell them to request the whole darn battalion get up here. Now. I have no idea how many Germans we got in this town. Could be a hundred."

"Yes, sir."

As Erickson made the call to company headquarters, Schäfer began spouting off again, pacing in a small circle, pointing at Jim.

Jim swallowed hard, then said to Bowerman, "Let's see if I can get him to come down off his high horse a bit. Maybe talk man-to-man with him, no weapons." He handed Bowerman his sidearm.

"Careful, Loot. Might be a really bad idea."

"Yeah. I know. Tell the major I'd like to work out a deal with him, respect his rank, honor his service."

Bowerman sighed but followed orders. Jim spread his hands, hoping to indicate to Schäfer his intent to try to end their standoff peacefully.

It didn't bear fruit. The SS officer responded with a sneering laugh and a shout, then launched into another diatribe. Bowerman waved the .45 at him to keep him from coming any closer to Jim. Whatever Schäfer said, Jim noticed his NCO seemed to want no part of it and stared wide-eyed at the SS officer as he continued his verbal onslaught.

"What's with this guy?" Jim said, feeling another wave of uneasiness ripple through his body.

"He says there's no way he'll surrender to ya. He and his men will fight to the death. Many will die. He says we're outnumbered."

Jim drew a deep breath to steady himself. "Well, let's find out what kind of a poker player he is. Tell him this, that our full battalion, including tanks and artillery, is only five or ten minutes behind us."

"It's a lot farther to our rear than that."

"I know, I know."

"You're gonna call his bluff, sir?"

Jim nodded. "And tell the major that yes, there may be a fight to the death, but it's going to be his men that do the dying. Not ours. It'll be his men that are outnumbered."

Bowerman addressed the major, but the German merely spit on the ground, puffed out his chest, and placed his hands on his hips as if to say, "try me."

Jim shrugged and spoke directly to Schäfer. "We'll burn down the town then. You'll have no place to hide."

"Sir, we don't have a flamethrower," Bowerman said in a low voice to Jim.

"He doesn't know that."

The sergeant passed the threat to Schäfer.

He continued to stand with his hands on his hips, glaring at the Americans.

Seconds ticked away. Each side stood its ground, posturing and metaphorically rattling its sabers.

"I'll tell you one thing," Jim said to Bowerman, "if his NCO's reaction to him is any indication, I don't think his men have bought into this notion of fighting to the death."

"I hope we don't have to find out, sir."

But the SS officer seemed to decide otherwise. He snapped an order to his NCO. The NCO hesitated, and received a slap in his face for his dalliance. Schäfer performed an about-face, as did the NCO. Over his shoulder, the officer shouted, "Wir kämpfen," and he moved back toward town.

"'We fight' was what he said," Bowerman translated.

Jim couldn't help but wonder if his confidence—perhaps overconfidence—born of the success at the crossroads hadn't tricked him into leading his platoon into the iconic box canyon of Western movie lore. The reality of death suddenly hovered over him like a buzzard circling above road kill.

He drew another deep breath, regretting the position he'd put himself in . . . his platoon in.

His heart hammering, he ran a flash assessment of his life—had he done enough with it to curry God's favor, to be allowed to survive, to fall in love, to father children, to watch a family blossom and carry forth his legacy?

He didn't dwell on the questions, however, because he had no answers. Instead, he forced himself to control his respiration and focus on the problem at hand. In the end, he fell back on a belief that had been ingrained in him since he was a child—God will take care of it.

And the solution came to him, like a shooting star tracing a trail through a black sky. "Halt," he yelled at the departing Germans.

Bowerman glanced his way, "What are ya doin', Loot?"

"I just realized what these guys fear more than us."

The two Germans stopped but didn't turn around.

"Tell them we won't fight," Jim said. "We'll withdraw and leave them alone."

"Sir, I don't get it."

"Tell them we'll withdraw and wait for the Soviets to show up. I'm guessing they can't be more than a couple of days east of here."

Bowerman let loose a muffled guffaw. "Fuckin' brilliant, sir . . . pardon my language." He called out Jim's message to the Germans, who turned slowly to face the two Americans.

"These guys have been in reverse gear since early '43 on the Eastern Front," Jim said, "you think the Red Army is going to be taking prisoners?"

"No, sir. And the Krauts damn well know that."

SS Sturmbannführer Schäfer fingered the Iron Cross hanging around his neck, tugged his field jacket into position, pulled himself fully erect, and strode back toward Jim with his NCO in tow. Bowerman again halted them about ten meters in front of Jim.

Schäfer said something. Bowerman translated.

"'You would leave us to the barbarians?' he said."

"How are these guys any different from barbarians?" Jim responded. "Don't translate that. Ask him if he'd reconsider surrendering to me."

Bowerman did.

The SS officer didn't respond immediately. Instead, he turned toward his NCO and said something. The NCO appeared to be startled, but then said Jawohl and began to back away. Schäfer pivoted back toward Jim. "Sturmbannführer Schäfer, Bataillonskommandeur, 3.SS-Panzerdivision, möchte sich vor Second Lieutenant Thayer, United States Army, ergeben."

He snapped off a crisp salute, moved his left hand to the Iron Cross at his neck, and stepped forward while extending his right hand to Jim as if offering to shake hands.

"Nein," Bowerman shouted.

Something malevolent and atavistic flashed in the German's eyes.

The deafening report of Jim's Colt .45, the one he'd given Bowerman, shattered the late afternoon stillness as the sergeant pulled its trigger. Schäfer stopped, stared wide-eyed at Jim and Bowerman, swayed on his feet, then crumpled to the street.

Almost simultaneously Bowerman yelled, "Get down," and pulled Jim to the ground. But then, nothing.

Thirty seconds passed. Jim and Bowerman stood.

"Stay back," Bowerman said. Keeping the .45 aimed at Schäfer's motionless body, he advanced toward it.

Jim remained in place, not fully comprehending what had just happened.

"Sir," Bowerman said, and motioned Jim forward.

Jim moved to where Bowerman stood. With the barrel of the pistol, the sergeant spread open the German's field jacket. "Look."

A gaping chest wound met Jim's eyes. And something else. At the bottom of a lanyard strung around the German's neck rested a stick grenade, or, as the Brits called it, a "potato masher" due to its appearance— a cylindrical explosive device at the base of a wooden stick.

"Oh, my Lord," Jim whispered. "How did you know?"

"I heard the bastard say somethin' to his NCO about a blast radius, which scared the bejesus outta the guy, and then Schäfer kept fiddlin' with —I thought—his Iron Cross, but I think he was really checkin' the lanyard holdin' the damn grenade. And once I saw him keepin' his hand inside his jacket while he was comin' toward us, I knew somethin' was up. He was gonna yank the 'tater masher free of the lanyard, pulling out the armin' cord, and blow us all to kingdom come."

"Sarge . . . sarge . . . I . . ." Jim could get no more words out. His head spun with a mélange of discordant, blurry images, black and white. He bent forward, put his hands on his knees, and drew in great gulps of air. He understood full well he'd been within three seconds of the end of his life.

"It's okay, Loot, it's okay." Bowerman rested his hand on Jim's shoulder.

Finally able to speak again, Jim said, "Get the rest of the platoon up here. We're either going to be fighting for our lives or taking prisoners within the next few seconds."

Bowerman signaled the men forward and they took up positions behind such cover as they could find—homes, walls, barrels. And they waited.

"See anything, Loot?" Bowerman asked.

"Nothing. I suspect when you shot the SS guy, you either scared the rest of the Krauts to death or brought their blood to a boil."

They waited some more.

After what seemed like half an hour, but probably was only a matter of minutes, Bowerman said, "Well, there's your answer."

A white flag on a stick poked out the door of a cafe.

"Tell them to come out, hands on their heads," Jim said.

Bowerman shouted the order in German.

A dozen soldiers filed out of the eatery.

Another white flag being waved back and forth appeared in the doorway of a bank. Bowerman repeated the order. This time, a group of perhaps thirty Germans, hands in the air, stepped from the building.

More white flags appeared. More SS soldiers spilled into the main street —really, the only street—of Hörbach. And they kept coming.

"Jumpin' Jehosaphat, sir," Bowerman said, "I didn't think an entire battalion was gonna be hidin' out here, I thought just a few survivors."

"How many you guess so far?" Jim asked.

"Gotta be several hundred."

"Okay. Tell them to lay down their weapons. Stack them in an area away from us. Then get them seated along the road. No talking. Post guards."

"Yes, sir," Bowerman responded. "On it."

And still the surrendering troops came.

JIM STUDIED the men as they streamed past him in dirty, tattered, threadbare field uniforms. Many stared at the Americans with hollow gazes. They seemed exhausted, hurting, hungry. Totally defeated.

"Sarge," Jim said, after Bowerman got the surrender semiorganized, "find an officer and get him over here. Ask him how many men are here and where they've come from."

Bowerman yanked an officer, an Obersturmführer, out of a line of prisoners and brought him to Jim. There he proceeded to enter into an extended conversation with the German.

After they'd finished, Bowerman spoke to Jim. "This guy, he's a first lieutenant, he says the SS-Panzerdivision Totenkopf has been in a fightin' retreat for almost two years. They've gone backward for over six hundred miles across the Russian steppe in the Ukraine, then into Poland, Czechoslovakia, Hungary. He thanks us for not killin' them. He says they're hungry and need clothes and medical attention. They're tired of fightin' and just wanna go home."

No different from the rest of us, Jim thought. "Tell him we'll do our best for them. Tell him to select his most severely wounded men and we'll try to get them to a field hospital. And tell Erickson to radio headquarters again and let them know we really need help, that we've got several hundred prisoners. We can't guard them all . . . not that they're gonna try anything."

A short time later, a major from regimental headquarters arrived in Hörbach.

"Heard you gentlemen needed some rank up here," he said to Jim. "That you had an SS officer who wouldn't surrender to a junior-grade."

Jim saluted the major. "Yes, sir, but, well, the officer decided to surrender after all." He inclined his head toward Schäfer's body still sprawled in the street. A couple of mangy dogs patrolled the periphery of where the German lay, and several crows hopped in an inspection tour around it. Bowerman shooed them away.

"No, shit, lieutenant. What happened?"

Jim told him the story, finishing with, "And now we've got a few hundred prisoners."

The major shook his head in stunned disbelief, then moved his gaze along the throngs of prisoners that Jim's platoon herded along the road. "I'll tell you one thing, lieutenant, you've got more than a few hundred.' When E Company gets here, we'll form the Krauts into groups of fifty each so we can get a more accurate count. In the meantime, make sure every one of them is disarmed. We don't need any more stunts like your SS buddy there pulled."

By dusk, with the arrival of E Company, the prisoners had been formed into smaller groups and counted. And recounted, because no one could believe the initial number. But it turned out to be accurate. Second Lieutenant Jim Thayer's platoon had taken almost eight hundred prisoners in the little town of Hörbach, Austria.

"Thayer," the major said, "you may have just earned yourself a medal.

So why don't you and your guys grab some chow and shuteye now and be ready to get back to your recon duties early tomorrow. I'll have Easy Company shuffle these POWs back to where they can be sorted out, fed, questioned, and given medical attention."

Jim and Bowerman moved the platoon to the other side of the town and settled in for the night.

"Post a couple of sentries on two-hour rotations tonight," Jim told Bowerman. "I don't expect anything, but there are still some fanatics out there who can't admit the war is virtually over. As we just found out."

"Will do, sir. Ya know, rumors are runnin' wild that an armistice or surrender will be signed any day now."

"I know. But remember, the game isn't over until the last out in the final inning."

"Ya gotta admit, though, here we are in the bottom of the ninth and the Germans got nobody on with two outs and two strikes on the batter."

Jim nodded. "One thing I will tell you, sergeant, I take a lot more pride in what happened in this little town than back at the crossroads. I don't like killing, I'd rather save lives. I know you had to shoot the SS officer—you saved my life—but when you can save *eight hundred* lives, now there's something everyone here can puff out his chest about."

"Well, I don't think nuthin' will ever top today, Loot. Let's hope the Krauts appreciate what we did for 'em."

11

Just east of Hörbach, Austria
May 3, 1945

"Who goes there?"

Nobody says that anymore, Mo thought. "Americans," he hollered back. *Well, one American.*

"How do I know that?" the voice retorted.

"How do I know *you're* American?"

"Who won the World Series last year?"

"How the hell would I know? I've been fighting a war, flying B-24s out of England. Besides, I'm from California. We don't have any major league baseball teams."

"You're a pilot?"

"No. I'm a goddamned stewardess flying for TWA. Now hold your fire. I'm Captain Maurice Nesmith, 448th Bombardment Group, United States Army Air Forces. I've got a German prisoner."

"But you don't know who won the World Series?"

Jesus. "No. Do you?"

"What company is Boogie Woogie Bugle Boy from?"

"Well, not yours. That's for sure."

"Do better than that or I'll shoot."

"Laverne, Maxene, and Patty said he was from Company B."

"Okay, captain—"

"And in case you were wondering, Boogie Woogie Bugle Boy was introduced in an Abbott and Costello film in '41."

"I said Okay. Move toward the sound of my voice with your arms in the air."

Major Voigt whispered to Mo, "How do you know that stuff about Boogie Bugle Boy?

Did you just make it up?"

"Like you making stuff up for the SS? Orders from Göring. No, I'm a big band fan. I heard the Andrews Sisters—that's who recorded the song —perform with Glenn Miller once. Chesterfield Cigarettes broadcast. Now walk ahead of me. Keep your hands on your head. Act like my captive."

"Jawohl," Voigt mumbled.

A flashlight beam scanned the two men as they moved toward the sound of the sentry's voice.

"I've got a Luftwaffe prisoner," Mo said. "He's walking ahead of me. Don't shoot."

Voigt and Mo stopped when the sentry holding the light came into view. A second soldier trained a rifle on them.

"I'm Captain Maurice Nesmith, United States Army Air Forces," Mo said. "Okay if I lower my hands?"

The sentry with the flashlight ran the beam over Mo, inspecting his face and uniform. "Got your dog tags?"

"Around my neck."

"Okay, put your arms down. Who's your prisoner?"

"A Luftwaffe major."

The flashlight beam scanned Voigt.

"Alright, sir," the guard said to Mo. "Follow me. Our lieutenant will be interested in meeting you . . . and your buddy. But tell him to keep his hands on his head."

The sentry led Mo and Voigt to an abandoned shed adjacent to the road. He called out to whoever was in the shed. A lieutenant stepped from the dilapidated structure looking a bit annoyed. Perhaps because his opportunity for sleep had been interrupted.

"What is it, private?" the lieutenant asked.

"Got some visitors, sir. Thought you might like to meet them."

The young officer stepped forward to get a closer look at Mo and Voigt.

"Who have we got here?" he asked.

While the lieutenant, a butter bar, examined the two newcomers, Mo got a closer view of him, a skinny kid who looked like he belonged in high school, not on a battlefield. But something in the lieutenant's demeanor—his intense gaze, his haggard face—told Mo the guy was a combat veteran.

Mo introduced himself and Voigt.

"I'm Lieutenant Jim Thayer, 71st Infantry Division," their greeter responded. "I'd be glad to take the prisoner off your hands, Captain Nesmith. We captured a bunch of SS troops this afternoon and are in the process of shuttling them back to battalion headquarters. We can throw your guy in with them."

Voigt swiveled his head to look askance at Mo.

"That might not be such a good idea, lieutenant," Mo responded.

"Oh? And why is that?"

"That, Jim—if I may call you that—is a three-beer story. Short version: an SS officer had a gun at the back of my head earlier today and was about to pull the trigger when Major Voigt showed up and saved my bacon."

"Yes, sir, it's okay to call me Jim. Sorry, I don't have even one beer, let alone three. But I'd be glad to share some Spam with you. Please." He gestured at the nearly collapsed shed.

"Thank you, Lieutenant Thayer," Voigt piped up. "I haven't eaten in quite awhile."

Jim's eyes widened in surprise.

"He spent a couple of years in the States," Mo said, "so he speaks excellent English."

They entered the shed, sat on some wooden planks, and divvied up two tins of Spam. Mo ran through the story of hooking up with Voigt in more detail. A kerosene lantern perched on a wooden box gave off a jiggly glow that lent the atmosphere of a campfire story to his tale . . . and attracted an endless cadre of orbiting insects.

After Mo had finished, Jim said to Voigt, "I can see why you might not be welcomed by the prisoners we took, especially if the SS guys you flim-flammed got caught and tossed in with them. But I am going to have to send you two back to battalion. We're still a combat unit and don't have the manpower to guard a prisoner. I can't have a noncombatant tagging along, either."

"With all due respect, Jim," Mo said, "I can handle a weapon. And I'll take responsibility for watching Major Voigt. But believe me, he's not a threat to us."

"I can't authorize that, captain."

"But you would obey the order of a superior officer, wouldn't you?" Mo smiled, not wanting the lieutenant to think he was coming on as a hard ass.

Jim shrugged. "Like I said, we're still in combat. You'd be a lot safer back at battalion."

"Maybe so, but I don't want Major Voigt treated like a run-of-the-mill POW. And besides, I can't help but feel hostilities are about over. I'd be willing to bet tomorrow will be a pretty damn uneventful day."

Jim sighed. "Could be. Okay, I'll accede to your 'order,' captain. You've still got your sidearm, right?"

"And Major Voigt's."

"Keep it. We'll get him a field jacket to throw over his Luftwaffe uniform, and find a pot for his head, so he won't be mistaken for a bad guy."

"Fair enough."

"Just stay out of the way, and everything should be fine. For now, I'll have the guys rustle you up some bedrolls and maybe we can all catch forty winks before we press on after sunup."

"Thank you, Lieutenant Thayer," Voigt said softly. "I appreciate your kindness, even though I'm the bad guy here."

"Not in my eyes," Mo interjected. "See you in the morning, Jim."

Just east of Hörbach, Austria
May 4, 1945

Mᴏ ᴀɴᴅ Mᴀᴊᴏʀ Vᴏɪɢᴛ had awakened well before sunrise and now sat together on a mossy, dew-drenched log and sipped what passed for coffee from metal mess cups.

"I know you spent time in Minnesota, major," Mo said, "but where in Germany are you from? Where'd you grow up?"

"Before I answer that, let me say I know you Americans don't stand on formality as much as we Germans do, so I would not be bothered, in fact would be honored, if you would call me Jürgen. And to answer your question, my home is in a place called Wildbad"—he pronounced it Veeld-baud —"a beautiful little town with a stream running through it in the Black Forest."

"Family?" Mo took a swig of his coffee, its warmth more welcome than its taste.

Jürgen smiled. "My wife is Karolina. She grew up in Stuttgart. She presented me the most wonderful gifts of my life, two dark-haired beauties, our twins, Ursula and Ute. They are six—no, seven—now. I want nothing more than to return to them, hug them once more, and hike through the woods with them and see who can be the first to spot a cuckoo." His voice drifted off, as though he was already back with them, enjoying a Germany that had existed before the war. He snapped back to the present and asked, "And you?" He lifted his cup of coffee to his lips, his hand trembling.

"Jürgen," Mo said, "are you hurt?"

"Nein, my friend. It is too much combat. I am weary of war, the killing, the dying, the destruction, the sorrow, the hopelessness."

"I know," Mo said softly, "I saw a lot of that on our side, too. Too much combat? We call that being 'flak happy' or—you'll love this—the 'Focke-Wulf jitters.'"

Jürgen smiled benignly.

Mo went on. "If you're a ground pounder, it's known as being shell shocked or having battle fatigue. It wears men down."

"Yes," Jürgen said quietly, "why could not we learn to settle our differences on the fußball field instead of the battlefield?"

"Do you suppose your Führer would have ever accepted that?" Mo realized a bit more anger than he intended had crept into his question.

Jürgen cast his gaze at the ground. "I suppose we Germans were too enamored with a man who had led us out of the gloom of the depression and the stranglehold of the Treaty of Versailles to realize the salvation he offered was only an illusion. I am afraid the German nation will tumble back into a pit of blackness now."

Jürgen fell silent, as though contemplating a future without hope.

Mo decided to change the subject. "Well, about me, you asked. I'm from California. Grew up on a citrus farm in a place called the San Fernando Valley. I don't have a wife or kids, but, like you, I want to return home. And then I want to find me a gal and start a family. I want to go back to school, too."

"You were in school when the war began?"

"Yes, I graduated from Cal Tech—the California Institute of Technology—with a degree in engineering. And I was just thinking, it was on a spring break a few years ago in San Diego that I saw B-24s landing and taking off at Lindbergh Field, and that's when I decided I wanted to learn how to fly them. So I did. And now I want to study aeronautical engineering."

"Will you go back to Cal Tech?"

"Maybe. But it's expensive. Perhaps I'll try a public university, maybe Michigan or Washington."

"I wish you well, my friend."

"But the jets," Mo said, "you must tell me about the jets. I guess you won't be shot for giving away military secrets, will you?"

"No, you Americans will have them soon enough . . . if you don't already." He took another swallow of coffee, his hand again quivering. After he'd finished the sip, he tossed the remainder of the coffee into the bushes and set the cup on the log. "Got a Lucky?" he asked.

"Lucky Strike? No." Mo reached into a pocket of his flight jacket and retrieved a pack of cigarettes. "A Chesterfield?" He shook one from the pack and extended it to Jürgen.

Jürgen smiled. "That is right. You listened to Glenn Miller broadcasts sponsored by Chesterfield." Shakily, he placed the cigarette in his mouth. Mo reached over with a lighter and lit it.

Jürgen took a long drag and exhaled, the smoke mingling with the fog of his breath in the chilly morning air.

"We called it die Schwable, the Swallow," he said. "As General Galland said after he first flew one, 'It is as if angels are pushing you.'"

"The jet?" Mo asked. "The Me-262?"

"Yes."

"I can't imagine. I'm a bomber pilot."

"You know, when the Me-262 first went into production in the spring of 1944, Hitler and that fat fool, Göring, insisted it be used as a bomber." Jürgen shook his head slowly as if recalling a disappointing memory.

"Why a bomber?"

"I am not sure. I suppose they saw it as an unstoppable means of delivering payback to the Allies for their devastating air campaign against Germany." He took another long puff from the Chesterfield and stared at Mo. "You killed hundreds of thousands of civilians, you know."

Mo didn't respond. Instead, he polished off his coffee—rapidly cooling —in two big gulps.

"But that is war, I suppose," Jürgen said. "Let us hope and pray it is over. Anyhow, many of our senior fighter pilots, led by General Galland, who commanded the German fighter force, realized the real value of the jets would be in employing them against your bombers. There was no way the piston-driven fighters escorting your bombers could stand up against the Me-262."

"I know that all too well," Mo mumbled rather gruffly.

"Galland and other senior Luftwaffe officers constantly locked horns with Göring. That culminated in what became known as the Fighter Pilots Revolt in January. That is when a group of Galland's allies confronted Göring and suggested he step down from his position as commander-in-chief of the Luftwaffe."

"I'm sure that was well received."

Jürgen issued a sardonic laugh. "Göring ordered the pilots executed, Galland included. But since most of the aviators had become national heroes by then, he later thought better of it. Instead, he offered Galland command of a squadron of jets configured as fighters, and pilots of his choosing, figuring they would all be killed in combat within a few months."

"Nice guy, your air force commander. So, did you become part of that squadron?"

"Yes, me and other experienced pilots—a lot of aces—all picked by General Galland. We became known as the Der Galland-Zirkus, the Galland Circus. But you know what? We proved a point. With the experience we had and the capabilities of the jet, we ended up with a four-to-one kill ratio over American aircraft."

Mo whistled softly.

"Even Göring was impressed. In fact, he admitted—much too late—that Galland was right. Die Schwable was better suited as a fighter than a bomber. And to everyone's surprise, Göring said he wanted to fly one in combat. But by that stage of the war, he was in no physical shape to do so."

The platoon around Mo and Jürgen began awakening. Yawns, groans, and muted curses broke the dawn silence.

"This guy, Galland—" Mo said.

"Adolf Galland," Jürgen interjected.

"Yes. He sounds like an interesting character."

Jürgen smiled. "Understatement. He was promoted to what would be your equivalent of a brigadier general when he was only thirty. He was the youngest general officer in the Wehrmacht. His men loved him. He was a superb pilot and a great leader, a man of integrity. But he did—how do you say it?—march to the beat of a different drummer."

Mo nodded.

"In 1937, he joined the Condor Legion and flew ground attack missions in the Spanish Civil War in support of Franco's Nationalists. His plane, a Heinkel He-51, an open-cockpit biplane, had a cartoon Mickey Mouse painted on its nose. And sometimes Galland went into combat with a cigar clamped between his teeth and wearing swimming trunks."

"Swimming trunks? Really?"

"Different drummer. But he was a truly exceptional pilot. He was eventually awarded a Knight's Cross with Oak Leaves, Swords, and Diamonds."

"Is that like an Iron Cross?"

"Bigger deal, my friend. You cannot get an award much higher than a Knight's Cross with Oak Leaves, Swords, and Diamonds."

"He had a few kills, I take it?"

"When he took command of the German fighter force, he had over ninety, but was barred from further combat at that point. Hitler did not want his generals getting killed. Galland was not happy about that. But he got some additional tallies once he took over JV-44. I guess he ended up with around a hundred."

"Good grief."

"Mostly Brits."

"And you. How many kills? Including *Rub-A-Dub*?"

"I am not in the same league as the greatest aces, nor would I want to be, I suppose. You know, there was one pilot, a Major Erich Hartmann, who had over three hundred and fifty kills. Primarily Soviets. They called him the Black Devil. To us, he was 'Bubi.' But let's not talk about kills anymore."

Jim strolled up to the two pilots. "I hope you slept well, gentlemen. We'll be departing just after sunrise . . . in about half an hour." He tossed each man a packet of K-rations. "Breakfast. Enjoy."

As Mo and Jürgen went to work on their "breakfasts," Mo said, "You told me yesterday you'd flown out of Munich. I thought our air forces had destroyed virtually all of the Luftwaffe bases."

"Yes. Your bombers have been quite efficient. Our squadron—the few planes we were able to get operational anyhow—was flying out of what was left of the Munich-Riem airport, once the most modern commercial terminal in the world. When it opened in 1939, it seemed to unlatch the gates to the world. From Bavaria, one could fly anywhere. How does the song go? Stairway to the Stars? Yes, it seemed like a stairway to the stars."

"There ya go. Glenn Miller and Ray Eberle. Ella Fitzgerald. The Ink Spots."

"Good times." Jürgen's voice, soft and empty, seemed to echo from the past.

"Maybe coming again."

"Not for Germany."

Mo felt a moment of sadness for Jürgen, but it hadn't been America that had started the war.

"So the squadron got to Munich?" he said, more of a question than a statement.

"We had to get away from Berlin. The Red Army was on our doorstep. Galland decided on Munich-Riem. I remember flying there in early April. The wonderful terminal and its classical architecture had been pockmarked by shrapnel and shells, its roof had been bombed away, water had pooled on the floor of the reception area, and all the glass had been blown from the windows in the control tower. So sad."

No, not so sad, Mo thought, *a testament to Allied air power.* "So you didn't have much to operate with?"

"We used an abandoned orphanage about two kilometers from the field as our headquarters, an old shed with camouflage netting draped over it for our alert shack, and we, ourselves, dug out blast pens for the jets—U-shaped earthen works. After a mission, we would help the mechanics push the aircraft into them, noses facing out. But we knew we were operating on borrowed time."

"But the Swallow, as you call it, sounds like it could have turned the tide of the war." Mo wondered how close the Germans had come to reversing their fortunes.

Jürgen shrugged. "Probably not. There were too many problems. We built over fourteen hundred of them, but only three hundred ever saw combat, and there were probably only two hundred that were airworthy at any one time. We were the last operational squadron in the Luftwaffe. We had twenty-five planes at one point, but never more than six were operational at once."

"What were the problems?"

"Fuel shortages, a dearth of good mechanics and airframe specialists, and the fact we had to keep relocating and hiding the planes as the Allies advanced. Also, the engines were junk. They were superbly engineered, but constructed of low-grade metals because we did not have access to the good stuff. A brand-new engine had a lifespan of twenty-eight hours. A rebuilt one, just ten."

Jürgen inhaled his Chesterfield, exhaled, coughed. But he now held the cigarette in a steadier grasp.

"With the lousy engines," he went on, "you never knew when they might quit on you. We learned to keep our hands off the throttle in a dogfight—an abhorrent thought to a fighter pilot—because rapid changes in the engine's internal speed would cause it to snuff out like a candle in a wind gust. So. The truth is we had a fearsome weapon but lacked the logistics to make it war worthy."

"I guess we, the Allies, dodged a bullet, so to speak."

"Maybe, maybe not. I think the Me-262 probably arrived too late in the war to make much difference even had it been a robust weapons system. But enough about the jet. Tell me about you. Like your plane's name. Americans love naming their planes, do they not? Why is that?"

Mo chuckled. "Esprit de corps, I guess. Better to be able to identify yourself as a crewman on *Rub-a-Dub-Dub* than on a B-24 bomber based at Seething, England."

Jürgen laughed. "*Rub-a-Dub-Dub*? What on earth is that?"

"Well, it's the plane you shot down."

Jürgen ceased his laughter. "I am sorry our acquaintance began that way. Truly. I trust your crew bailed out safely."

"As far as I know. I stayed with the aircraft a bit longer, trying to make sure it didn't pile into a village that appeared in its path."

Jürgen gazed at Mo intently. Then he reached out and laid a hand on his forearm. "You are an honorable man, Mo. You would have been welcomed into the Luftwaffe."

"Wrong team," Mo responded.

"But brothers in the air."

"Maybe in another time and place."

"Yes. So tell me about *Rub-a-Dub-Dub*. The name. I do not understand it." Jürgen sat back and stubbed out his Chesterfield. "I know all your American bombers have names and cartoon nose art. For those of us in the Luftwaffe who understand English, many are humorous, some even a little, how do you say, suggestive?"

Mo chuckled. "Our wives and sweethearts wouldn't necessarily approve of some of the images and names we christen our planes with."

"No. But some are rather clever. And do not tell the Gestapo I said that. I seem to recall one called *Hitler's Hearse* and another one named *Plunder Bus*. A play on words. Oh, and there was a B-17 that went by *Wabbit Twacks*. What on earth is that all about?"

"Have you ever heard of Elmer Fudd?"

Jürgen shook his head.

"Elmer Fudd is a cartoon character. With a speech impediment. He can't pronounce r's. And he's always hunting a cartoon rabbit, or wabbit, as he calls it. Bugs Bunny."

"I guess I needed to be more immersed in your culture."

"Elmer and Bugs probably came along after you left the States."

"But what about your plane, *Rub-a-Dub-Dub*?"

"My *former* plane?"

Jürgen sighed. "Yes. Former."

"Well, to answer your question, there's an old nursery rhyme, English, I think, that goes something like, 'Rub-a-dub-dub, three men in a tub; the butcher, the baker, the candlestick maker.' So on the crew of our B-24—the tub—we had a butcher, a baker, and—"

"And a candlestick maker," Jürgen said brightly.

"No. Not a candlestick maker. A furniture maker from North Carolina. Hamilton Morris from Hickory. He was our tail gunner." Mo remembered something and shook his head. A sad remembrance. "He was yelling through the interphone that trying to shoot down your damn German jets was like trying to blast lightning bolts out of the sky. Anyhow, we decided a furniture maker was close enough to a candlestick maker that we'd name our 'tub' after the nursery rhyme."

"Let us hope, captain, that in the future we do not have to worry about shooting lightning bolts from the sky or punching holes in bombers in which butchers, bakers, and furniture makers ride . . . or even wabbits." He smiled at Mo.

"Or even wabbits," Mo agreed.

Dim morning light at last filtered into where Mo and Jürgen sat. From the surrounding forest came the first peeps of early-awakening birds.

Jim appeared and signaled to the two men it was time to depart. They stood.

"Gentlemen, you are welcome to ride with me in my Jeep," Jim said. He spoke to Jürgen. "Remember, sir, you are still technically a prisoner, so you will not have a weapon." And then to Mo. "You are responsible for him, Captain Nesmith, so I hope you are comfortable with your decision not to turn him over to battalion."

"I am, lieutenant. We'll be fine."

"As far as our mission today goes, I don't expect any trouble. We've been tasked to search for a big ammo depot that is supposedly hidden someplace in the area, although we don't have any specifics as to where that might be. Anyhow, since battalion is to our immediate rear now, I don't expect we'll have anybody sneaking up from behind us. We'll have our two half-tracks lead the way when we shove off and we'll be Tail-End-Charlie in the Jeep, if I may use Air Forces lingo."

Mo nodded and flashed a quick smile.

Jim addressed Jürgen again. "Keep the pot on your head and the field jacket buttoned up. I don't want anybody mistaking you for a German who's snuck into our ranks." He laughed lightly. "I've seen enough death to last me for a lifetime, and the last thing I want is to have to deal with anymore now that we're about finished with this nastiness."

"I agree, lieutenant," Jürgen said. "No more death."

12

The hamlet of Parzham
Western Austria
May 4, 1945

Frieda Mayr stood by the window of the cottage she and Karl shared, nibbling on a slice of Schinken while peering out at the sunlit early morning and wondering if Karl would return today. He'd promised to send someone from the DP Movement Center he commanded to check on her in his absence, but no one had shown up yesterday. *Maybe today*, she thought. *On the other hand, Karl could be back by evening, so what difference would it make?*

She didn't like being alone, but at least it wouldn't be for long. Karl had promised her "only a day or two." And he'd reassured her that the rumors wafting through the village like smoke from distant fires carried no bases in truth. The German Reich remained strong, and the Allies knew their best —no, their only—weapon was the spread of fear through the civilian population, not with explosives but with words.

Still, it was Karl's description of their enemies as brutal and ruthless and barbaric that frightened her . . . if they ever did show up. He told her what they did to women. Warned her. They took them captive, held them as slaves—sex slaves—then discarded them once they had fulfilled the Allies' carnal needs. But they didn't just toss them away or let them go. They eviscerated them, cut off their arms and legs and breasts and fed them to pigs and dogs. It was that kind of bestiality that the German Wehrmacht fought against, would rally against, and would ultimately prevail against.

She walked to the front door, opened it, drew in a lungful of fresh, cool air, and shielded her eyes against the low, slanting rays of the sun. It was just beginning to lift above the roofs of the small homes and buildings nestled shoulder-to-shoulder along the hamlet's "main" street. Smoke rose vertically from a few chimneys in the stillness of the disappearing dawn.

But something unusual met her gaze and she gasped, not understanding. A number of the homes displayed white flags—linens, bedsheets, towels—on makeshift poles or draped from balconies. She snapped her hand over her mouth, stunned. White flags of surrender? Capitulation? She didn't understand.

An ox cart clattered along the road in front of the cottage. Old Lukas, an ancient farmer who'd apparently been a fixture in Parzham for decades, sat in the seat of the wagon urging on an ox that looked older than Methuselah. Frieda darted to intercept the elderly man.

"Lukas, my friend, what is happening?" She pointed into the village at the flags.

Lukas pulled back on the reins and the ox halted.

"My dear, you haven't heard? The Americans are coming."

"No, no," she said, her voice shrill and constricted. "Rumors. Rumors."

"Not rumors. Americans are in Hörbach. An SS battalion surrendered to them there yesterday. I know. I saw them with my own eyes. I went there this morning to deliver some vegetables to an old friend. The town was filled with American soldiers."

"No, Lukas. That cannot be true. My—" she wondered what she should call Karl and decided on husband "—husband told me the Germans will soon launch a major counterattack and that the Russians and Allies will have their offensives blunted and be pushed out of the Greater German Reich."

Lukas removed a wide-brimmed straw hat—one that looked more like a colander than a hat—from his head, ran his fingers through his thick, white hair, then placed the hat back on his head.

"That may be difficult to do, my dear, now that most of the Wehrmacht has been taken prisoner by or surrendered to the Allies and Russians."

"Hörbach, you said? The Americans are in Hörbach?" Frieda asked, not accepting what Lukas had just told her.

He nodded.

"Mein Gott, mein Gott. That is only eight kilometers from here." Terror suddenly rippled through her body like a powerful eddy in a river. Her bowels loosened. "I'm going to be sick, Lukas, I must go." She turned and sprinted toward the cottage.

"White flag, my dear, white flag," Lukas called after her. "The Americans, they will not harm you."

They will dismember me. She made it to the toilet with no time to spare. She sat there for a long while, panting, her heart hammering like an artillery barrage. She had no idea what to do. She wondered if she had the courage to take her own life. She had no gun, but she could slash her wrists, set herself ablaze, or fling herself at the Americans with such fierceness and abandon they would think she was attacking them and be forced to shoot her. *Yes, yes, I can do that.* She imagined—well, hoped—such a death would be swift and relatively painless.

She composed herself, washed her hands, brushed her hair, and walked to the kitchen. She withdrew a large butcher knife from a drawer, then stepped back outside into the morning sun. Birds swooped in pursuit of insects for breakfast, greening tree leaves rustled in a soft breeze, and honeybees rode lazy thermals from flowerbed to flowerbed. Knife at her side, she waited for the Americans.

She attempted to reconcile what Karl had told her with what Lukas had just related. Had Karl lied or just been mistaken? It gnawed at her that no one from the DP Movement Center had come to check on her. Could Karl have lied about that, too, about arranging for an officer to drop by and ascertain her welfare? Her comfortable little world, which had seemed so sturdy only yesterday, was crumbling into pieces like a medieval parchment.

Her hand holding the knife began to tremble. Her knees wobbled as if she stood on stilts. Clenching her jaw, she resolved not to let the Americans take her alive, defile her, brutalize her. Tears filled her eyes as she wondered why Karl had left her alone. *He must have known, he must have known.* She stifled a sob. Then she heard them.

The Americans. The clatter of tracked vehicles. The thrum of gasoline engines. She watched as two tracked vehicles—wheels in front, metal treads in the rear—rattled down the lane that ran in front of her cottage. A Jeep followed.

She said a prayer, drew a deep breath, and moved closer to the edge of the road. The two tracked vehicles, full of soldiers—yes, Americans—rumbled past her. She gasped. Even seeing the enemy with her own eyes, she couldn't believe it. The Jeep, bringing up the rear of the little column, approached her and stopped.

Four men sat in it. Two in front, two in back. The driver, an NCO she presumed, got out and walked toward her.

"Grüß Gott," he said.

He speaks German? Austrian German? The knife quivered violently in her hand as she tried to raise the weapon. Her knees buckled as she attempted to execute her planned attack. She tripped over a cobblestone and sprawled onto the road, the knife skittering away from her, out of reach. Her world went black.

But light returned. She opened her eyes and stared into the blueness of the overhead. Her throbbing head felt as if it were being cradled in someone's arms. A voice spoke to her in German.

"Are you all right, Fräulein?"

The American soldier. "Don't kill me, please don't kill me," she whimpered, her words coming out as more of a croak than a genuine plea.

"Don't be afraid of us. We are not going to hurt you. You've no need for a knife."

"You can have me," she whimpered, "do with me as you please. But I beg you, leave me whole. I will do your bidding. Always. You can trust me."

She sensed someone dabbing at her head with a rag or cloth. The American-accented voice spoke again. "Nasty cut you've got there. We'll get a bandage on it, then help you back to your house."

"You aren't going to . . . use me?" she whispered. "Kill me?" Her breath came in short, sharp gasps. Fear still gripped her with the fierceness of an angry gorilla.

Three men stood over her now, officers, apparently, while the soldier she presumed to be an NCO tended to the wound on her head. One of the officers appeared rail thin and quite young. The second looked older, a pilot maybe. The third seemed older than the other two. Perhaps he was the one in charge. He remained silent as the NCO talked to the young officer.

The NCO spoke to her again. In broken German. "Don't worry, Fräulein. We will do you no harm. Why are you so frightened of us?"

"My husband warned me. That our enemies are animals. Barbaric."

"I don't think your husband knows us very well. Is he present?"

She shook her head.

"Well, no matter. We'll help you back to your house, then be on our way."

Two sets of arms helped her stand. With the NCO on one side of her, and the older officer on the other, they helped her back into the cottage. She remained stiff and tense, and she knew the two men sensed that. She remained far from convinced they meant her no harm.

They settled her into a threadbare armchair.

"May I get you a cup of water, Fräulein?" the officer—the one who hadn't previously spoken—asked in almost perfect German.

She stared at him, stunned. "You are German?"

He nodded. He spread open the field jacket he wore so she could see the Luftwaffe wings on his flight uniform. "Major Jürgen Voigt, Jagdverband 44."

"A traitor," she whispered.

Jürgen sighed. "No. A prisoner of war. But I surrendered willingly. The war is over, Fräulein. Germany has lost. A formal surrender is only days, if not hours, away. My primary duty now is to assist the Americans in gaining as much territory and gathering as much equipment as they can from the Reich before the Red Army can gobble it up. Now that we are here, you and your fellow townsfolk should be safe from the Soviets, yes?"

She nodded, but remained unsure she was truly safe. Her thoughts continued to be scrambled. She still could not believe the Americans had appeared so swiftly.

Major Voigt walked to the kitchen. On the way, he stopped and examined some military plaques and framed documents that hung on the pine-paneled walls. In the kitchen, he retrieved a porcelain cup and filled it with water. He returned to where Frieda sat, knelt by her side, and handed her the cup. "I see that your husband is in the SS. A Hauptsturmführer Karl Jagensdorf."

"Yes, but he is not my husband. He is my . . . betrothed." A sense of pride swelled within her.

"I see. Do you know where he is?"

"No."

"It's all right, Fräulein. You won't be giving away any secrets. As I said, the war is all but over."

Then is my Karl still alive? Fear once again grasped her in a chest-crushing grip. "He . . . he said he was going to Innsbruck for a meeting."

In English, Jürgen spoke to the NCO, then in German to Frieda. "It's likely that Innsbruck has already fallen to the Americans, or is about to. If your SS officer is wise and honorable, I suspect he has surrendered and is safe."

"He is that, sir. He is a fine gentleman. Do you think he will be treated well by the Americans?"

"I do." He stood. "I must take your leave now, Fräulein. Be well."

He turned to go, but the NCO stopped him. They entered into a brief conversation. Jürgen pivoted back to Frieda.

"I wonder," he said, "if you could tell me what the Hauptsturmführer did, what his job was?"

She hesitated, still uncertain about speaking to the Americans. And a German who helped them. On the other hand, Karl's job had been an honorable one, helping others. "He commanded a DP Movement Center."

"Oh, and what is that, if I may ask?"

"An organization that helps displaced persons—war refugees—find places of shelter or new homes."

"Commendable. Do you know where this center is located?" The Luft-waffe's officer's tone of voice sounded somehow skeptical.

"Not specifically. Karl never told me. But it must be someplace nearby. Perhaps in or near the town of Gunskirchen."

"And that is where?"

"About three kilometers east of here." She paused, then went on. "The people in the center—what will become of them if the German Wehrmacht is no longer there to help them?"

"If we come across the center, I'm sure the Americans will render whatever assistance they can to the refugees, so do not worry. One more question. Did the Hauptsturmführer ever mention anything about an ammunition depot? We are searching for one that we were informed may be somewhere in the area."

"No, never. He only talked about the DP Center, and not much about that."

"So, he never hinted at any other spots where troops or supplies might have been located nearby?"

"No. You understand, I had no need to know of such things."

The Luftwaffe officer nodded and stood. He thanked her for her help, clicked his heels—like an old-school gentlemen would—and departed with the American NCO.

She sat alone in the empty cottage, her head pulsating, her thoughts jumbled, her emotions scrambled. She felt abandoned, but managed to convince herself that Karl would somehow return for her. He would carry her off to Landshut and they would resume their lives together, allowing memories of the war to fade into the dust of time. They would have children and grandchildren, travel the world, embrace friends, and grow old together. They would be soulmates and lovers even as they stepped into eternity.

He was such a good man.

Her chin dipped against her chest as she nodded off in the warmth of the spring sun that now beamed through a window into the interior of the cottage.

All will be well with the world, she thought.

13

East of Parzham, Austria
May 4, 1945

Jim moved his Jeep to the front of the patrol and studied a map while Bowerman drove.

"These maps are worthless," he groused. "Half the roads around here aren't even on them, and the ones that are aren't necessarily depicted correctly."

"We're just gonna have to go potluck then, I guess," Bowerman said, "pick roads at random, drive down 'em for a bit, and see what we can find. If anything."

"Well, with no intel, I don't have any better ideas."

The Jeep bounced and jumped along a rutted dirt road, the so-called main road, as the platoon headed southeast out of Parzham. Jim struggled to stay in his seat. Behind the Jeep, the half-tracks wallowed along like baby hippos negotiating rugged terrain.

In the rear of the Jeep, Major Voigt leaned forward and asked Bowerman a question. "Sergeant, what did you think of the Fräulein's portrayal of the SS officer she lives with?"

"She didn't seem to know much." He had to raise his voice to be heard over the rattling of the Jeep and the growl of its engine.

"I do not think she does. But I found her description of his job, well, somewhat puzzling."

"Sir?"

"I have never heard of the Wehrmacht, particularly the SS running a . . . what did she call it?"

"A Displaced Persons Movement Center."

"Yes. Odd."

The Jeep slammed into a large pothole and all the riders became briefly airborne.

"Shit, sorry," Bowerman said.

After the ride smoothed out, Jim turned to Major Voigt. "So you don't think the SS officer was running such an operation?"

"As I said, it just sounded a bit unusual. Especially with hostilities virtually at an end."

"So he could have been in charge of something else?" Jim said.

"Quite so."

"Like an ammunition depot?"

"Why not?"

"But the Fräulein had no idea where 'her' officer worked?"

"She did not seem to."

"She could have been bluffing."

"Of course. But if she was, she was very good at it."

"Maybe," Bowerman said, injecting himself into the conversation, "we should go back and ask the Fräulein a few more questions. Perhaps a bit more forcefully."

"No," Jim responded, "our assignment is to find an ammo depot, not act like the Gestapo."

Another few minutes brought them to a narrow track that connected perpendicularly to the road they'd been following. "Let's try this one," Jim said. The tiny convoy turned left and rolled across a greening meadow sprinkled with colorful wildflowers.

From the meadow, the patrol edged into a stand of hardwoods—beech and oak—and moved carefully along a narrow path, barely wide enough for vehicles.

"Don't look like this has been used much," Bowerman said.

"Yeah," Jim agreed, "soon as we get to a wide spot, turn around."

They popped out into another meadow, performed a one-eighty, and headed back to the road they'd originally been on.

Several more trips down side roads and lanes brought similar results. Nothing. Sometimes the roads merely petered out, forcing the patrol to back out. Other times, the paths would lead to a dead end—a creek, a cliff, a stone wall. Jim's frustration mounted steadily.

The morning, under a burning sun, grew noticeably warmer. No friendly white cumulus showed up to block its warming rays.

Jim, exasperated at the lack of progress, wiped sweat from his brow and tossed the map into the footwell of the Jeep. "Worthless," he grumbled. "There's a spiderweb of roads and lanes and paths around here and nothing is marked or mapped. The war could be over before we ever turn up anything."

Up ahead, a road branched off to the right and appeared to climb toward a forested hill.

"Whaddaya think, sir?" Bowerman said. "Try it? It looks like it's had a little traffic on it. I mean, at least it's been used recently."

"Sure. Go for it."

The patrol once again rolled off the primary road and headed toward . . . what? The Jeep and half-tracks plunged into the cooling shadows of the forest and followed the road around the brow of the hill and then into a shallow vale where a small stream burbled busily over a rocky bed. Sunshine glinted, like white sparks, off the surface of the water. The road turned to parallel the creek and eventually brought the patrol into a tiny clearing and a small, undoubtedly private, sawmill.

Jim signaled for the vehicles to stop and shut off their engines. They did. He remained seated in the Jeep, listening. From deep in the woods came the ring of an ax biting into timber. The sound ceased, and shortly a man wearing a flannel shirt, leather pants, and sturdy work boots appeared. A broad-brimmed, low-crowned Tyrolean hat covered a tangle of stringy gray hair. He carried a double-bladed ax that rested on his shoulder.

He approached the Jeep but halted some distance from it.

Jim dismounted and, with Bowerman at his side, walked toward the man who seemed neither threatening nor welcoming. He did, however, appear circumspect of his visitors.

Jim spoke to Bowerman. "Reminds me of home, of Oregon."

"How so?"

"The heavy timber, the smell of fresh-cut logs, of sawdust."

"Grüß Gott," Bowerman said to the man with the ax.

The man nodded but didn't return the greeting.

Bowerman continued speaking to him in German and the man listened intently. After Bowerman had finished, the man responded with a rather lengthy statement.

While he talked, Jim scanned the small operation. He saw what he assumed to be the house where the logger lived. In an adjacent shed, he spotted additional double-bladed axes, a couple of crosscut saws—what loggers in the Pacific Northwest called "misery whips"—and a stable that housed a trio of oxen. Yokes and chains hung on the wall of the shed. The oxen, Jim figured, were used to drag the timber the logger cut from the forest to the sawmill. The sawmill itself boasted a large vertical saw that appeared to be powered by a waterwheel. A set of exquisitely crafted wooden gears linked the waterwheel to the levers and pulleys that drove the saw. To Jim, it seemed amazingly clever.

As the logger continued to talk, a figure emerged from the house and walked toward the gathering. As it drew closer, it morphed into a young woman, perhaps in her twenties. She was dressed similarly to the man in leather pants and boots. She moved to a position next to the man. She appeared lithe but muscular, albeit a bit underfed.

Jim swatted away swarms of flies—probably attracted by the piles of ox dung that dotted the grounds around the mill—as he waited for the man to complete telling Bowerman whatever it was he was relating.

Finally finished, Bowerman translated for Jim.

"The old coot's name is Otto. This is his sawmill. He and his daughter, Amelie, run the thing. His wife died 'bout ten years ago, and the Germans drafted his son, Oskar, into the Wehrmacht, so just he and Amelie are left."

"What happened to his son?" Jim asked.

Bowerman addressed the question to Otto.

Otto shrugged and spoke briefly, a wistful look forming on his weather-beaten face.

"He doesn't know. He ain't heard from him in several years."

"Tell him we're sorry," Jim said.

Bowerman spoke again to Otto, who looked at Jim and began talking once more, a hint of anger in his inflection.

After he'd finished, Bowerman said, "He hates Germans. He said he'll be happy when they leave and Austria can become Austria again. Not part of the fuckin'—his word—German Reich."

"Tell him they should be leaving soon, that the war is just about over. And ask him—just out of my curiosity—how he operates his mill."

The question launched Otto into another extended explanation.

When he'd finished, Bowerman explained to Jim.

"He says he cuts down the timber—mostly pine, but some oak and spruce, too—and uses the oxen to drag the logs out of the woods to the mill. Amelie runs the saw and cuts the logs into boards. The boards can be fashioned into poles or stakes, or just left as boards. His clients are farmers and townspeople who live nearby. He says they don't make much money, but enough to get by on. At least until the Germans showed up.

"They, the Wehrmacht, helped themselves to whatever provisions they wanted—food, money, supplies—and told him it was his 'contribution' to the Greater German Reich. Or thievin' Huns, he calls them."

Jim studied Otto and Amelie. They didn't appear to be starving, but seemed clearly emaciated. Their faces were drawn and creased, probably from both lack of proper nourishment and difficult labor in the harsh environment of the woods.

"Tell him," Jim said, "I salute his and his daughter's hard work. Explain to him it reminds me of my home in Oregon and the great forests there."

Otto smiled as Bowerman spoke, then he turned to Jim. "Ory-gone," he said, "Ja, ja. Dooglas fir. Here, too. Up, up." He pointed in the direction of the Alps.

"Yes, Dooglas fir," Jim responded. "Higher elevations?"

Otto nodded, although Jim wasn't sure he'd understood completely. He reached into his pocket and extracted another Hershey bar. He handed it to

Otto, saying, "It's not much, but maybe it'll give you and your daughter a little extra energy today."

Bowerman translated.

Otto wasted no time in opening the chocolate, breaking the bar in half, and sharing it with Amelie. "Danke, danke," he said. "So gut, so gut."

"You got an endless supply of those things, lieutenant?" Mo asked from the Jeep.

"Last one," Jim said. He turned to Bowerman. "Okay, time to get down to business here. Ask Otto if he knows anything about an ammo depot in the area."

Otto shook his head as the sergeant asked the question, then spoke.

"He says no," Bowerman said, "but he wonders since the Germans are on their way out, if we wouldn't like to stay here and help protect him and his daughter from the Russian pigs, since he hears rumors they're going to replace the Krauts."

"Tell him, no. We must press on. But tell him to be careful and keep a close watch on anyone else coming down this road."

Jim climbed back into the Jeep as Bowerman finished speaking with Otto and Amelie.

As the sergeant took his position in the Jeep, Otto walked to where Jim sat and spoke in German.

"What did he say?" Jim asked Bowerman.

From the rear seat, Jürgen said, "He said he wants to tell us that the Germans, a few months ago, were here and made him and Amelie work extra hours to cut much lumber for them. Even some of the soldiers pitched in to help."

"Does he know what the lumber was to be used for?"

Jürgen and Otto exchanged sentences.

"No," Jürgen said, "just that they needed a lot of it quickly."

"Does he know where it went?"

"Not that, either. All he knows is he and Amelie worked hard and got no pay. Then, just as suddenly as they showed up, the Germans were gone."

Jim sat back in his seat and thought about it. He turned to the two officers in the rear. "So, does that sound like something that could be used to help construct an ammo depot?"

"No," Mo said, "I think you'd want something more substantial than wooden storage facilities. You'd probably want to build concrete bunkers reinforced with steel."

"But you would need troops to guard such a place," Jürgen said, "so maybe the wood could have been used to construct barracks."

Bowerman chimed in, "Ya know, wood might do it for bunkers, though, if ya was buildin' an underground storage depot. Ya know, to shore up walls and stuff."

"Well, any of those are good possibilities, gentlemen. But we still don't have any idea where to look."

"But it makes the likelihood there's a storage depot around here someplace seem a lot more plausible," Mo offered.

"Ask Otto where the nearest concrete plant is," Jim said.

Jürgen did, then said, "He is not sure, but thinks it would be in a bigger town where there would be more business. So perhaps in Wels, but more likely Linz."

"Which direction would that be?" Jim asked.

"North of here," Jürgen said, without consulting Otto.

"Okay, north it is," Jim said to Bowerman. "Let's go."

"Onward and downward," Bowerman muttered.

He cranked up the Jeep and, half-tracks following, headed back to the titular main road. Bouncing and jouncing and hopping, of course. A bone-cracking ride

They reconnoitered a half dozen more side roads—paths really—but to no avail.

Back on the primary road, Jim caught a glimpse of something glinting in the sun several hundred meters ahead of them and signaled for the vehicles to halt.

"That doesn't look right," he said to Bowerman.

"I see it, sir. Could be sunlight reflectin' off field glasses. Certainly somethin' shiny that don't belong."

The men waited and watched. The reflective glint moved, then disappeared.

"Let's move up on foot and see what's going on," Jim said.

Jim and Bowerman walked slowly toward where they'd seen the brightness. Jim, .45 in hand, took the right side of the road, Bowerman, his Thompson at the ready, walked on the left. As they neared the spot the reflection had come from, a helmeted figure rose from the tall grass bordering the road on the right. He held a rifle aloft with both his hands over his head. He yelled something that Jim didn't understand. It didn't sound like German.

"Holy cow jumped over the moon," Bowerman exclaimed. "A Ruskie."

Jim saw it now. A dirty brown uniform. A heavy, round steel helmet, also brown.

"Hey, GI," the Red Army soldier yelled. "Ve Vriend."

Other soldiers rose from the grass, one wearing a round fur hat with a red star insignia.

"Yes, friend," Bowerman called back in response.

"You 'Mericun, dah?" the Russian asked.

"American. 71st Infantry Division."

The Russian smiled. He kept his rifle held high as five other soldiers joined him, also holding their weapons above their heads.

"You understand Russian?" Jim asked Bowerman.

"No."

Jim motioned for the Russians to lower their weapons.

"Do you suppose the main Russian force has gotten this far west?" Bowerman said, "or do ya think this is just an advance patrol?"

"I suspect it's just a recon force. Only six guys and lightly armed."

The Russian who appeared to be in command of the small group stepped forward, said something in Russian, and shook hands with Jim and Bowerman. He appeared to be about thirty, lean and sunburned with an old wound on his cheek, and gnarled hands scratched and splotched with mud.

"Vriend, good zee," he said. He smiled again, revealing missing teeth.

"Yes, good to see you, too," Jim said. "Where are you going?"

The Russian cocked his head, apparently not understanding.

"What you do?" Jim tried.

"Look vor Deutsch. Kill Deutsch. You zee?"

Jim turned to Bowerman. "I think these guys are some kind of elite squad, living off the land and reconnoitering well in advance of the main

Red Army. I suspect we'd better keep them away from our logger friend and his daughter back there. These guys might not find their place, but I'm not sure good things would happen if they did."

"I agree, Loot. I don't think the Ruskies have much sympathy for anything German. Especially if they find a young lady livin' with just her dad in an isolated spot. No matter that Otto and Amelie are technically Austrian. I don't think that would make no never mind to these guys. Let's try to send 'em in a different direction."

"Roger that. Got any ideas?"

"Let me try, Boss."

"You're on."

Bowerman spoke to the Russian commander. "Many Deutsch soldiers that way." He turned and pointed to the northwest. "We see."

"Minnie?"

"Beaucoup. Viele." He opened and closed both hands twice to show twenty fingers.

The Russian seemed not to understand the hand signals.

"Try dvadtsat'," Jürgen said. He and Mo had left the Jeep and joined the confab with the Russians.

"*You* know Russian?" Jim asked, surprised.

"Nein, just to count a little bit."

Jim hoped the Russians didn't detect Jürgen's German accent. He decided they probably didn't since they seemed not to understand English. "Keep your jacket buttoned up," he reminded the Luftwaffe officer.

But the Red Army commander did seem to understand dvadtsat' and repeated the word.

"Dah, dvadtsat'," Jürgen confirmed. He turned and pointed the same direction Bowerman had. "Desyat' kilometer that way." He'd obviously picked up on the ploy Bowerman had come up with.

The Russian grinned broadly, stepped forward, and grasped Jürgen in a hearty bear hug. He released him, then signaled his men to move off down the road. "Bol'shoye hpasibo," he called over his shoulder as the little cadre strode away.

"What did you tell him?" Jim said to the German.

"Ten kilometers. That should keep them busy for awhile."

"Does he know he just embraced his mortal enemy?"

"Let us keep that our little secret."

Jim chuckled.

Jim's platoon once again rolled down the road, heading in the opposite direction the Russians had. He slumped back in the passenger seat of the Jeep, growing weary of the unit's fruitless search. The warming rays of the sun seemed to be subtlety nudging him into the land of Wynken, Blynken, and Nod.

"I'm ready to call it a day," he said to Bowerman. "It's almost noon. Let's take a long lunch break, relax, grab a smoke or two, and maybe the war will be over by later this afternoon."

"No argument from me, Loot."

They rolled past a faintly visible road on the left that led into a pine forest.

"Hold on," Bowerman said, "that looks interestin'."

"Like all the rest," Jim responded, not finding it at all interesting. All he could see were two parallel tracks, not recently used, that disappeared into a heavy stand of Austrian pines.

"No. Well, maybe. Let's make it our last hoorah for the mornin' and see what happens."

Jim grunted his assent. "Okay, sarge. We'll take the Jeep and let the rest of the platoon stand down. Grab the radio from Private Erickson and we'll go take a look. Let's just say I don't have high hopes."

He turned to the two aviators in the back seat of the Jeep. "You gentlemen like to accompany us, or are you ready for a break?"

"In for a dime, in for a dollar," Mo responded.

"Me, too," Jürgen said.

Five minutes later they found themselves creeping through the piney woods along an old vehicle track that grew fainter and fainter the deeper into the copse they plunged. Overhead, thick intertwining pine boughs blotted out the sunshine and cast the floor of the forest into deep, midday dusk.

After several more minutes, Jim said, "Hold up, shut off the engine."

Bowerman did and they sat in silence, listening.

"That's odd," Jim said.

"What?" Bowerman asked.

"Nothing. No sounds. Not even birds."

"Yeah, weird." Bowerman placed his Thompson on his lap.

Jim withdrew his Colt from its holster. He turned to look at Mo and Jürgen. He didn't say anything and they merely nodded in response to his tacit question.

"Okay," he said to Bowerman, keeping his voice low.

The sergeant restarted the engine. At a snail's pace, they continued down the dark road.

GUNSKIRCHEN LAGER

UPPER AUSTRIA

14

Gunskirchen, Austria
May 4, 1945

Bowerman held the Jeep at such a slow speed that the bumps and dips in the track they followed went unnoticed. Jim thought he caught movement deep in the pines once and lifted his Colt .45 into firing position. But nothing materialized. Maybe a soft breeze had merely moved the branch of a tree and caused a shadow to dance in the sunlight. He lowered his weapon. Bowerman continued to ease the Jeep along in the barely visible ruts.

Finally, the track became impassable, blocked by pines that stood like dark, towering spikes in the duff-covered forest floor. Bowerman parked the Jeep after turning it around, just in case they had to make a rapid exit back along the path they'd been following. The men dismounted.

Jim drew a deep breath. Stopped. Wrinkled his nose.

"What on earth?" he whispered.

A whiff of a stink unlike anything he'd ever encountered seared his nostrils.

"Not an ammo depot, that's for damn sure," Bowerman muttered.

"God, must be an old slaughterhouse around here," Mo said, his words barely audible.

A puff of a breeze wafted the reek away and the men moved on, pushing deeper—cautiously—into the pine forest. The thick canopy of the trees held the woods in deep shadow, a dimness that seemed unnatural on a bright spring day, almost as if they had entered uncharted land, a place devoid of light and life.

Jim thought of a medieval history class he'd taken at the University of Oregon. In ancient times, maps often carried sketches of mythical beasts to represent the guardians of unexplored territories. To warn of such dangers, mapmakers sometimes entered the inscription "Here Be Dragons." He wondered, idly, strangely, if they were stepping into a place where "there be dragons."

The men continued silently through the eerie dusk, treading softly over the pulpy floor of the forest. Jim sensed they had, indeed, entered a land where mythical creatures lurked, though he couldn't imagine for the life of him in what form they might be. He knew only—but had no idea why—that they were there.

Again, a fetid breath of air drifted over the men. They halted, puzzled, repulsed, unsure of what lay ahead.

Then a dragon stepped from the gloom. No, not a dragon. A human. No, not a human. Jim stared, stunned, realizing he couldn't classify it. A former human, perhaps? Skeletal. Crepe paper skin. Unwashed, Filthy. Stinking. Tatters of cloth hanging from its frame like wind-shredded flags on a stormy coast.

It—Jim had no idea whether it was a man or a woman—stumbled toward him, bony arms outstretched, hands gnarled, fingers curled like talons. Its mouth moved, but only a dry rasp reached Jim's ears.

More cadaverous beings materialized from the gloaming, some hobbling, some crawling, others walking, then falling, then picking themselves up only to fall again. All around them, motionless bodies lay in the forest. Not a few. Hundreds. Corpses.

Jim holstered his weapon, took a step back, unable to speak.

And then the stench swarmed over him. Permeating. Deep. Choking. He gagged, retreated another step. The reek engulfed him. Urine. Feces.

Vomit. Filth. Blood. Decay. And if they had odors—hopelessness, despair, anguish, despondency.

Jim slammed his forearm over his nose, but nothing prevented the smothering, choking stink from worming its way into his soul. He gagged again.

Bowerman spoke, his voice grating, choking. "Loot, Loot, my God, what is this, these things . . . these people?"

Jim didn't have an answer. He had no idea what they'd stumbled across.

The individual he'd first seen stood within a few feet of him. Bloody excrement stained his legs, welts and sores covered his arms, lice clung to his thin hair like morning dew on a patch of grass. He pointed a skeletal finger at Jim's canteen.

"Viz," the person rasped, "viz."

"Good God almighty," Mo said, "good God almighty." He took a few steps back, then turned and vomited onto the forest floor.

Jim extended his canteen to the emaciated being who'd requested it. The person took one swallow, choked, spit out the water, then collapsed onto the ground in front of Jim and wrapped his or her pencil-thin arms around Jim's ankles.

"Köszönöm, köszönöm," the person repeated in a scratchy, barely audible voice.

"He says thank you," another croaking voice said, this one from a man who had appeared from behind the individual at Jim's feet. The second person, like the first, appeared to be nothing more than a scarecrow, a caricature of a human being, though the scarecrows Jim had seen had been better dressed.

Jim looked around, attempting to assimilate what was happening, what he and the others had stumbled upon. The walking dead kept coming. Except not all walked. Some crawled. Others sat against tree trunks, too exhausted to move. No, not too exhausted—too close to death to move.

An overpowering stench continued to fill the air. Jim had smelled muddy barnyards before and absorbed the stink of freshly fertilized pastures. But compared to the reek that had replaced the oxygen where he now stood, such places would have been worthy of the pearly gates. He continued to hold his forearm tight beneath his nose, not that it helped. The stench would not relax its assault on his gag reflex.

The man who had spoken to him, stared at him, his gaze unfocused, neither grateful nor fearful. Blank. It mimicked what GIs had come to know as the "thousand-yard stare"—the vacant gaze of a traumatized combat soldier who fixated on a distant nothingness.

"WHO ARE YOU?" Jim finally croaked out. "Who are these people?"

Next to him, Jim heard one of "these people" begging Bowerman for a cigarette. Bowerman fumbled for one, handed it to the skeleton-with-skin who stood before him. The figure promptly slammed it into its mouth. Not to smoke it. To eat it.

"Hungarians, mostly," came the man's answer to Jim's question. His voice carried a sandpaper edge. "Hungarian Jews."

"Why are you here? What is this place?"

More and more people appeared. They pressed in on all sides of Jim, Bowerman, Mo, and Jürgen. It seemed they all wished to touch the men, to make certain they were real, not mirages or apparitions. Others wanted to shake their hands, hug them. Cloaked in their filth and vermin, and the rags that substituted for clothing, they appeared otherworldly. Not human. Only the tears in their eyes betrayed them as human.

"The Germans sent us here," the man responded to Jim. "We are . . . were . . . prisoners, you see."

"This is a prison camp? A work camp?"

"No."

Jim chanced to remove his hand from beneath his nose, but the overpowering stink of open latrines, decaying bodies, and seeping wounds caused him to retch. He clapped his hand over his nose again. This time with so much force he almost bloodied it.

"No," he blurted, "not a work camp?"

The Hungarian gestured with his hand at the carnal-house landscape. "Does it look like we could work? The Nazis sent us here to die. This is a death camp, pure and simple. That was its only function. It's called Gunskirchen Lager."

Jim nodded, at a loss for words. He scanned his surroundings again. Though he had initially thought he'd seen hundreds of bodies lying unburied in the mud and excrement that blanketed the ground, he now realized it was thousands.

He drew a shallow breath, removed his hand from his nose again, and asked Bowerman to contact headquarters for him on the radiotelephone. Jim's hand trembled as he took the handset from Bowerman and spoke to a corporal on the other end. He explained what they'd found and where.

"Are you requesting the assistance of another platoon, lieutenant?" came the response from the corporal.

"Did you not hear what I said," Jim snapped, latent anger at what he'd discovered bubbling to the surface of his psyche. "No, I don't want another damn platoon. I want at least a company. No . . . two companies. All the medics and docs you can find. All the rations and water you can jam into trucks. All the transportation you can round up. Listen closely. There are thousands of people here. Thousands. Many are dead. Many more will die before help can even get here. So we need assistance fast. Really fast. Over and out."

Jim asked the Hungarian his name.

"Zágon," he said.

"Jim," Jim responded, clamping his hand over his chest in an identifying gesture. "Where is the main camp? You at least had barracks . . . I hope."

"This way, follow please. But before we walk, could I have something to eat? Maybe piece of chocolate, or sausage bite? I have not for three days eaten."

"Nothing?"

"The guards left us three days past. Before they go, they give us each—in their infinite kindness—one lump of sugar. And loaf of moldy bread for seven or eight to share." Zágon issued a derisive snort.

Jim fished a dried fruit bar out of his K-rations packet and handed it to Zágon. The Hungarian bit off a small piece and swallowed it whole without chewing. He repeated the action several times. Within seconds the bar had disappeared.

Bowerman, Mo, and Jürgen also doled out K-rations to starving prisoners, some of whom did not handle the renewed, and abrupt, intake of food at all well. They would cram whatever they were given into their mouths, choking and gagging but forcing it down. To Jim's horror, several collapsed into the reeking gumbo of mud and filth and simply died. He realized too late their esophagi, likely constricted by starvation, simply could not handle the sudden reintroduction of solid food. Yes, they were starving to death. But if they ate too much, too quickly, they died anyhow.

Zágon led Jim and his men toward the main camp, waving his arms to part a path through what had become a teeming mass of malodorous humanity. It seemed they all wanted to touch, or at least glimpse, their liberators, their saviors. Those who could no longer stand merely sat in the quagmire of death that blanketed the ground and issued weak waves.

In the distance, a barbed wire fence materialized. Jim presumed it marked the boundary of the camp. They made slow progress toward the enclosure, pushing through the throngs of skeletal humanity that surrounded them, and stepping over dead bodies. Zágon noted bitterly that the last act of the dead had been to escape their prison and at least die as free men or women.

"You told me you came from Hungary," Jim said as they continued to slog through the muck. "What did you do there, what kind of work?"

"I was professor in university. I learn English so I could do research. Most Hungarians here are doctors, lawyers, scientists. So speak little English. But Nazis, they saw us only as criminals."

"Criminals? Why?"

"Because we worship under Star of David, not Christian cross."

Jim hoped—at least wanted to believe—that was an indictment of Nazis, not Christians.

"When did you arrive here?"

"Not long past. Few weeks. Before that we were in place called Mauthausen, a concentration camp east of here, maybe fifty-five kilometers. Very big. That was primary camp. But scores of littler camps in area, too. Many, many prisoners."

"Do you know how many?" Jim's boots made strange sucking-squishing sounds as he plodded behind Zágon through the mire, a foul quicksand of death. The only other noise that hung in the barely breathable air seemed to be the murmur of the newly liberated souls, sometimes punctuated by the cries of the sick begging for care, or the dying pleading for release from the agony of their existence.

Zágon shook his head in a negative response to Jim's query. When he did, Jim could see open sores on the back of his neck, lice wriggling through rivulets of blood and pus that seeped from them. "The Nazis did not confide with me," Zágon answered, an acidic edge to his sandpapery words, "but rumors told of maybe two hundred thousand men, women, and children coming to Mauthausen complex since it be open in 1938."

"How many here, in this place, Gunskirchen Lager, any idea?"

Zágon shrugged. "Thousands dead already. Gone. Many thousands, I think, sent here. We die fast, you know. Get to prison camp, maybe you survive for few months. Die early, if lucky. You know, before Nazis could work you to death, starve you, freeze you, throw you on electric fence, make medical experiments on you."

"Good God," Jim muttered. "Hold up, please." He suddenly felt as if he'd been flung into a spinning, airless universe. He knelt and bowed his head in order to keep from blacking out.

"Ya alright, Loot?" Jim felt Bowerman's hand on his shoulder.

"Yeah, yeah. Give me a minute." Slowly he regained his bearings, the sights and sounds and smells surrounding him coming back into focus and perception—the reality of having stumbled into a living nightmare. He stood. "Okay, let's move on."

Zágon appeared to take a detour as they approached the entrance to the cantonment. Jim saw why and retched again. His stomach roiled and bile rose in his throat as he watched four or five people, no more than bags of bones, clawing frantically into the bloody, cut-away cavity of a dead horse —something probably left by the Germans.

It was obvious the animal had died several days previously—swarms of flies orbited it, parades of maggots lined its wounds, dozens of crows pecked at its eyes—but despite that, the hunger-crazed prisoners ripped the entrails from the animal and jammed the rotting viscera into their mouths. Blood and tissue slathered their chins, hyenas at a kill. Humans transformed.

Jim closed his eyes, hoping to blot the image from his mind, his memory, his soul. He wanted to bury the scenes he'd witnessed over the last half hour someplace so deep in his brain that his synapses would never be able to reach them, to recover them, to dredge them up, to pull them to the surface where they could be remembered, envisioned, talked about. Never.

They stepped into the main camp. And Jim understood what he had seen outside the fence had been only a teaser. Inside, there was not just a scattering of bodies. There were stacks, piles, mounds, as if the dead human beings had been no more than sacks of potatoes or cordwood to be tossed into heaps for storage.

"After the Germans, the SS, fled, we had no strength, no tools, to bury the dead," Zágon explained, his statement more a plea for absolution than a declaration.

15

Gunskirchen Lager, Austria
May 4, 1945

"This can't be," Bowerman muttered as he entered the sprawling enclosure behind Jim. "Tell me this ain't real, Loot." He kept one hand clamped over his nose and mouth, a futile attempt to stave off the penetrating reek.

Thousands of starving people continued to cluster around the men, begging for food and cigarettes, thanking them, falling at their feet to wrap their arms around their saviors' legs.

Adding to the horror of the dimly lit netherworld into which they'd stepped, Jim caught sight of at least two human carcasses—what little was left of them—entangled in the barbed wire fence. Their final resting place, he thought, an homage to their last desperate act, an attempt to escape their brutal incarceration and pass into the next world as free souls.

Jim wanted out, away from this sewer of depravity that festered in an Austrian forest, a putrid prison of ghastly existence and agonizing death. He wanted to be a million miles from it, where its sights and sounds and smells would never find him, never wriggle to life in his memories, never pursue him in his worst nightmares, never haunt him for even a fleeting moment. Yet he knew he couldn't flee from where he stood, wouldn't, for he and Bowerman and Mo and Jürgen represented the only link to sanity and hope and compassion these people had. At least at this moment.

"Tell the people," he said softly to Zágon, "that help is coming. Soon. Food, water, medicine."

Zágon responded, waving his arms and yelling at the throng to be silent for a moment. He then announced what Jim had told him. His words were met with hoarse cheers, cries of gratitude, and bony-handed, barely audible applause.

"With me, come," Zágon said to Jim.

Jim followed as they pushed—gently—through the crowd. People clapped Jim on the back, reached to touch his uniform, croaked out thank you's in half a dozen different languages. Jim and Zágon traipsed through the mud and filth that layered the camp like a slimy carpet and reached a group, ten or twelve, of one-story frame buildings.

"This is where we lived, slept, died," Zágon said, gesturing at the barracks-like structures. "No, allow me to correct. We did not live in these hovels, we merely existed, as if we were spiders, flies, or lice."

Jim leaned into one of the buildings, through a transparent wall of stink, and peered around, his eyes watering. Hollow-cheeked, glassy-eyed beings stared back through the dank air, most unable to move or rise from where they rested on a muddy, feces-coated floor. Several of the inmates managed weak waves. Jim lifted his hand in a friendly return gesture and backed out.

"We slept on top of each other," Zágon said, "often three-deep. Sometimes in night, someone beneath you die. But we too weak to move them, so we continue to sleep . . . or try. In morning, we drag them out. And leave them. Germans sometimes buried them in mass graves. You know, hide evidence. But after SS leave, no more bury."

Jim could not find the words to respond. He merely shook his head and allowed a tear to slide down his cheek.

Zágon continued to speak. "Each building maybe designed to shelter four hundred, four hundred-fifty people. So camp expected to hold, I guess, forty-five hundred."

"How many were here altogether, do you think?" Jim asked, his throat so constricted by emotion he could barely get his question out.

"Not hundreds. Thousands."

Jim stared.

Zágon shrugged. "Maybe ten thousand. I not know. Perhaps twenty thousand. So many died."

Jim closed his eyes, still unable to process what he had stumbled into. It just kept getting worse.

He felt a light tug on his sleeve. He opened his eyes and looked down into the skeletal, sore-encrusted face of a young boy, perhaps twelve or fourteen. More bones than meat. More bones, almost, than skin. He hugged Jim, buried his face in his uniform, and muttered, "Na zdrowie, na zdrowie," and disappeared.

"Polish," Zágon said.

"Oh," Jim responded.

Zágon pointed toward the northern perimeter of the camp. "Latrine there. Twenty holes. For whole camp. Impossible. Almost everyone had diarrhea. You know, typhoid fever, dysentery. This place was human Petri dish for disease."

"So I suppose not everyone made it to . . . the holes . . . in time."

Zágon stared at the ground, the ooze, in which they stood and didn't respond immediately. After several moments he lifted his head and transferred a rheumy, scarlet-tinted gaze to Jim. He seemed a man defeated, not saved.

"No," he said, "they did not. And if you relieved yourself anywhere other than at latrine—not something you could control, you understand—you were shot by SS sentries."

"Shot? For not being able to make it to the latrine?"

"Those were orders guards had. Some seemed to enjoy. Sport, you know. Kill a Jew while he takes a shit."

The depravity seemed unimaginable to Jim. "But diarrhea. Didn't they understand?"

"You think that mattered? You think they cared?" Zágon tipped his head back and stared at the sky, stared at nothing. "They let bodies lay where they fell, in their blood, in their shit, in their piss. Excrement became their burial shroud, their funeral dress." Acerbity edged his words, suppressed fury clipped them.

Jim again scanned the horror surrounding him, knowing he would forever be unable to grasp it, or even begin to understand it. Which is why he wanted to forget it.

"Jagensdorf's Jägers, they were called," Zágon continued, "the animals who shot us. In English, Jagensdorf's hunters. Yes, animals. They were animals. We were something less."

"Who or what is a Jagensdorf?"

"Hauptsturmführer Jagensdorf, commandant of Gunskirchen Lager. Perhaps he was what in your Christianity is known as Satan." Zágon's words came out as a low, scratchy-throated growl.

"Jagensdorf?"

"Yes."

Jim turned toward where the rest of his group remained, and shouted, "Major Voigt." He motioned for the Luftwaffe officer to come to him.

Jürgen, who hadn't uttered a word since they'd discovered the prisoners, approached. He reached Jim and stood, tight lipped and rigid jawed, before him. His eyes registered something Jim couldn't describe—shock, humiliation, disbelief, anger, fathomless sorrow, guilt. Jim didn't know. Maybe all of them.

"Yes, lieutenant?"

"What was the name of the SS officer the young girl back in Parzham gave you? Her husband or lover or whoever he was?"

"Hauptsturmführer Jagensdorf."

"Do you remember his first name?"

Jürgen squeezed his eyes shut, then popped them open. "Karl."

Jim addressed his next question to Zágon. "Was the commandant's name Karl Jagensdorf?"

Zágon shook his head. "I was not on first-name basis with him." He craned his neck and swiveled his skull-like head as though looking for something.

Apparently he spotted it. "Murtuska," he called out, and beckoned to someone.

Out of the throngs of milling, emaciated living dead, a buxom—obviously well-fed—woman strode. She appeared better clothed than the rest, or at least not as shabby. The crowd parted as she moved in Zágon's direction. Jim read disdain in the glares of many. It seemed obvious to him what Murtuska was, or had been.

Zágon apparently sensed Jim's reaction to the woman. "She was one of the few who was on, how you say, 'friendly terms' with guards," he whispered.

She arrived where Zágon stood and they engaged in a brief conversation in Hungarian. Finished, Zágon spoke to Jim. "She says commandant's given name was Karl."

"Jesus," muttered Jim. He looked at Jürgen. "You suppose that gal in Parzham didn't know? Didn't know who she was shacked up with? A butcher?"

"What do you think? I doubt she is barely out of her teens, if that." Jürgen paused, swallowed hard, then went on. "Lieutenant, I hope you do not think we are all like this, the kind of human beings who could engage in something like this." He gestured at the tortured humanity surrounding them. "I hope you know there exists decency in the German people. That this depravity is an anomaly."

"You're sure? I've heard rumors . . ."

Jürgen hung his head, seemingly at a loss for a response.

"I'm sorry," Jim said, "I didn't mean that as a blanket indictment."

In a barely audible voice, Jürgen responded, "Well, maybe you should have."

"Not now, not my place. You're a standup guy from what I've heard, major. Let's worry about your fellow soldiers later. In the meantime, I've got a job for you. Come on." He walked with Jürgen to where Bowerman and Mo stood.

"Sarge," Jim said, "I want you and Major Voigt to take the Jeep and go back to Parzham and bring our little Austrian Fräulein here. I want her to see how an SS officer runs a—what did she call it?"

"DP Movement Center," Bowerman snapped.

"Yeah, let's make sure she understands what a DP Movement Center is."

"You sure you want to do that?" Mo chimed in. "She's just a kid, you know."

"You standing up for her, captain?" Jim realized his anger had gotten the best of him, but he didn't care. He wanted to lash out at someone. Major

Voigt, he realized, was a straight shooter, so that left Fräulein Frieda Mayr as the only other convenient German—or at least German sympathizer—that offered a target for his fury.

"No, lieutenant," Mo responded to Jim, "I'm not standing up for her. Maybe you're right. Maybe she should see what the German Reich and the SS really stand for. Let her carry a message back to others in this country who welcomed the presence of the German Wehrmacht and their damned ideology."

"Go get her, sarge," Jim said.

16

The hamlet of Parzham
Western Austria
May 4, 1945

Frieda stood by the window of her cottage and watched the endless parade of American troops and vehicles that moved along the road fronting her home. *How could Karl have been so wrong?* she wondered, telling her the nearness of Allied forces was all rumor and propaganda, that the German Reich remained powerful and would soon oust their enemies from German and Austrian soil. *Surely he had been misled by his superiors.*

Her heart rate ratcheted upward as more and more infantry marched along the road, a haze of dust hanging in the wake of their trek. Heavy trucks and armor rumbled over the cobblestones, too, shaking the earth and chewing the road to pieces. The dishes on the shelves in her house clinked and clattered as though in a death rattle.

But her thoughts focused not on that, only on Karl. *Where is he? What has happened to him? Why has he not returned?* She realized with agonizing, stomach-churning certainty he must be hurt or captive. Otherwise he would have come for her.

She backed away from the window and collapsed into a chair, sobbing, struggling to breathe, her world disintegrating around her. She considered trying to make her way to her brother's home in Wels, but was terrified to venture out on her own. Among the enemy.

The Americans and the German she'd met earlier seemed decent enough. But perhaps they were not representative of the soldiers who now flooded into her country. Karl had warned her of their barbarism and brutality. And he knew. She trusted Karl. She had no reason not to . . . didn't she?

But now she had no Karl. She remained alone. Vulnerable. Her tears continued and her body trembled. Karl had called her his Häschen, his little bunny. And now the wolves were at the bunny's doorstep. Ravenous.

"Karl, Karl," she whispered through her sobs, "why did you leave me? I love you so much. I need you. I need you."

Loud knocking at her front door startled her. She gasped. Fought to control her breathing. *The wolves,* she thought, *they've come for me.* She moved her gaze toward the kitchen, searching for a weapon. A knife. A serving fork. A mallet. Anything.

"Fräulein Mayr," a voice said in German, "it's Major Jürgen Voigt, Luft-waffe, we met earlier today. Could you come to the door, please? We mean you no harm."

We? She peered through the diaphanous lace that covered the small window in the door. The German-speaking American who had accompa-nied Major Voigt earlier stood beside him. She pushed the curtain aside and checked to make sure no additional soldiers lurked on either side of the door. She spotted no one. She opened the door.

"Thank you, Fräulein Mayr," Major Voigt said. Frieda noted his face appeared taught and drawn. He seemed less at ease than earlier. The American glared at her. She read something in his stare that sent a ripple of unease through her being.

She took a step back from the two men. "What is it you want?" she said, a slight quiver in her voice.

"We would like you to come with us, to see something," the German said. He seemed to have a great deal of freedom for a prisoner of war.

"Something?"

"We believe we have discovered the place where your . . . betrothed worked."

"Oh, my. You found Karl? He is okay?" She clapped her hand over her mouth.

"No, we did not find Karl, Hauptsturmführer Jagensdorf, only the place where we think he worked, the facility he commanded."

"The movement center?"

"Yes, the movement center. We thought you should see it."

"Yes, yes. Of course. I will come with you. Perhaps someone there knows something more of Karl."

"Yeah, they probably do," the American responded in a curt tone.

"We are ready to go then?" Frieda asked. "I so want to find out about Karl."

"I would advise you to grab a kerchief, Fräulein," Major Voigt said, "not for your head, but perhaps to tie over your nose and mouth."

"Sir?" She didn't understand.

"I will warn you, the place where we are going smells very, very bad."

"The movement center?"

"Lots of unwashed bodies," the American chimed in. There remained a steeliness in his glare.

"I see." She stepped back into the cottage and re-emerged clutching a blue-and-white striped kerchief that she stuffed into the pocket of her dress.

The two men escorted her to the Jeep. They helped her into the rear of the open vehicle. The American climbed into the driver's seat, the German into the front passenger seat.

A large army truck stuffed with unshaven, unwashed, tough-looking American soldiers rumbled past. A few of them waved, a few others issued admiring whistles. At least she thought that's what they sounded like. Perhaps the Americans weren't the monsters Karl had painted them to be. Maybe that was something else about which he had been misled.

Frieda, Major Voigt, and the American bounced along in the Jeep, slowed by the American military traffic, for about fifteen minutes. Frieda thought other than the influx of Allied soldiers, it seemed a perfect spring day—a few puffy white clouds set in a cobalt sky; soft, warm breezes bearing bees and dragonflies over emerald pastures; steady-winged hawks riding the upward spiral of thermals over low hills.

Nearing the town of Gunskirchen, the Jeep turned off the primary road they'd been following and bobbled into a field along a barely discernible track. The American drove more slowly as they approached the perimeter of a pine forest. He eased the vehicle into the gloominess of the woods, the pines standing like an army of mute sentinels. Frieda felt a strange unease.

Then a stench unlike anything she'd ever experienced, or even imagined, smashed into her with the power of a flash flood. She gagged. Then choked.

"Put on your kerchief, Fräulein," Major Voigt said.

Without hesitation, she did. The Jeep halted, unable to proceed any farther into the dim forest.

"My God, what is that smell?" she asked.

"You'll see," the American said. "Come on. Follow us."

17

Gunskirchen Lager, Austria
May 4, 1945

They dismounted from the Jeep. They had not taken more than a dozen steps when Frieda spotted clusters of figures staggering and stumbling through the wooded gloom—skeletal walking dead with sores and wounds festering on their bodies, tattered clothing hanging on them like well-used cleaning rags, and hollow-eyed stares registering unfathomable despair. Her psyche recoiled.

One of the creatures stumbled and fell. Frieda screamed when she saw what it had tripped over. A decomposing body. She screamed again as she spotted more and more human carcasses littering the landscape like gruesome mushrooms. Sickening. Nauseating. And the stench. The stench would have penetrated an iron barrier.

She ripped the cotton mask from her face, leaned over, and vomited. And vomited again. And again. After several minutes, only dry heaves remained.

The German major rested a hand on her shoulder. "Here," he said, and offered her a drink of water from a canteen.

She took a sip, her chest still heaving from her extended regurgitation. She managed finally to straighten up. She spit the water from her mouth.

"What is this?" she screamed. "What have you brought me to? This hell hole, this human garbage pit, this . . . this . . . slaughterhouse? You pigs! You pigs!"

"Fräulein, please," the Luftwaffe officer said softly. "This is not the Americans' doing. This is where your Karl worked. This is what he commanded."

"No, no," she continued screaming. "You lie. He helped people. He was a good man. Don't put this on him. This is not his work. This is a shameless charade, a frame-up, a cruel trick. Why do you wish to demean my Karl? He was kind. Not this, not this."

She flung herself at the German, flailing at him with her fists, pounding his chest, loosing a string of invectives she thought impossible—vicious, unladylike words she previously would never have considered uttering. But now she yelled them with all her might. The major did not retreat or flinch from her attack, nor did he strike back. He merely held her at arm's length, not allowing the full intensity of her blows to reach him.

After what seemed like forever, but more likely was only a minute or two, her strength waned and her emotionally fueled fury abated. She fell to her knees, sobbing, unable to control the convulsions that rippled through her body. Blackness whirled around her, engulfing her, and she toppled forward.

Jim and Jürgen helped Frieda back to her feet after she regained consciousness.

"Tell her we're sorry," Jim said to Jürgen, "but there's more we want her to see. She needs to understand what went on here."

"She is very young, very naïve," Jürgen said. "Do you think it is right for her to view such . . . depravity?"

"There's nothing right about any of this," Jim snapped, moving his arm in a sweeping gesture at the appalling scene surrounding them. "And I want whoever is responsible for the barbaric treatment of these people caught.

Brought to justice. Unfortunately, this young woman is the only outside connection we have to the SOB who ran this place."

"She has been lied to, taken advantage of. She likely does not know anything."

Jim nodded, knowing Jürgen had a point. "At least she should be witness to what happened here. She needs to understand this isn't some elaborate, cruel sham to make her SS officer and his cronies look bad. It isn't made up. It isn't Allied propaganda. I know it's hard on you, too, major. But it is what it is. I have a feeling that what we're going to discover is that this is but a peek through a rip in a curtain—" He stopped speaking, fearing his emotions were getting the better of him.

"I understand, lieutenant. I share your feelings, your anger." Jim read in Jürgen's eyes that he truly did.

Against his better judgment, Jim drew a deep breath, then continued. "What I wanted to say is that I believe we're going to uncover a plot so devastating it would put a Greek tragedy to shame. I think we're on the verge of unearthing a genocidal scheme that will cast a shadow over German society for generations. I'm sorry, I don't mean to throw spears at you, sir."

"But maybe I deserve them. Perhaps all of us who never swore allegiance to the Party deserve them for not standing up to the man we let commandeer our nation."

"The trouble is, you realize such things only in hindsight, never as they're happening, never as you're going down the road."

"Maybe," Jürgen said, his words almost a whisper, "the road was just too dark."

"It had to have been," Jim said softly, though he couldn't really imagine, couldn't really envision, living in a police state where the ideology of a despot was the only credo acceptable, and dissenting beliefs and actions were deemed punishable by imprisonment . . . or worse.

He changed the direction of the conversation. "Well, come on, help me get Fräulein Mayr into the camp so she can see what Hauptsturmführer Jagensdorf's Displaced Persons Movement Center truly looks like."

With Jim on one side of Frieda and Jürgen on the other, they guided her toward the camp's entrance. Jürgen spoke quietly to her, but she continued to sob and mutter what Jim assumed were protestations.

Bowerman moved up to walk beside Jim and gestured at the additional American troops and trucks that had appeared since he was dispatched to fetch Frieda. "Looks like a little help has arrived."

"A couple of additional companies showed up within the last half hour. They brought medics, MPs, a few rations, a little water. And the 761st Tank Battalion is on the way, too."

"That Negro outfit?"

"Yep. They're gonna help us get some German water tank wagons in here, then they'll start commandeering horses and wagons from the locals and loading them with all the food they can find. Some residents of Gunskirchen told us there's a big warehouse about five kilometers from here stocked with dried noodles, potatoes, soups, and meats."

"Five kilometers?" Bowerman muttered. "While people here starved to death? Goddamned SS." He spat into the mud and goo at his feet.

Frieda continued to stumble along between Jim and Jürgen, her chest heaving with silent sobs. She tried to avert her eyes from the horror surrounding her. And with her right hand she struggled to keep the kerchief clamped over her nose to interdict the reek that filled the air. Her efforts, Jim knew, would prove futile.

He understood. They had all crossed the River Styx and stepped into a netherworld of horrors so reprehensible they could never be interred. A stench so pervasive it ate into your soul. Moldering bodies so numerous they'd cram your nightmares for a lifetime. Disease-ridden, skeletal beings so countless they would haunt you through eternity. Jim understood.

Mo approached the group of men and Frieda. "Well, a little good news. I just heard that some grunts found a German supply train—food and everything—not far from here. There's a captain in one of the companies who was a locomotive engineer with the New York Central, and he and an Austrian brakeman . . . well, brake lady . . . are gonna drive the train onto a siding just outside of the camp."

"Okay," Jim said, "but do me a favor, captain. Find out who's in charge of that and make sure there are plenty of MPs on the siding when the train arrives. The people in here are going to be like sharks when they find out there's a train with food coming in."

"I'll take care of it, lieutenant." Mo trotted off.

Jim spotted Zágon and signaled for him to come to where he and Jürgen stood with Frieda.

Frieda recoiled as the man, undoubtedly appearing like a zombie to her, approached.

Jürgen told her she would be safe, that the man wouldn't hurt her, that he'd been a professor in Hungary.

After Zágon reached them, Jim said to him, "Please tell the Fräulein here what went on in this camp, what kind of place it was. Major Voigt—" he nodded at Jürgen "—will translate."

Through rheumy eyes, Zágon studied Frieda, then began to speak in slow, measured tones. "People sent here to die," he said, then continued to repeat much of what he had told Jim earlier. He paused frequently to allow Jürgen time to translate.

Frieda stood motionless, her eyes wide with shock or disbelief, Jim couldn't decipher which.

After Zágon had finished his story, Jim said, "Tell her, please, who the commander of this camp was."

"The commandant of this place, Gunskirchen Lager," he said, "was SS Hauptsturmführer Karl Jagensdorf."

"Nein, nein, nein," Frieda cried. Once more her body became wracked with great, heaving sobs.

The men watched her in silence. Jürgen rested a comforting hand on her shoulder. Gradually, her crying ceased. In a hoarse voice, she asked a question of Zágon.

"She wants to know if you can describe Jagensdorf?" Jürgen said.

Zágon nodded. "Tall and blond with cold, blue eyes. Erudite perhaps, but cruel."

Frieda fainted, but Jürgen held her erect. "I think she has had enough," he said. "You have made your point, lieutenant."

"I need to ask her one more thing," Jim said. "I need to ask her if she has any idea—now that we all know who this man she was living with really was—where he might have gone."

Frieda came to almost immediately, and Jürgen put the question to her. She responded with soft, broken words.

"All she knows," Jürgen said after she'd finished speaking, "is that he said he was going to Innsbruck. He left yesterday. She has heard nothing since."

"Well, Innsbruck surrendered to the 103rd Infantry Division yesterday," Jim said. "So he didn't go there. I think we can be pretty certain he's headed deeper into the Tyrol with the rest of the Krauts."

Zágon entered into the exchange between Jim and Jürgen. "One of the ladies on 'friendly terms' with guards here told me they leave day before yesterday, late. Say they go to meet Jagensdorf, escape deep into mountains."

"That means the sons of bitches are gonna skate then," Bowerman growled. "Damn it."

Nobody spoke for a moment. The only sound that coursed around them were the plaintive wails of a young boy who knelt in the mud at the feet of a corpse—a friend, a relative, close family?—and beseeched that it be given a proper burial in an individual grave, not dumped into a mass burial pit. *Even in death*, Jim thought, *these people find no veneration*.

"We should try somethin'," Bowerman said, "anything. We can't let the bastards responsible for this hell hole get away."

"I feel the same way, sarge," Jim responded, "but that kind of mission isn't in our charter. We're an infantry platoon. The bottom line is I have no authority to issue an order to go after these guys."

"Not to mention they've got a head start on us by a day or more," Mo added. "And we don't even know for sure where they're headed."

Jim chuckled.

"What?" Mo asked.

"Just chuckling at your use of the term 'we.' You seemed to have adapted quickly to your new status as a ground pounder, despite the fact you're a flyboy."

"Hey," Bowerman said, "now there's a thought. Captain Nesmith *ain't* one of us. So he could sure do his own thing, if he wanted to, like go on a hunt."

"By himself? That'd be crazy."

"He could 'borrow' a Jeep."

"Sarge, come on. He's not going after a bunch of Nazis by himself."

"As much as I'd like to," Mo muttered.

"Perhaps he could convince a willin' NCO to go along," Bowerman said, winking at Jim.

"Sarge, for crying out loud, you just can't—why are you so hell-bent on going after these guys anyhow?"

Bowerman remained mute for a moment, then said, "My mother's maiden name was Weinberg, if that gives ya a clue."

Jim surveyed once more the misery, the gruesomeness, the shocking legacy of barbarity that sprawled for acres in all directions from where he stood.

He turned to Bowerman. "You know, the war's almost over," he said quietly.

Bowerman eyed him intently before speaking. "Are ya suggesting I—"

"I'm not suggesting anything, sergeant. I'm just saying the war's almost over." He paused. "For instance—just making this up on the fly, you understand—if a Jeep or something were to go missing for a few days, I doubt anyone would get their knickers in a twist. Anyhow, that said, I think Fräulein Mayr has been through enough today. Why don't you and Captain Nesmith take her back to her home." A command, not a question.

"In the Jeep?"

"Of course, in the Jeep."

Jürgen, who'd been supporting Frieda, spoke up. "If you do not mind, I would like to go along, too."

"Not a good idea," Jim said. "Technically, you're a prisoner of war."

"Ah, but as you just said, the war is almost over. So, if there is no more war, maybe I would not be a prisoner of war any longer. Technically."

"I don't think it works that way, Major Voigt."

"I see. Well, if say, a prisoner of war went missing—similar to a Jeep going missing—with the war winding down, who would get twisted knickers?"

"I never said a Jeep was going to go missing. Or a POW. All you're asking is to escort Fräulein Mayr home, right?"

"Correct, lieutenant."

"As her translator?"

"Correct."

"Then I guess it's okay." Jim spoke to Mo. "He's still your prisoner, captain."

"He's proved a model one, so far," Mo responded.

"Okay, get going, gentleman. Try not to get lost. And be careful. There are still a lot of Germans running around out there."

"Then it's a good thing we got one with us," Bowerman said.

Jim flashed a transitory smile. "And one more thing, just in case you have to make any lengthy detours—" he cleared his throat in an over-dramatic fashion "—I'd make sure the Jeep you use has a full tank of gas and auxiliary cans."

"Yes, sir," Bowerman responded. He faced Jim, paused, then snapped off a smart salute.

Jim returned it, wondering if the two would ever exchange the courtesy again. He realized he'd just given his tacit blessing to an unsanctioned pursuit. Militarily, heads could roll. Especially his. Morally, maybe that was the price to be paid. But if it was, so be it. The depths of depravity into which he and his men had stepped could not be ignored. Those responsible must—he repeated the word to himself, *must*—be held accountable.

He would not ignore his military duties, but neither would he ignore the heinous crimes that had been committed here, the thousands who had been tortured and murdered as though nothing more than cattle in a slaughterhouse. No, he thought, they had not even been that. Killing cattle served a purpose. What had occurred at Gunskirchen served no purpose . . . other than to support the twisted philosophy of madmen and satisfy the warped pleasures of sadists. There was no way he would turn a blind eye to such degeneracy, no way he would not green-light an effort, however nontraditional or unofficial, to chase down the deviates responsible.

"Godspeed," he whispered, as the three men and Frieda receded into the funereal miasma that shrouded Gunskirchen Lager.

UPPER AUSTRIA

18

Leaving Gunskirchen Lager, Austria
May 4, 1945

Once the Jeep departed the dim forest and the stench and horrors of what the Americans had shown her, Frieda drew a deep breath. She tilted her head back, allowing the sun to caress her face. Sparrows and robins, free and happy, flitted through the spring sky, melodious representatives of the goodness she knew prevailed in life. Surely the grisly miasma she had just experienced, whether staged or somehow real, was but a dark aberration of human existence.

The freshness of the air she inhaled wouldn't do one thing, however, and that, she realized, was to blot away the stink that had settled into her clothing. The stench of the camp had embedded itself into every fiber of the attire she wore. Every item would have to be destroyed. Burned.

Her thoughts flipped again to Karl. She remained confused and hurt by his absence. She knew he loved her, would never abandon her—but where was he, what had happened to him? She needed him now more than ever. And despite what she had been told about his role in the atrocity she had been dragged to view, she knew it wasn't true. She knew him too well, recognized his honesty and compassion, understood his deep feelings for her.

Wanting a distraction from her brooding, she closed her eyes and listened to—not understanding—the conversation of the men who bore her home. The two Americans rode in the front seats of the Jeep, and she and Major Voigt in the rear. She caught the name Hauptsturmführer Jagensdorf a couple of times. The dialogue seemed intense, earnest, and she wondered if her Karl was the topic of the discussion.

"About what do you talk?" she whispered to the major during a lull in the conversation.

He seemed hesitant to answer her. He leaned forward and spoke to the two Americans.

Then he sat back and answered Frieda. "We would like to find your . . . betrothed, and, well, speak to him. About what he might know in regard to Gunskirchen."

"He had nothing to do with the horribleness you showed me. I know Karl. He is a gentleman, a noble German soldier."

"Yes. Then perhaps he could tell us how his name came to be associated with that camp. He did flee from the Americans, you understand."

"Of course. He is frightened. Defeated."

The major nodded. "In truth, it may be of no matter, because we do not know where he and his fellow soldiers went. And wherever it is, they have over a twenty-four-hour head start on us, so it would be almost impossible to overtake them."

"You do not think he went to Innsbruck?"

"No, the Allies have taken Innsbruck. If anyplace, we guess he would be fleeing deep into the Tyrol, into the highest mountains of Austria."

"Oh, maybe he goes then to the Grossglockner."

"And that is?"

"The highest mountain in the country. Thirty-eight hundred meters."

"Where is it located? From here?"

"To the southwest. Well over a hundred kilometers."

The German leaned forward and conversed with the Americans again. The GI driving the Jeep seemed to get upset, maybe angry. The American flyer shook his head several times, perhaps in disappointment.

The Luftwaffe officer spoke to Frieda again. "We think it is probably futile to go in pursuit of Hauptsturmführer Jagensdorf. Even if the roads are clogged with retreating Wehrmacht, he could be deep in the Tyrol by now. He is just too far ahead of us to be caught."

"But what if there are road accidents or bombed-out bridges? He might be unable to travel." Frieda realized her only chance of finding out what had happened to her lover lay with these three men. A frisson of excitement rippled through her at the thought of seeing Karl again. With him lay her future, her life, her destiny. She must reach him. Or at least find someone who could tell her what had become of him or where he had gone.

"True. But we would be stalled by the same impediments. And again I remind you, he is many hours ahead of us."

The Jeep clattered and whined along the cobblestone road leading to her home. She had no intention of staying there, however, now that she saw a way of discovering, with any luck at all, what had become of Karl.

"He may be far ahead of us," she said, "but he would be using the main highways. There are other roads and trails that do not appear on any maps that could be used to bypass the primary routes . . . and gain ground on someone you might be trying to overtake."

"I am sure. But that does not help us. We do not know these secondary ways any more than Hauptsturmführer Jagensdorf does."

"Ah, yes, major. But I do."

She held the Luftwaffe officer in her gaze and read the surprise in his eyes. She continued to press her advantage. "With my brother and father, I have hiked the trails and back roads in the Tyrol since I was seven. I know many different ways—short routes, quick routes, dead ends, dangerous passages. I could lead you through the foothills of the Alps and get you to a point on the main route into the mountains where you could intercept someone." She paused, hoping to make her next point more dramatic. "Someone even with a good lead on you."

She thought she saw a glow in the major's eyes. At least she hoped one might be there.

Once again the major conversed with the Americans. After he'd finished, the American sergeant brought the Jeep to a stop on the side of the road. He turned to face her and spoke to her in his fairly good German.

"You understand, Fräulein, that we wish to find Hauptsturmführer Jagensdorf for reasons other than you do?"

"I do. But I think—if we find him—you will discover he is a different man from what you have been led to believe."

"That I doubt, Fräulein. So I believe, should we indeed go in pursuit of 'your' officer, as you call him, you should prepare yourself for an outcome that might not be so pleasant."

She could not imagine that, but nodded in agreement all the same. "Are we going, then?" she asked, a tremor of excitement reverberating in her voice. *Oh my, but Karl will be so surprised and so thrilled to see me. Please let him be alive.* She lifted a silent prayer to Mother Mary, the Blessed Virgin she had in recent years allowed to vanish from her life. Maybe Mary had waited for her with infinite patience, waited for her to return.

"Yes," the American said, "if you can give us directions, we shall try to find Hauptsturmführer Jagensdorf."

Frieda felt tempted to squeal with delight, but the presence of the soldiers intimidated her. She gave them only a broad smile instead. None of them returned it.

The sergeant drove the Jeep a bit farther along the road and stopped in front of her cottage. "Best you get some warm clothes and hiking shoes," he said.

She darted into her home and returned shortly wearing a dark woolen sweater, trail boots, and a fresh gray kerchief on her head. She carried a long, heavy coat, several blankets, and a kerosene lantern. She handed the blankets and lantern to Major Voigt.

"I found this, too," she said, and gave him a large folding map—*REICH-SKARTE—Süddeutschland, 1939.* "It includes western Austria," she said.

"Wunderbar." He showed the map to the Americans.

"I thought you said *you* knew ways to bypass the main roads," the sergeant said.

"I do."

"So why do we need a road map?"

"Because it will show us where we can intersect with the primary highways." She took the map from Major Voigt, unfolded it, and brought it to the sergeant.

"We are here," she said, and pointed to a spot on the map. "If we take the road we are on about two kilometers west, there's a dirt road that leads off to the left, to the south. It will take us into the foothills of the mountains. Then there's another track here—" she pointed at the map again "—a pretty rough one, that will take us around the brow of a large ridge and then down into a narrow valley. There's a little-used roadway in the valley that connects to the main highway here." Again she jabbed at the map.

"How much time do you think that would save us?" the sergeant asked.

She shrugged. "I do not know exactly, but many hours. If the main roads are clogged, maybe a half day. Perhaps an entire day if the primary highway is totally blocked."

"Let's get going then," the American said.

She climbed into the Jeep. They waited for several minutes before pulling back onto the cobblestone road to allow another American convoy to rattle past them, pushing deeper into Austria. Once the unit had passed, the sergeant pushed the Jeep westward, hopping, wobbling, and bouncing over the pulverized stones.

THEY HADN'T MOVED FAR along the road when Fräulein Mayr, Frieda being her given name, Mo recalled, signaled that the turnoff they were to take was coming up.

Bowerman slowed the Jeep. "Uh, oh," he said.

Mo spotted the reason for his concern. Two MPs guarded the dirt road that Frieda had wanted them to turn onto.

"Guess I'm the senior American officer here," Mo said. "I'll handle this."

Bowerman pulled the Jeep to a stop where the MPs stood. Mo dismounted and approached them.

"Halt," one of them yelled. "Identify yourself."

"Captain Maurice Nesmith, United States Army Air Forces."

"ID." A demand, not a question.

He displayed his dog tags.

Both MPs saluted. "Had to be sure, sir," the other MP said.

"I understand." Mo studied the two Military Policemen. They appeared quite young, corporals, probably fairly new to the theater. He decided his rank would probably carry the day, if required.

"We're under orders to prevent anyone from going down this road," the MP who had first challenged Mo said. He sported a wispy mustache and an unshaven face with tiny pimples. "Too many Krauts trying to skedaddle into the Alps."

"Well, obviously we're not Krauts trying to skedaddle into the Alps," Mo said. Jürgen snorted a laugh from the backseat of the Jeep. "But we have our orders, too, and we need to take this road."

"You have written orders, sir?"

"No. Do you?"

"Our company commander gave us our directive."

"Mine came from the commander of the 71st Infantry Division. Look, I really don't want to play 'mine is bigger than yours' here. I need to get into the Tyrol as quickly as I can. We're on the trail of a Nazi war criminal who's fleeing into the Alps, so we need to move pretty fast."

"Who's we, sir?" the other MP spoke again. Mo guessed him to be the senior of the two guards. Stout and ruddy-faced, probably a farm kid.

Mo gestured at the Jeep's occupants one by one. "Master Sergeant Henry Bowerman, 71st Division. Major Jürgen Voigt, POW, German Luftwaffe. He's the one who can identify the Nazi we're after. And Fräulein Frieda Mayr, our translator." He hoped the MPs wouldn't ask her a question in English.

"But you, you're obviously not 71st Division are you, captain?" the senior MP said.

"No. I was a pilot with the 448th Bombardment Group out of England, but I've been working with the OSS to help identify war criminals."

"OSS?"

"Office of Strategic Services. Basically, it's a group of spies headed by General 'Wild Bill' Donovan. You've probably heard of him. But I can't tell you much more about him or the OSS, you understand." *Because I don't know any more.* "I'd really hate to have to contact General Donovan and tell him we're being held up on our quest by a couple of sentries." *Of course, I've never met Donovan, nor do I have any way of contacting him.*

"Hey, look guys," Bowerman said from the Jeep, "if we were the bad guys and wanted to blast our way into the Alps, you'd be dead by now." He plucked his Thompson submachine gun from the floor of the Jeep and held it aloft for the MPs to see.

The two NCOs glanced at each other, then waved the Jeep on with no further questions.

"You're a great bullshitter," Bowerman said to Mo as they bounced along the dirt road headed south.

"I'm a pilot. We have lots of great war stories. What did you expect?"

Jürgen leaned forward. "I would expect to hear that you had probably been good buddies with Roosevelt, too." He smirked.

Mo laughed. "Naw, if it comes to telling more tall tales, I'd rather tell one about how my superb airmanship allowed a reciprocating engine bomber to shoot down a German in a jet."

Jürgen sighed and sat back. "P-51," he mumbled.

As the Jeep climbed toward the foothills of the Alps, the pasturelands and clumps of pines and oaks gave way to stands of fir and larch. The sun sank toward the western horizon, painting the landscape in broad ribbons of yellow and orange. A sudden mountain breeze triggered wind waves that rippled through small fields of spring wheat dotting the upland.

"Reminds me a bit of home," Jürgen said to Mo. "When you come to visit me after this foolishness is over, you will see. We can hunt, fish, hike. Drink beer."

"And tell lies about our aviation skills," Mo added.

The two men laughed, as only a couple of comrades-in-arms who had once fought each other could—two men who'd in the past been sworn enemies, but now against all odds shared a bond as deep as brothers.

Jürgen clapped Mo on the shoulder.

Bowerman spotted something in the distance and braked the Jeep. "Whoa, whoa, whoa."

"What?" Mo said.

"Jerries, about a hundred meters ahead." He snatched the Thompson off the floorboard.

Mo pulled his .45 from his shoulder holster.

The Germans, ten or twelve, advanced on the Jeep, but not in a threatening manner. They kept their weapons slung and raised their hands over their heads.

Bowerman stepped from the Jeep and leveled his submachine gun at them.

"Wir geben auf. Nicht schießen," they yelled.

Jürgen clambered from the Jeep. "Don't shoot," he shouted at Bowerman. "They want to surrender."

"I know," Bowerman snapped, "but we ain't takin' no damn prisoners."

Jürgen stepped forward and initiated a conversation with the soldiers. After concluding a lengthy back and forth, he explained to Mo and Bowerman. "They are mostly kids. They were conscripted into the army just a few months ago and given hardly any training. They were handed weapons and told to go fight. Now they just want to go home. They had been on the main road leading into the Tyrol yesterday, but traffic there came to a complete halt, so they decided to strike out on their own. They ended up here, tired, hungry, and lost."

"Can't help 'em," Bowerman growled. "Did ya tell 'em we're on a special mission?"

"I did. And that we had no extra food. I told them the Allied lines were back in the direction we had come from several kilometers. They could go there and surrender."

"Good," Mo chimed in. "Tell them to leave their weapons with us. We might be able to use the extra firepower. Oh, and ask them if, by chance, they encountered any SS outfits when they were on the main road."

Jürgen spoke to the Germans again, then turned back to Mo and Bowerman.

"Interesting," he said. "They encountered a small unit of SS yesterday led by a Hauptsturmführer whose name they cannot remember. But they said he was a real bastard. Would not share any rations with them. Asked them why they had not stayed to fight—"

"Even though *he* was on the run, huh?" Bowerman said.

"Yes."

"Can they offer a description of the guy?" Mo asked.

Jürgen addressed the soldiers once more, then spoke to Mo. "Other than he was tall and blond, no. But they said he told them he had commanded some sort of transportation center."

"Well, maybe there is a God after all," Bowerman said.

"Okay, send these guys on their way," Mo said to Jürgen. "Then tell our gal Frieda what we found out and see if she knows the quickest way to get back to the highway in a spot where we might surprise our SS buddy.

Jürgen complied, dispatching the Germans northward amid a flood of Dankes and Auf Wiedersehens. Then he spoke to Frieda.

Mo gestured at a nearby pasture. "We'll bed down here tonight and move out at sunup. Could be an interesting day tomorrow."

19

Wels, Austria
May 5, 1945

Jim and his platoon spent the night bivouacked outside the perimeter of Gunskirchen Lager. Shortly after sunup, Jim received a summons to the town of Wels, roughly seven kilometers east of Gunskirchen. A major, Cameron Coffman, who identified himself as the 71st Division's Public Relations Officer said he was in Wels and wished to speak with Jim.

Jim hitched a ride in a Jeep that belonged to one of the regiment's liaison officers from the operations staff and arrived in Wels late in the morning. The town appeared to have been largely untouched by the war. A few of the little Gingerbread-style homes and shops displayed pockmarks stitched by rifle or machine-gun fire, and isolated craters from bombs or artillery shells dotted the streets of the tidy village, but overall, the evidence suggested there had been minimal fighting in Wels.

The 66th Infantry Regiment of the 71st had set up a temporary command post in an office building fronting a large town square. That's where Major Coffman greeted Jim. "Just call me Cam," the major said as Jim dismounted from the Jeep.

Jim saluted and introduced himself. The two officers shook hands. "Looks like you guys have attracted quite an audience," Jim said.

Thousands of civilians milled about in the square, examining the regiment's vehicles, marveling at the equipment they carried, and telling the soldiers there were no Nazis among them, the town's residents.

"Yep. And we've heard all those assurances before," Cam noted, "all across Germany. In every town we took there were only folks who loved Americans and hated Hitler."

"All of the Nazis, gone with the wind," Jim added with a note of sarcasm. He'd heard the same thing, over and over.

"Right," Cam responded. "Well, come on. There's a little bakery on the other side of the square where we can sit and talk. If you don't mind, I'd like to go over your experiences at the death camp."

"Sir, I don't know . . . I'm not sure I can talk about—"

"It's okay, Jim." Cam laid a reassuring hand on his shoulder. "If you can't, you can't. I understand. It's not an order, just a request. I was there, too, late yesterday afternoon."

"Oh."

"Yes," he said quietly. "And I know I'll carry some images that will probably haunt me for the rest of my days. So I understand your reticence." He fell silent for a moment, then said, "I recall a man in one of the barracks too weak to move lying in his own shit. I saw a little girl doubled over in pain from starvation, bawling for help. There was a rabbi tripping and falling over a dead body as he scurried toward me to kiss the back of my hand. And a woman too weak to stand crawling to me and patting my muddy combat boots . . . as if they were the sandals Jesus might have worn." Cam's voice trailed off and he could only shake his head.

"Why?" Jim asked. "Why would human beings do what we saw to other human beings?"

"You know, lieutenant, we will still be asking that question when we are old men. And we will still not have the answer."

They reached the bakery—Bäckerei—and sat outside. The proprietor brought them a fresh-baked loaf of dark bread and, as a bonus, two steaming cups of real coffee, the first Jim had enjoyed in months.

"I'll try to tell you a few things I remember, major," he said. "But then I want to forget them. Forever."

"Nobody would blame you."

Jim took a sip of his coffee, then related to Cam what he could recall. Some memories, he realized, he had already suppressed.

"Thank you," Cam said after Jim had finished. "I'm going to issue a news release to the press about what was uncovered here. But I won't use your name so you won't be bombarded with questions. And you know—I'll give you a heads-up here—there will be a few people who won't ever believe what we witnessed. 'Too horrible,' they will say, 'you just made it up.'"

"Really?"

"I've been in this business awhile. I've seen it all, all the different reactions to tragedies." Cam nodded at Jim's now empty coffee cup. "More?"

"Please."

Jim cut some slices off the loaf of bread and parceled them out between him and the major.

"Well, I've got some info for *you*, about Gunskirchen Lager and the bastard who ran it," Cam said.

"Hauptsturmführer Jagensdorf?"

"Yes, that bastard." The major took a bite of the bread, finished his coffee, then signaled the owner of the shop for refills. The town's residents continued to prowl the square, mingling with the GIs, sometimes asking for chocolate or chewing gum, and asking questions about life in the States. Cam plucked a pack of Lucky Strikes from his jacket pocket, offered Jim one—he declined—then lit up.

"Let me begin with Gunskirchen Lager," he said. "Over the past twenty-four hours we've learned a few things. Construction began last December. At the end of March, the Germans declared it an independent sub-camp of the Mauthausen complex. You've heard of Mauthausen?"

"Yes, one of the prisoners mentioned it."

"The complex consisted of almost one hundred satellite camps. We don't have an exact tally yet."

Jim issued a soft whistle of astonishment.

"At Gunskirchen, eleven barracks, using timber felled locally, were built. One was used to accommodate the SS guards who ran the place. The other ten housed prisoners."

"Who built the camp?"

"Prisoners from Mauthausen. Poles, French, Russians, Belgians. In mid-April, the commander of Mauthausen decided to transfer inmates living in a tent camp at Mauthausen to Gunskirchen. Many of them died on the march to the sub-camp. Then, maybe two hundred a day passed away after they arrived."

"How many were transferred altogether, do you have any idea?"

"We can only estimate, but maybe as many as twenty thousand. Most were Hungarian Jews."

"So, twenty thousand people jammed into a camp designed to hold—?"

"Four or five thousand."

Jim hesitated to ask the next question, but did anyhow. "Deaths?"

"We'll never know exactly. Reliable records weren't kept. Big surprise. But maybe as many as five thousand."

"In a little over two weeks?"

Cam nodded. Jim read in the major's eyes how deep the atrocities at Gunskirchen Lager had burrowed into the man's soul. *Five thousand*, Jim thought. He shoved his cup away, wondering if it was divine intercession or merely a roll of the cosmic dice that had delivered him here—to a neat Austrian village on a bright spring day—to sip coffee and nibble on bread as the greatest conflict in the history of mankind sputtered to an end on the European continent.

"Hauptsturmführer Jagensdorf," Jim said, "what did you learn about him?"

"Born in Landshut, Bavaria, in 1913 to an aristocratic family. Joined the SS in '35. He arrived at the Mauthausen complex shortly after it opened in 1938. Over the years, he earned positions of increasing responsibility. He was given command of Gunskirchen Lager in April."

"Not because he was a nice guy, I'm guessing."

Cam leaned toward Jim and lowered his voice. "Let me tell you. At Mauthausen, there were the 'one hundred and eighty-six steps.' One hundred and eighty-six uneven steps that led from a stone quarry up a steep incline.

Dutch Jews wearing wooden-soled sandals were forced to carry huge blocks of granite on their backs up the stairway. In the process, they were whipped and taunted, and sometimes forced to race. If they stumbled, they were shot.

"Even if they completed the 'race,' at the top of the stairs they'd be exhorted to push the prisoner in front of them off a clifftop. If they didn't, they were shot. It got so bad that some of the prisoners made suicide pacts. They'd link hands and voluntarily leap to their deaths off the cliff. 'Parachutists,' Jagensdorf called them. He told the guards he wanted more 'parachutists.'"

Jim stared out at the bustling town square.

"There's more," Cam said.

"Of course there is," Jim muttered.

"There was 'the post.'"

Jim waited.

"Jagensdorf loved 'the post.' He'd order a prisoner's arms tied behind his back, then hang the victim by his wrists from a post just high enough so his feet couldn't reach the ground. He'd leave the victim like that for hours. Usually the prisoner would pass out from the intense pain caused by the rupture of the tendons in his shoulders.

"After the ordeal—according to reports we heard—Jagensdorf would sometimes visit the victim, smile, pat him on the cheek and tell him he did well. But, the SS officer would go on to explain, since his ruined tendons left him unable to move his arms, he could no longer work, and therefore would need to be removed from the camp."

Jim gazed intently at the major. "Shot, I assume."

"Or gassed."

Jim closed his eyes. He wondered if he'd done right by allowing three good men to go in pursuit of Hauptsturmführer Karl Jagensdorf. On the one hand, it seemed abhorrent not to hunt down such an animal. On the other, he doubted Bowerman, Mo, and the German officer realized they were chasing a true barbarian. A being that had escaped from the abyss.

Jim opened his eyes. He noticed the crowds in the square had suddenly begun to melt away, scurrying down streets and alleys back into their shops and homes, closing doors and shuttering windows. In the brightness and

warmth of a sunny spring afternoon, the residents of Wels were aban-
doning the town square.

"What's going on?" Jim asked.

Cam looked around. "I don't know." He stood to get a better view.

They both spotted it at the same time. Like a flood tide of humanity—
such as it was—the former inmates of Gunskirechen flowed into the
square. Following several different cobblestone avenues, they spilled into
Wels. Very few walked upright. Using crude crutches or twisted walking
sticks, most hobbled. Some crawled. Others were tugged on thrown-
together sleds, or pulled in rickety wooden wagons or carts.

Except for the bump and rattle of their conveyances over the stones,
they moved silently—a legion of cadaverous scarecrows come to life. Many,
in truth, barely clinging to life.

Their tattered clothes—perhaps unwashed for years and crawling with
lice, fleas, and chiggers—fluttered like shredded battle flags on their emaciated, twisted bodies. Sores and scabs flecked their heads and torsos. Feces
and urine stained their legs.

Mid-twentieth-century lepers, Jim thought.

They arrived, it seemed, not so much to view their liberators, the American GIs, as to confirm their freedom, to verify they no longer faced the
existence of slaughterhouse animals.

Cam hammered on the door of the now-closed bakery. The proprietor
opened it. The major stepped in and returned with an armload of bread
and pastries. He and Jim plunged into the mass of starving refugees,
breaking off small pieces of the eats and placing them in the clutching, dirt-
encrusted hands of those who reached for them. The stench of the camp
remained with them, encasing them in an invisible fog.

They remained silent, not speaking, not even offering thanks. Jim read
no joy in their faces, no signs of relief, no vestiges of hope. There seemed
only puzzlement and shock. Shock at what had suddenly transpired in
their lives after suffering an extended reign of terror and torture and agony.
A bestial subsistence in which the only deliverance arrived amid the
thunder of hoofs from a Pale Horse.

For the next two hours, Jim, Cam, and hundreds of other GIs continued
to do what they could for the Gunskirchen refugees, but eventually the

Americans ran out of food, candy, gum, and cigarettes. Medics worked on the most critically ill and wounded of the former prisoners, but even then, many took their last wheezing breaths in the Wels town square.

Near four o'clock, the refugees from Gunskirchen began to compress toward one side of the square. From the other side of the quad, the sound of rhythmic marching echoed off the buildings lining a broad street. A column of German soldiers, perhaps two or three hundred, paraded into the square.

"Troops from the garrison here that surrendered yesterday," Cam said to Jim.

The Germans assembled in orderly ranks directly across from the congregate of the living dead . . . the living dead from France, Poland, Russia, Yugoslavia, Hungary, the Balkans, the Low Countries.

American MPs kept watch over the Germans who stood in perfect military formation, their bodies erect, their uniforms pressed, their stomachs undoubtedly full.

Across from them, maybe twenty-five meters distant, huddled the filthy, disheveled, hopeless legacy of the brutality of the German Reich.

A strange quietness entombed the square. The two groups remained immobile. No one spoke. No one shouted. No one shook a fist. It seemed as if time itself had been suspended—as if two disparate factions, actors in the greatest tragedy of human existence, were making a silent, un-applauded curtain call for the benefit of posterity.

Cam whispered to Jim. "I think what we're witnessing is something mankind may never see again. I'm awestruck."

Jim was, too. He moved away from the major and walked down the front rank of Germans. He gazed into their eyes. The Wehrmacht soldiers kept their stares caged, straight ahead, not looking back at Jim. But he read in their eyes the same arrogance that had existed since the rise of the Third Reich. He wondered if it would always be there, always exist in the psyche of these people who thought themselves the Herrenvolk, the Master Race.

He walked to the other side of the square and took a last look at the faces of those the Nazis had humbled and tortured and murdered for so many years. Now, however, *they* had become the free people of the world, the Germans, the incarcerated.

He thought—or maybe it was just his wishful imagination—he'd witnessed just a flicker of hope in a few of the stares of the former prisoners. But he wasn't sure. Yet, he knew there had to be at least a glimmer of optimism. There must be. Otherwise, what had been the purpose of his journey through war-ravaged Europe? Why had he endured? Why had he buried so many fellow soldiers? Why had he killed?

Yes, he was certain he'd caught a glimpse of hope in a couple of their vacant gazes. Pinpoints of light in the darkness, tiny glows of distant fires on a black horizon, the first glints of a winter sunrise in frigid dawn.

Within another hour, the square had emptied. Transportation had been secured for the German soldiers. They were on their way to prison. For the refugees of Gunskirchen, every wheeled vehicle within reach had been commandeered. They were on their way to freedom. Though Jim knew freedom—true freedom, peace—would be slow to come. If ever.

AUSTRIAN ALPS

20

In the foothills of the Alps
East of Salzburg, Austria
May 5, 1945

The day, as many of the previous had, dawned bright and cool. Mo and Bowerman had arisen early. Jürgen and Frieda weren't far behind. After a quick K-ration breakfast—chopped ham and eggs in cans and dried fruit bars—they set out southward in the Jeep. Frieda, using the map, had pointed out their route before they left, though she seemed a bit uncertain. Mo hoped she wasn't blowing smoke up their asses, that she really did know a shortcut to the main road, and that her equivocation stemmed from not having been in the area for several years. He decided there was only one way to find out, so they continued on their quest.

Despite the roughness of the road, they made good time initially as Bowerman pushed the Jeep to its limits. He squeezed all the power he could out of its sixty-horsepower engine and constantly rammed the gear shift stick back and forth, running up and down through the three forward speeds.

For all that, Mo doubted the Jeep ever topped forty miles per hour. The road was just too rugged. "Wish I had my bomber," he yelled to Jürgen in the rear seat.

"Wish I had my jet," came the response.

Mo shook his head. "Maybe not. We'd probably just shoot each other down."

"Come on, sirs," Bowerman hollered. "Neither one of ya could stay airborne very long over this terrain. Gotta leave it to the infantry to complete the tough missions."

"All yours, Sergeant Bowerman," Mo said.

They jounced on, gradually climbing, leaving the oak, beech, and pine forests behind and pushing into denser stands of fir and spruce. Silvery streams, fed by mountain snowmelt, splashed their way through small valleys and draws, and here and there eddied into quiet pools that provided patient kingfishers hardy meals. In several spots, the Jeep was forced to ford flowing water, but the streams proved always to be shallow, with the vehicle finding good traction.

By mid-morning, Mo and his 'team' arrived at a crossroads. Of sorts. The intersecting road barely qualified as one. Rocky, narrow, and rutted, it seemed virtually impassable.

Mo asked Jürgen to ask Frieda if this is where they should turn.

He did, and she clambered out of the Jeep and paced up and down the narrow lanes of the intersection for several minutes, appearing to examine them closely. Then, shielding her eyes from the sun with her hand, she scanned the western horizon. She motioned for Jürgen to join her. Extending her arm and sweeping it back and forth, she seemed to point something out to him as she talked.

He rejoined the men at the Jeep. "She says she is certain this is the way that will lead us over that big ridge there." He gestured westward. "She warns the track will get very narrow and hard to follow, since it is rarely used. But she says it will save us a great deal of time in getting to the next valley where there's a road we can follow to the main highway leading to the Tyrol."

"Which is the one we think most of the Wehrmacht will be following," Mo said, seeking confirmation from Jürgen.

Jürgen nodded.

"Okay, let's mount up and keep rolling," Mo commanded. "How are we for gas?" he asked Bowerman.

"Extra can strapped to the rear. It's full."

They settled back into the Jeep and pushed on, albeit at a much slower pace. As Frieda had warned, the track became narrower, with tree boughs and underbrush encroaching on it from both sides. Parts of the route had washed out, and the ruts that defined the so-called road did not follow a straight line but rather wound this way and that. They reminded Mo of the trails Sidewinder snakes etched in the California desert.

Bowerman fought the steering wheel in a never-ending battle to keep the Jeep from slewing off the track into tangles of bushes and brambles. Mo and the other passengers gripped whatever parts of the vehicle they could to keep from being pitched from their seats. It occurred to him this was a strange way for a B-24 pilot to be fighting a war—riding in a bucking bronco army Jeep and "commanding" a search party consisting of an infantry sergeant, a German Luftwaffe POW, and an Austrian Fräulein.

"Hey, Jürgen," he said, "don't you think this is strange? An army air forces captain, a Luftwaffe major, an infantry grunt, and an Austrian gal off chasing a bunch of Waffen SS prison guards?"

Jürgen didn't answer right away. Then he smiled and said, "What is *not* strange about a global war that kills millions of people and changes nothing, my friend?"

"Point taken. Perhaps you should write a book about it when all this is finished."

"No. The victors will write the books and define the history. Not the Germans. So I'll leave that to others. You and I? As I said earlier, we will get together when all this is past and tell lies, drink beer, and go fishing."

Mo couldn't think of a better resolution.

The track the Jeep followed steepened. Bowerman dropped the range selector into low and the vehicle climbed like an iron mule. They reached the top of the precipitous ascent. Below them, a rushing stream, its banks littered with old deadfalls and forest debris, thundered through a deep cut in the land.

"Well, no friggin' way we can ford that," Bowerman said. He got out of the Jeep and studied what lay ahead of them. "Looks like there are ruts running parallel to the creek." He turned to Jürgen. "Could ya ask the lady if she knows if there's a bridge we can cross . . . maybe further upstream?"

Jürgen, Frieda, and Mo joined Bowerman in surveying the surrounding landscape. Mo realized if there was no way to cross the stream, there was no way they could reach the ridge that lay ahead of them. And if they couldn't get to the ridge, that meant they couldn't get to the valley on the other side of it. No valley, no road to the highway, and no way to interdict the SS goons.

Frieda gazed long and hard at the stream, at the rutted track running beside it, and at the wooded hills encircling them. Far above the little ad hoc search party, a pair of large hawks orbited in the cloud-flecked sky. Mo wished he had their view of the topography that lay ahead.

After speaking with Frieda, Jürgen said, "Fräulein Mayr recalls a wooden bridge over the stream about two or three kilometers from here. She believes it should be strong enough and wide enough for the Jeep."

"*Should* be?" Bowerman said.

"Let's go find out," Mo said.

They scrambled back into the Jeep, and Bowerman herded it along, slithering and sliding, over the barely visible rutted track for another fifteen minutes.

"There," he exclaimed, "right ahead of us."

Mo stood in the Jeep, clinging to the windscreen frame to keep his balance as he attempted to get a better view. Sure enough, what looked like a crude wooden bridge appeared about a hundred meters ahead. But as the Jeep drew closer to the structure, the Air Forces officer sank back into his seat and uttered a silent curse.

Bowerman brought the vehicle to an abrupt halt adjacent to the bridge —or at least what used to be a bridge. Two massive fir trees, shorn of limbs, that had formerly served as the main beams of the structure, had collapsed into the rushing water below.

The quartet again dismounted from the Jeep and went to inspect the now defunct wooden span.

"Looks like a flood—probably a combination of heavy rain and snowmelt—washed away the banks that supported the beams," Jürgen said, "and that was the end of the bridge."

"And the end of our great adventure," Mo groaned.

"Sometimes you get the bear, sometimes the bear gets you," Bowerman said. He slammed his fist onto the hood of the Jeep, creating a small explosion of dust.

"I am sorry," Jürgen chimed in, "truly. I know we were after some of my fellow Germans, but they deserved to be caught and they deserved to be made to stand before a judge."

Frieda stood by silently, head down, obviously disappointed she would be unable to reconnect with "her" Karl.

A gruff voice came from behind the group and startled them. "Grüß Gott."

Mo fumbled for the .45 in his shoulder holster. Bowerman snatched his Thompson from the floor of the Jeep.

A bearded elderly man sat on a boulder at the edge of the forest. A shotgun rested on his lap. He made no threatening move. In fact, his eyes seemed to convey a sense of puzzlement as he watched Mo and the others.

Mo and Bowerman put their weapons away. Mo studied the man. Elderly perhaps didn't begin to describe him. Ancient, maybe. A gray, untrimmed beard fell to his chest. His face displayed as many wrinkles and creases as the surrounding terrain. A low-crowned, wide-brimmed hat that looked as though it had been chewed on by goats sat canted on his head. Well-worn lederhosen extended to his knees where they fit over the tops of ratty woolen stockings. A moth-eaten sweater and muddy hiking boots completed his ensemble.

"Grüß Gott," Jürgen said, responding to the man's traditional Austrian greeting.

The man stood, placed his shotgun—something that looked to be from the turn of the century—on the big rock, and approached Jürgen. A long conversation in German followed a tentative handshake. Mo thought Jürgen seemed to struggle a bit understanding the man's words, perhaps because the old gentleman spoke German with a dialect unfamiliar to Jürgen.

Their discussion went on for quite some time. Frieda appeared to be listening intently and occasionally interrupted with a question or a statement.

Finished, Jürgen turned to Mo and Bowerman. "Perhaps some good news. This is Herr Klaus, Bruno Klaus—" Jürgen gestured at the old man "—and he says there is a place farther upstream where we can cross."

Mo and Bowerman stepped forward to shake hands with Bruno. "Where does he come from?" Mo asked.

"He says he belongs to a group of Austrians known as the Wächter der Berge, or Guardians of the Mountains, who live in a remote valley. He would not say where. Frieda says she has heard of them, but always thought they were a myth, an old wives' tale. I guess not. Bruno says the Wächter der Berge goes back many, many years."

"What do they do?" Mo said.

"As I understand it, they protect these mountains from poachers, interlopers, people who want to cut the trees. They look out for their family interests. They apparently have their own set of laws and codes and enforce them with a great deal of vigor.

"And they have no love for Nazis. A Wehrmacht patrol wandered into their valley last autumn and demanded the Guardians turn over to them a cache of food. Meat and vegetables that were meant for the winter.

"Two of the soldiers raped a young woman who lived with her parents in the settlement. Rather than risk additional harm to their wives or children, the Guardians elected not to seek retribution, and they also gave in to the soldiers' demands for food. That meant the people in the valley hovered on the brink of starvation when the snow and cold came. So they still carry with them, and probably always will, a keen sense of hatred for Nazis."

"I see. Well, tell him we offer our condolences for their suffering, and that *we* mean no harm to him or his fellow Guardians. Tell him, too, we appreciate him informing us about the bridge."

"I am afraid, captain, it is not exactly a bridge," Jürgen said.

"Sir?"

"I gather it is more like a fallen log that spans the creek."

"So, no Jeep?" Bowerman said, his face contorted in dismay.

Jürgen shook his head. "People only."

"Shit. So much for our fifty-cal that's mounted on the Jeep."

"We'll go with what we have," Mo responded. "Sarge has his Thompson and we've got the rifles the German soldiers surrendered to us. By the way, those are certainly different-looking things." With a pistol-style grip behind the trigger and a long, curved magazine feeding into the chamber from underneath, the weapon bore little resemblance to any combat rifle Mo had ever seen. He turned to Jürgen. "What the heck are they?"

"SturmGewehr," Jürgen said. "That translates to 'assault rifle.' Something new. On full automatic you can empty that thirty-round magazine in three seconds."

Mo allowed his mouth to hang open. Finally he said, "Boy howdy. Are you kidding me?"

"Nein." Jürgen smiled, perhaps revealing a smidgen of Teutonic pride.

"So you know how to use them?"

"Jawohl."

"Good. You can be our weapons bearer."

"Sir," Bowerman interjected, "with all due respect, he's still our enemy. He's a POW."

"Technically, yes. But he's proved otherwise to me. And since I'm not answering to any specific command authority here, I'm designating him—assuming he agrees—as our arms carrier."

Jürgen smiled. "Do not worry, sergeant. I shall not shoot you in the back. I want Hauptsturmführer Jagensdorf as much as you do. He does not represent my country. I am not so sure he even represents humanity."

They climbed back into the Jeep and took it down the narrowing path as far as they could. Bruno, walking, led the way. Despite being bent with age and relying on a walking stick, he proved able to move more rapidly through the thickening underbrush than the Jeep. At last the track became impassable for the vehicle.

"End of the road," Bowerman said.

"Okay," Mo responded. "Let's make sure we've got all the supplies we can carry and push on. Major Voigt, how many rifles are you comfortable toting?"

"They are heavy, but I can sling one over each shoulder. And I can cram a lot of extra magazines into my pockets."

"I'll tote one, too. It'll be nice to have an automatic weapon. I assume you can give me a quick lesson on how to fire the thing."

Jürgen nodded.

A short hike brought them to the fallen log spanning the creek, an ancient spruce stripped of limbs and planed flat on the walking surface. It seemed to offer a passable albeit narrow way over the thrashing water below.

Bruno went first, pointing out the best and safest places to step. Bowerman crossed next, then Jürgen. On the other side of the "bridge," Jürgen waited for Frieda with an extended arm while Mo guided her onto the log. She appeared unafraid and moved easily over the fallen tree. Mo crossed last.

On the other side, Jürgen and Bruno entered into another extended conversation. Upon completion of their discussion, Jürgen spoke to Mo and Bowerman. "Bruno is worried about our safety. He says the Germans are bad—I guess he means me." He gave a little laugh. "So he would like to accompany us on our mission."

"No, no, no," Mo said. "Please give him our heartfelt thanks for what he's done for us. But as tough and resilient as he seems, I can't take an elderly man, a civilian, into combat. If there is any shooting, that old blunderbuss of his would be useless against Wehrmacht weaponry. Tell him we hold him and his fellow Guardians in the highest esteem, but that it's more important he return to his family and neighbors and care for them."

Bruno appeared to understand, nodded a farewell, and sent the tiny group on its way with a hand-sketched map of how to reach the valley road.

They moved along a narrow path, edging ever higher into a dense alpine forest and thick undergrowth rife with rhododendrons, edelweiss, and heather. The air cooled and a busy wind urged the tops of the evergreens into a rhythmic ballet.

The track appeared little used and no other hikers appeared. After an hour, maybe more, of holding a steady pace, the group reached the crest of the trail and began a winding descent into a shaded valley far below. Another hour brought them to the valley, a narrow slash in the land quilted with trees and farmland.

An additional fifteen minutes delivered them to the road they sought. Frieda spoke to Jürgen. He translated for the group. "The Fräulein says this road will intersect with the main highway to the Tyrol about ten kilometers south of here. She does not think any soldiers will try to come this way, since the route in this direction dead ends at the head of the valley not far north of here."

Mo studied the road. Only an occasional farm truck or horse-drawn cart moved along it. "We'll stay off the road as much as we can as we head toward the highway," he said. "The less attention we draw to ourselves, the better. We don't need any of the locals mentioning to the troops on the highway that a group of . . . I don't know . . . armed militia appear to be headed in their direction. Not that they would, but I don't want to take any chances."

They remained off the roadway as much as the topography would allow. Instead, they slogged through pastures and snaked through woodlands. From time to time, they had to edge closer to the road. If they encountered a vehicle or spotted someone on foot, they merely waved and smiled and kept moving.

By late afternoon, they came within sight of the intersection. The mouth of the valley broadened into relatively flat terrain with low, rolling hills. Grasslands, vegetable farms, and fruit orchards dotted the landscape. A steady flow of Wehrmacht traffic, both vehicles and soldiers on foot, crept along a broad, paved highway.

Mo halted the group and scanned the road junction and topography. "Let's hope Jagensdorf and his Merry Men haven't passed by yet. I'm not sure how we're supposed to recognize the bastards, but I'm guessing they'll still be decked out in their distinctive SS garb. And I know our little Fräulein here will be able to spot Jagensdorf."

"Sir, if I may?" Bowerman said.

"Go ahead."

"I think a good place to set up watch might be in that little orchard down there." He pointed at a stand of what Mo took to be apple trees. The grove stood adjacent to, and perhaps twenty meters off, the primary road below them. "Plenty of trees to hide behind. But I don't think the Krauts are especially alert anymore. They certainly ain't gonna be expectin' any Americans to be around here."

"I'm with ya, sarge. Let's fan out as we approach the orchard and move as quietly as we can. We don't have to keep totally hidden, but we should probably try to continue to carry a low profile. You know, attempt to look like orchard workers or something. Major Voigt, you might want to strip off your GI jacket now. Stay with Fräulein Mayr and give us a shout if she spots Jagensdorf. Oh, and it might be a good idea to jam a magazine into one of those German assault rifles and be prepared to give us some support if needed."

"Perhaps, captain," Voigt said, "I should take the lead if we do intercept Hauptsturmführer Jagensdorf, you know, make a German-to-German approach. That might appear less threatening to him, at least initially, and make him more inclined not to challenge it. Maybe."

"Yeah, big maybe. But it's worth a try. You're on, major." Mo didn't know if it would work, but he didn't have any better ideas, and they possessed only limited manpower and firepower, so . . .

"Will the Americans try to kill Karl?" Frieda asked Major Voigt as they walked toward the orchard. She realized apprehension threaded her words. But she still didn't trust the Americans. They had been good to her, but they also seemed to have prejudged Karl as evil.

"Not if he obeys their commands."

"But why do they want him? Surely you don't believe all those terrible things those awful people at that camp accused him of?"

"It is not for me to judge, Fräulein. But it is hard to believe that those who accused him would have made things up about an SS officer picked at random."

"But you, you are German. Do you think a fellow soldier could have been responsible for what we saw back there? Karl is an officer like you."

"No, my dear, he is not an officer like me." She detected a tinge of anger in the major's words. "He is a member of the Schutzstaffel, political soldiers who have sworn an oath of absolute loyalty and obedience to der Führer. I took no such vow. Mine was to my country, to the Luftwaffe, and to my family."

"But you both fought against the Americans, the Brits, the French. Our enemies. I don't see how you are different."

She watched the Luftwaffe officer appear to struggle with his response.

An awkward feeling enveloped her, as though she was a child about to be lectured by a parent. A child who had not yet been exposed to a bigger world that perhaps lay beyond what she had so far experienced. She drew a deep breath. A strange, fleeting feeling coursed through her—that maybe her view of the world was limited by the prism of her love for Karl through which she viewed it. *But so what? What is wrong with that? With love? Love is the bond that will hold me and Karl together forever.*

The major spoke again. "I must be honest with you, Fräulein. Men in the SS are schooled in racial hatred and taught to harden their hearts to human suffering. That is not something to which all in the Wehrmacht subscribe. I include myself in that group."

Frieda stared at the officer, unwilling to accept what he had said. She looked away and trudged in silence beside him.

A short walk brought them into the orchard. Mo and the sergeant picked out trees behind which to kneel and use as observation points. Major Voigt led Frieda to a stack of wooden crates that could be used for concealment.

Overhead, the sun slid inexorably westward, readying itself to disappear behind a distant mountain range that sat in jagged bas-relief against a velvet horizon. The Wehrmacht units moving along the road had thinned, likely in preparation for bedding down for the night. Clusters of troops and vehicles now came along only every few minutes. Frieda realized it wouldn't be much longer before dusk would settle over the valley, making it virtually impossible to recognize anyone on the road.

Major Voigt whispered to her, "If you spot Karl, tell me. I will go to him. Please, stay here, behind the tree, out of sight. I do not wish to place you in jeopardy."

"Jeopardy," she hissed, "why would I be in—"

"Shh, Fräulein." The major placed his forefinger over his lips. "Lower your voice. Do not call attention to us. I beg you to listen to me. Do as I say. It is for your own good."

She fell silent, sulking, not understanding the concern these men were displaying over Karl harming her. Harming anyone. Crickets began to tune up, welcoming the impending twilight. She watched the few Wehrmacht stragglers who remained move along the highway, and wondered if Karl might slip by unnoticed in the dark of night. No, she would not let that happen. She would stay awake all night if necessary.

But then he was there. Striding along the road in his handsome green-gray uniform and his calf-length jackboots, now muddy and dusty from his travels. A number of rough-looking men accompanied him.

"Oh, my," she squealed, and burst from her hiding place.

Jürgen reached for her but she slipped his grasp and stumbled onto the road.

"Karl, Karl," she cried and sprinted toward him.

He drew his sidearm and aimed it at her.

21

***

At a crossroads near Werfen, Austria
May 5, 1945

Frieda flung herself at Karl, who lowered his pistol but seemed strangely unreceptive to her arrival. She wrapped her arms around him and pushed her face into his chest. He smelled of dust and smoke and sweat.

"Oh, Karl," she whispered, "I was so worried. So worried that something had happened to you."

"What are you doing here?" he said. His tone sounded harsh.

"I came to find you."

"Alone?"

She took a step back from him and looked up into his face—the same chiseled features she'd fallen in love with. But somehow they looked more severe than she remembered. Perhaps, though, that could be attributed to the failing light.

"I . . . I came with others," she stammered.

He raised his sidearm again and extended his arm, leveling the weapon at the orchard she had come from. "Who?"

"A . . . a Luftwaffe officer."

"Luftwaffe? What are you doing with a Luftwaffe officer? Are there more besides him?" Karl seemed rattled.

She started to answer, but Major Voigt stepped into view, his arms raised. "I am Major Jürgen Voigt, Luftwaffe Jagdverband 44."

Karl trained his pistol on him. "What are you doing here, a Luftwaffe major? Why are you with Fräulein Mayr?"

Frieda noted the SS men accompanying Karl had assumed kneeling positions with their rifles aimed at the orchard. She didn't understand what was going on.

"You are, I presume, Hauptsturmführer Karl Jagensdorf, Waffen SS?" Voigt said.

"Why do you ask?" Karl said.

"There has perhaps been a misunderstanding regarding your duties of recent."

"Yes?"

"Fräulein Mayr tells us—"

"*Us*? Who might *us* be?"

"Please, Hauptsturmführer, allow me to finish."

"Be quick about it then." He waved his handgun at Major Voigt.

"Fräulein Mayr tells us you were the commandant of a DP Movement Center. That you arranged transportation for displaced persons, moving them to areas of the Reich less affected by the war. Helping them, in effect, to get a new start in their lives."

Karl smiled. "Of course."

Frieda relaxed.

"Unfortunately," Major Voigt said, "we have heard different stories."

"There you are with *we* again."

"Then let me say *I*. I have heard different stories."

"And what might those be? And from whom?" He kept his sidearm pointed at the major.

"There was a . . . well, let me say, a detention facility near Gunskirchen of which you were identified as being the commander."

Karl laughed. "By Jews no doubt. Jews will say anything to deflect from themselves the blame for what has happened to our great nation. Surely you know that, major. Surely you understand the lengths those subhumans will go to in order to sidestep responsibility for their own fates."

"Yes, yes. That may be. But I assume you must have in your possession documentation—orders from the Reich, or official messages perhaps—that would establish you as commandant of a DP Movement Center."

"Lost in the haste to flee the Allies, I'm afraid."

"I see."

An uneasy silence—except for the tweet of an early-on-the-job night-bird—settled over the intersection.

"Maybe you should have waited for the Allies, the Americans in particular, to arrive," Major Voigt said. "They most likely would have been sympathetic to your efforts to assist displaced people."

"Ah, but the Jews would have stepped forward and lied about me, you know that."

"But at your facility, the movement center, they would have seen evidence of your efforts to assist people."

Frieda whispered to Karl, interrupting his conversation with Major Voigt. "You were fleeing without me. Why? I thought you would come for me, take me with you, that we would leave together." Her world, her little world, viewed through her prism of love, seemed to be imploding as she stood next to the man who had said they would be together forever. Her head spun with the impossibility of what was happening.

But Karl ignored her and held his focus on the Luftwaffe officer. "Yes, they would have seen the evidence," he snapped, his words knife-like. He paused briefly, then went on. "So, we have talked enough. You should leave now. You and whoever *we* is." He waved his pistol in a dismissive motion.

"I do not think I can do that, Hauptsturmführer. There are some questions you must answer."

"No. There is nothing I *must* do but continue on to the Tyrol. Unless you have a large force backing you up, major, I suggest we say Auf Wiedersehen and go our separate ways."

Karl grasped Frieda's arm tightly. Stunned, she felt the muzzle of his handgun press against the side of her temple.

"Fräulein Mayr will be accompanying me," Karl added.

"She is young and innocent," the major retorted. "Let her go and we will be on our way."

"Oh, no, I cannot do that, my friend. She is my little Häschen. I cannot leave her." He put his mouth next to her ear and whispered, "You know that, don't you, my dear?"

She didn't. She didn't know this man at all. Her legs offered no more strength than strands of spaghetti. She felt as if she were being sucked into a black whirlpool.

"JESUS, MARY, AND JOSEPH," Bowerman whispered to Mo in the darkness of the orchard. "Why couldn't that little bitch have stayed put, like Major Voigt told her? What the hell do we do now?"

Mo felt as if he'd been coldcocked, like when *Rub-a-Dub-Dub* had been suddenly blasted from the sky. "Let him go," he said, resigned to his decision. "We're outnumbered, outgunned, and that Jagensdorf bastard has a hostage now." Mo had counted seven SS NCO guards with Jagensdorf. Two carried submachine guns, the rest, combat rifles. Even with Bowerman's Tommy gun and him with an assault rifle, they wouldn't stand much of a chance against the SS force. More to the point, Fräulein Mayr would be the first casualty if they attempted to take Jagensdorf by force. He couldn't see sacrificing the young woman, even if she had been the unwitting lover of an SS butcher. Beyond that, the element of surprise had evaporated, too. They'd lost the opportunity to perform a quick hit and run—ambush the SS weasels, snatch Jagensdorf, and take off like scalded cats. If only Fräulein Mayr hadn't been so impetuous, so foolish.

"Shit, shit, shit," Mo muttered. "All this effort for nothing."

Jürgen returned and joined them in the now dark orchard. "I am so sorry," he said. "After the Fräulein ran out on the road, there was not much I could do . . . except try to save her, and I could not do that, either."

"Not your fault, major," Mo said.

They knelt in the shelter of the trees and watched Jagensdorf and his men move on down the highway. The SS officer kept his handgun nestled against Frieda's head while the guards, rifles at the ready, scanned the surrounding area for additional threats.

"Nothin' like watchin' a mass murderer make a clean fuckin' getaway," Bowerman growled, and spat into the darkness.

May 6, 1945

THEY SLEPT OVERNIGHT in the orchard and took turns standing watch, just to make certain no one stumbled upon them. At sunrise, they departed and headed back up the valley. Mo had no doubt each of them felt a singular depression at having failed to take into custody—or maybe even "eliminate"—an SS officer who on all counts would qualify as a war criminal. Not only that, they'd allowed him to gain a hostage, a young woman who had been the responsibility of their little posse—himself, Sergeant Bowerman, and Major Voigt.

By late morning, they had another problem. They'd reached the upper end of the valley, a dead end, obviously having missed the turnoff that would have led them back over the ridge.

"I don't know where in the hell we are," Mo said.

"Yeah, you flyboys," chided Bowerman. "Well, let's backtrack. I think I can figure out where to turn to get us out of here."

Steep wooded slopes surrounded them on three sides. The ridge they'd come over to get to the valley rose sharply on their left, while a towering, snow-capped peak poked toward the sky on their right.

"Wo ist das Fräulein?" a gruff but familiar voice said.

Bruno, stooped but spry, emerged from a trail leading into a dense stand of fir and spruce. With his walking stick in hand and his ancient shotgun slung over his shoulder, he gave the appearance of a character escaped from a fairy tale.

"Grüß Gott," Jürgen said, and they dived into a long conversation. Bruno's bushy eyebrows wiggled up and down like alabaster caterpillars as he alternately scowled and grimaced at what he was being told by Jürgen. He appeared to ask the major a number of questions, then swung his arm in a sweeping gesture at the massive mountain that stood southwest of them.

Jürgen appeared puzzled and stepped back to talk with Mo and Bowerman.

"Our friend, Bruno, says that if we are still interested in intercepting the Germans and freeing the Fräulein, he knows a way."

"I ain't so sure the Fräulein wants to be saved," Bowerman said.

"Well, she may not realize it or understand it, but she needs to get away from that rat bastard," Mo interjected. "Anyhow, what does Bruno propose? I saw him gesturing in the direction of that rocky mammoth that looks like the Matterhorn. There's no way we can get around that, or over it, and get ahead of those SS weasels again."

"Our Wächter der Berge friend here takes issue with that," Jürgen said. "He says there is a hidden path that can get us to the other side of the mountain quickly."

"Hidden path?" Mo said.

Jürgen shrugged. "That is what he tells me."

"And we don't need mountain climbing equipment?"

"No, but he did say we will want warm jackets or coats. And gloves, if we have them."

"What about it, major?" Mo said. "You've been the guy talking with him. Can we trust him?"

"He got us this far, did he not?"

Mo gazed again at the prominence looming in the distance. It looked like a granite incisor the size of Rhode Island. "Well, nothing ventured . . . let's go."

Jürgen talked again with Bruno who nodded and motioned for the men to follow him. They plunged into a deep green forest and began climbing a precipitous, muddy trail. Despite his age and presumed infirmities, Bruno soon left Mo, Jürgen, and Bowerman panting in his wake.

"I thought this weren't gonna involve mountain climbin'," Bowerman said between gasps for air.

"This isn't mountain climbing, it's hiking," Mo responded, himself fighting for oxygen.

Bruno returned to the men, a puzzled look on his face, and spoke to Jürgen.

After he'd finished, Bowerman snapped, "I understood that. He wants to know how we can fight Germans if we can't keep up with an eighty-year-old man."

Jürgen laughed. "Yes, he said that."

"Tell him we're good at killin', but not so much at marchin'," Bowerman said.

Jürgen did. Bruno smiled and answered.

"He said he will march slower so that we can keep up with him and maybe kill Germans together," Jürgen told Bowerman. "I guess he doesn't realize I'm German," he added.

"Tell him to get goin'," Bowerman barked, probably slightly embarrassed.

After an exhausting climb, they began to descend. The mountain, now cloud-capped, loomed over them like a benevolent god.

"How in the hell do we get over or around that peak if we're going down?" Mo asked, truly puzzled.

Jürgen asked Bruno, then said to Mo, "He reminds us he told us this is a *hidden* way, a secret passage."

22

In the eastern Alps
Austria
May 6, 1945

The exhausted group, led by Bruno, continued a gradual descent. Mo realized their earlier long, hard climb had brought them above the timberline, for now only stunted trees and scrubby grasses dotted the rocky landscape.

The higher elevation, coupled with the absence of laboring up the steep trail, allowed a chill to envelop Mo. He signaled for a halt and suggested they pull on sweaters—those who had one—and button their jackets snugly. While Bruno, who appeared unaffected by the lower temperatures, waited, the rest of the men prepared to ward off the Alpine chilliness.

Bruno said something to Jürgen, who translated. "He said we might want to put on gloves, too."

"Orphan Annie's fanny," Mo said, "next he'll be asking if we have sled dogs."

Jürgen translated. Bruno chuckled, a phlegmy laugh, then said something in response.

"It is a passageway," Jürgen explained, "called der unterirdische Eisweg, a place nobody but the Wächter der Berge knows about."

Bowerman apparently understood. "An underground *ice* way?" Mo detected a note of awe in his voice.

Jürgen nodded. "It is not far, he says."

Mo and Jürgen extracted gloves from the pockets of their flight jackets and tugged them on. Bowerman didn't have any. "It's friggin' May," he grumped, "why would I have mittens. Shit, I'll bare-knuckle it."

The sky had grown overcast, and scudding clouds wrapped the top of the mountain in a fuzzy, gray cloak. A rumble of thunder reverberated off other peaks in the area and rippled through unseen valleys and canyons.

A short hike brought them to the narrow entrance of what looked like a cave. Beside it stood a crudely constructed wooden storage cabinet, camouflaged by fir boughs, about a meter high. Bruno pried open the cabinet, reached in, and pulled out two carbide lamps—acetylene gas lamps. He lit them, kept one, and handed the other to Jürgen along with an extended verbal discourse.

"He says," Jürgen told the others after Bruno had finished, "he will go into the iceway first. The sergeant and captain should follow. I will bring up the rear and keep watch in case any ice giants attempt to sneak up on us."

"Wait, wait, wait," Bowerman exclaimed. "What?"

Jürgen grinned. "It is a legend. For many years, people would not enter here for they feared a race of ice giants lived beneath these mountains."

"So what exactly are we entering?" Mo asked.

"As I understand it, first, a limestone cave that has been carved out over the millennia beneath the mountain. It is coated in ice. Next comes an ice tunnel. Literally, a natural passage through a glacier that clings to the mountain. Mostly beneath it, I gather."

"This just keeps gettin' better 'n better," Bowerman groused.

"Finally, on the other side of the glacier, Bruno's Guardians have dug and blasted out a short tunnel that opens up on the far side of the mountain."

"How about that?" Mo said, a rhetorical question. "Well, what say we go in search of some ice giants."

Bruno pushed his shotgun through the cave entrance, then wriggled through himself. Bowerman followed. Mo and Jürgen handed the assault rifles they carried to the sergeant, then they, too, squirmed through the hole.

On the other side of the entrance, Bruno and Jürgen extended their lanterns out in front of them and illuminated a scene Mo could never have imagined. He could have sworn his heart skipped a beat. Maybe two.

"Oh my god," he said.

"Holy effin' cow!" Bowerman whispered.

They stood inside a massive grotto slathered with layers of ice, azure and aquamarine. A cerulean universe. Giant icicles, like crystal stalactites, hung from the cavern's ceilings. Mounds of rime, like great frozen phalluses, rose from the uneven floor. The turquoise light danced and shimmered in the flickering glow of the carbide lamps.

"This is absolutely unbelievable," Jürgen said, almost in a whisper. "I had no idea something like this existed . . . so close to Germany."

Bruno spoke, apparently explaining something.

Jürgen translated. "He says this was discovered by the Guardians about twenty-five years ago. He has heard there may be other such ice caverns in the Alps, but he is not familiar with them. He and the Guardians have kept this one secret."

"Does he have any idea what goes on in here, what process occurs, to make this so . . . so magnificent?" Mo asked.

Jürgen asked, then responded to Mo. "He thinks a bit of thawing takes place every summer. That allows a tiny ice melt and also a bit of water from above to seep into the cave. In the winter, everything refreezes and an awesome variety of formations is created. It is an ever-changing icescape."

"Mind blowin'," Bowerman said.

"It's beyond spectacular," Mo added.

Bruno motioned for them to follow and he picked his way along narrow but slippery paths through a labyrinth of natural ice sculptures. The light morphed into a deep indigo as they pushed farther and farther into the cave—or, what seemed to Mo, a series of caves. In spots, the passage became almost claustrophobic as the icy walls of the cavern pushed in on them from both sides. In a few places, they had to duck-walk to get beneath the ice-draped roof of the cave. The footing varied between frozen gravel—threaded with icy rivulets—and solid ice.

The cold began to seep through Mo's outer jacket. Involuntary shivers rippled through his body. His exhalations became visible—tiny puffs of steam that formed a cotton-candy string of pearls in his wake.

They moved in silence through the blue universe for perhaps fifteen minutes before reaching a blue-white wall of ice. A dead end appeared.

Bruno pointed down and to the left at a fairly large opening, a hole, in the ice barrier. At the edge of the hole, he sat on his butt and slid into the gap. A solid thunk echoed through the cavern after he disappeared. Mo assumed that meant Bruno had landed safely on his feet in wherever it was he was taking them.

Bowerman and Mo followed suit with Jürgen bringing up the rear. They ended up in another cavern. *Well, cavern of sorts*, Mo thought. This one appeared different from the ice caves they had just journeyed through. Above where they stood appeared a smooth, arcing ceiling of ice. It seemed to Mo as if they were beneath a frozen river. Then he realized they were. He remembered what they had been told, that they'd be passing *underneath* a glacier.

They pushed on, having to stoop as they moved through a shimmering underpass in the ice. The footing remained glassy, but felt rough, the result, perhaps, Mo thought, of the seasonal freeze-thaw cycles Bruno had described—water dripping from the glacier in the summer, then refreezing with the advent of winter. In a few spots they were forced to crawl. That necessitated pushing their rifles, and Bowerman's Tommy gun, in front of them over the frozen surface.

An eerie oppressiveness wrapped itself around Mo as he thought of the frozen river that hung above them—a flow of compressed snow and ice, hundreds of feet thick, sliding inexorably, in ultra-slow-motion, down the flank of an Alpine mountain . . . as it had for centuries.

Does it ever become too weak, too fissure-riddled, too structurally unstable to support its own weight? No, no, don't go there. Mo crimped his eyes shut and continued to put one foot in front of the other as he concentrated on getting through the subterranean—subglacial?—passage.

They reached the end of their transit. Mo opened his eyes, blinked, and drew a deep breath. Fresh air, not icy. The aquamarine glow of the ice had transformed into the subdued gray light of a sunless Alpine afternoon. The sub-glacial passage they had been following opened into a short, cramped passage that obviously had been hacked out and dynamited by men. Bare rock, slippery with dampness and moss, squeezed in on the men from both the left and the right.

At last they stepped back into the open, into light rain. Below them, the topography sloped into a dense forest of fir and spruce dotted with larch. Bruno spoke to Jürgen.

Then Jürgen translated for Mo and Bowerman. "Bruno says he will take us on a trail through the forest that bends around the western flank of the mountain, then down a ravine that spills into the valley where the main road to the Tyrol runs. He thinks we can reach the highway by late afternoon and that we might be able to intercept the man we seek there."

"Except the 'man we seek' won't be surprised again," Mo said. "He knows we're after him now."

"But he might think we have given up and retreated, so maybe he drops his guard," Jürgen offered.

"Mmm, I don't know," Mo said. "I think the reason he took the Fräulein is because he realizes he's been IDed as the commandant of that death camp and that he's going to be pursued into the bowels of hell, if necessary. I doubt he'll let his guard down."

"That Austrian chick is his ace-in-the-hole now," Bowerman said.

"Yeah, and the poor gal doesn't even realize she's a hostage, or potential hostage," Mo said, "she thinks that bastard really loves her."

"I believe she has her doubts now," Jürgen said.

"I would sure as shit hope so," Bowerman said. "But that aside, how in the hell do we grab him and save her? We're outnumbered two to one, and he's got a shield."

"I don't know," Mo said. "We can't repeat the stunt we tried earlier. That didn't work. And the Fräulein has undoubtedly told him there are only three of us. I'm at a loss, guys. We probably didn't think this through very well and ended up painting ourselves into a corner. We got carried away by our emotions."

"It was more 'n that, cap'n," Bowerman growled. "We all saw that camp. The depravity. The stench. The hopelessness."

"You're right. I suppose we got carried away by our sense of morality, but the bottom line is we bit off more than we could chew. Look, let's get going. We've got a couple of hours yet to ponder this and come up with a plan . . . if we can."

With Bruno guiding them, they moved into the darkness of the forest. The rain ceased, but water droplets continued to splash down on them, sliding from the saturated boughs of the evergreens that hung over them like the wings of dark angels.

On the highway to the Tyrol

THEY'D SPENT the night in a vacant schoolhouse, and now Frieda and Karl and the other soldiers trudged along the highway leading deeper into the Alps.

"You frightened me last night," Frieda said to Karl. "You seemed so . . . I don't know . . . different."

Karl smiled. "Yes, I'm afraid I was. You surprised me. The Luftwaffe major surprised me. All the false accusations he brought with him upset me. I apologize, I truly do, for overreacting, for pointing a gun at you. It was an unforgivable act. I would never hurt you. But I was confused and acted stupidly. I hope you will forgive me, my dear."

"I do. I do. But I was so worried about you. When you didn't return—"

"Yes, I know. Everything happened so fast. The Americans arrived so . . . unexpectedly. I was cut off from you. I had no way of reaching you. I, too, was worried . . . about you. My superiors lied to me. They led me astray regarding how rapidly the Allies were advancing. Fed me falsehoods about the reach of their air forces, the speed of their armor, the sheer numbers of divisions that were slicing through Germany. Lies, lies, lies. Unforgivable."

"But we will be okay, Karl, no? We will be able to go to your home when this is over and live in peace? And care for one another? And enjoy life?"

"Of course. But first we must make certain the Allies do not intercept us and attempt to levy charges against me that have no basis in truth, my Häschen. The Jews, you know. After that, all will be well. I promise you."

She searched for comforting reassurance in his answer, in his facial expression, but couldn't find it. His words seemed hollowed of sincerity, as if he were saying only what he was expected to say, and not reaching into his heart.

The shadow of a burgeoning cloud darkened the road they followed and she wondered if the afternoon would bring thunder and rain. Or if it was just her mood that led her to worry over that.

"Do . . . do you think our enemies will try again to stop you?" she stammered.

He fixed her in his gaze. "I was wondering, my dear, how they were able to find me to begin with. Tell me, how many were there with you? Who were they? How were they able to get ahead of me, you know, find their way through the mountains? They must have had a guide, no?"

It seemed to her an accusatory question. Yes, she had helped the Americans in their pursuit of Karl, but she had done so out of her love for him, not to aid in his capture, which is obviously what the Americans had wanted from the start. She had never wished to see him taken prisoner, but only to be with him. *How could I have been so stupid?*

"A guide," Karl snapped at her, "I asked you if the men who pursued me had help finding their way?"

"Yes, yes. They had a guide, an old Austrian who said he belonged to a group called Wächter der Berge. He knew secret ways, hidden trails."

"Ah, I see. And how many men pursued me?"

"Only three, not counting the elderly man from the mountains—the Luftwaffe officer, an American airman, and a sergeant from, I think it is called, the infantry."

"Americans?"

"Yes."

"And you came with them, the Americans?" There seemed a hard, sharp edge to his words.

"I wanted so much to find you."

"Of course."

He signaled for the men with him to halt, and gathered them around him at the side of the road. Rag-tag German soldiers continued to stream past them in small groups, all intent on fleeing the Allies and finding safety in the high mountains.

Karl spoke at length to his men, and Frieda listened. He explained they needed to move faster, that he thought the Americans would try again to interdict them and take them prisoner. He ordered them in a sharp tone to commandeer a motorized vehicle, a truck, anything that could carry them more rapidly into the Alps. The men saluted and dispersed at a trot. He returned to Frieda.

"Since those who pursue me," he said, "have a shepherd, someone knowledgeable about these mountains, I think they will try again to outflank and capture me. They will believe that I think I've outdistanced them, that they stand no chance of catching me or getting ahead of me, and that I will have dropped my guard. Well, my dear, thanks to what you have told me, I have not. In fact, I will turn the tables on them. At the next major crossroads, if we can move rapidly enough, I will prepare an SS welcome for them, one with warmth and fervor." He fixed her in an icy stare, one without fervor and clearly lacking warmth.

She managed only a weak smile.

His men returned twenty minutes later with a battered farm truck, one with an uncovered bed behind the cab, but large enough to accommodate all of them. Karl elected to drive and helped Frieda into the front seat beside him.

He sat with the gearshift lever in neutral, and the engine coughing and sputtering at idle, while the men squirmed into defensive positions in the bed. Freida leaned close to Karl and locked him in her gaze. "You do love me, don't you?" she whispered.

He draped his arm over her shoulders. "Very, very much. Now listen to me, my dear. Stay near to me. Do not stray far. There are dangers we will yet face and I must be able to have you within my reach to protect you. Do you understand?"

She nodded. But she wasn't sure she did. For all his proclamations, Karl seemed oddly distant. Deep within her, she sensed the flicker of a tiny warning light. She couldn't explain it, didn't know from where it came, but knew it was there.

23

In the eastern Alps
Austria
May 6, 1945

Mo, Bowerman, and Jürgen moved steadily through the Alpine forest, laboring to keep pace with Bruno. The clouds had parted in the wake of the rain, allowing slivers of sunshine to knife through the trees and create a quilt-work of subdued shadow and vivid brightness.

The men discussed their options of capturing Jagensdorf and simultaneously freeing Fräulein Mayr, and realized there weren't many. Well, to be honest, Mo finally concluded, there weren't any. The SS bastards had all the advantages, they had none. They'd blown, or at least the Fräulein had blown, their only chance of grabbing the SS officer the previous evening. They'd held the element of surprise before she'd darted from hiding and alerted Jagensdorf.

It seemed to Mo they were on a fool's errand now, and as noble as it might be, he could not envision it ending well.

They pushed on, their conversations trailing off as they ran out of ideas. He allowed his gaze to wander into the deep woods surrounding them, a kaleidoscope of sun and shadow. He glimpsed, or thought he did, fleeting forms appear and reappear, but nothing clearly defined. He asked Jürgen to ask Bruno what they might be, if anything at all.

He heard Bruno chuckle and saw him wave his hand dismissively when Jürgen asked.

Jürgen said, "There are many things in the forest, Bruno says. Mischievous gnomes hiding behind trees, evil witches searching for lost children, or maybe even Krampus, preparing an ambush."

"Krampus?"

"A legendary horned creature—black and hairy with cloven hooves and a long, pointed tongue. Children are terrified of him, especially around Christmastime." Jürgen chuckled. "When I was small, I recall being scared to death of Krampus."

"I would have been, too."

"Or, more likely," Jürgen went on, "according to Bruno, what you are seeing is a bear or a stag. There are many of those. But no Germans, he says, so do not worry. You are safe."

"Maybe we could enlist Krampus to help us go after Jagensdorf."

"I'd second that," Bowerman chimed in. "Maybe ol' Krampus could end this goddamned war in a day or two."

That's when the idea came to Mo. He called out for Bruno to halt. The men gathered next to Mo.

"Sergeant Bowerman reminded me," he said, "the war isn't over yet, is it? I mean technically. Yeah, the Germans have all but given up, are fleeing in droves, and fighting is nonexistent, but there has been no official cease-fire or peace treaty signed, has there?"

"No, sir." Bowerman stared at Mo. "What are you thinkin'?"

"I'm thinking we ambush the bastards. Take out the damn guards before they know what hit 'em, but give Jagensdorf a chance to surrender."

"You think he will?"

"No."

"Then what?"

Mo gave Bowerman a squinty-eyed stare. "We'll figure something out."

"Yes, sir. We will. Tommy and us." He patted the submachine gun he carried.

Mo turned to Jürgen. "I'm sorry, sir. I don't think we have any other options."

The German officer stared at his feet. "I know."

"I'd understand if you don't want to be part of what I'm proposing."

Jürgen, holding his gaze on his boots, shook his head. "I cannot. I witnessed the same thing you saw in Gunskirchen, and it was beyond appalling. But I cannot take up arms against my fellow Wehrmacht in a military operation, an ambush."

"They aren't exactly your fellow Wehrmacht, they're SS," Mo responded. "They're murderers. But I get it. They are your fellow country-men. You are German. They are German. But unlike you, they have no honor. Still, I respect your decision, sir."

"Thank you, my friend," Jurgen whispered. "But I will still support you however I can. I will carry the rifles. I will make sure they are prepared to fire with full magazines. And if you allow me your pistol, I will defend you and the sergeant to the death . . . if necessary."

Mo patted him on the shoulder. "I know you will. But let's hope it doesn't come to that. When all this is over, and the world has drawn a deep breath and regained its senses, I want to catch a rainbow trout in a rushing stream in the Black Forest with a good guy who was my former enemy."

Jürgen looked up and smiled. "I know where the rainbows hide."

Mo nodded.

Jürgen held him in his gaze. "There is one thing perhaps you forget."

"Yes?"

"The Fräulein. Jagensdorf will try to use her as a hostage."

"Hopefully, in the confusion and surprise of an ambush, he won't have a chance."

"But if he does, I will try to distract him and save her."

Mo returned Jürgen's steady stare. "Which is why you are different from your SS countrymen. Which is why I think of you as a friend."

Bruno, who had been waiting quietly while the men talked, asked Jürgen a question. Jürgen said, "He wants to know what we are discussing. Should I tell him?"

Mo thought about it. Overhead, a crow cawed, and a gust of wind whisked a flurry of rainwater from the branches of a fir. "Sure," Mo said after pondering the question. "Why not? He knows what we're after and why. Might as well let him in on the details."

Jürgen spoke to Bruno at length. A smile spread over the old man's face as he listened, then he seemed to put forth an earnest proposal to Jürgen.

When Bruno had finished, Jürgen told Mo and Bowerman what he had said. "He wants to help. He understands we are outnumbered and fears for our lives. He says he can gather as many as ten or twelve men of the Wächter der Berge and support our ambush. It would also offer them a chance to even the score with the Nazis after they left his family and friends to almost starve last winter. And after they raped one of their young women."

Mo held up his hand to signal Jürgen to stop. "No. Tell Bruno I respect him very much. But I can't drag a bunch of . . . . I don't know . . . militia men in leather pants carrying blunderbusses into battle against the Wehrmacht. I'm willing to put my life on the line to get that SS goon, but I won't put the lives of a bunch of civilians at risk. Besides, there's not enough time left for him to muster his army. Please relay that to him in respectful words. We are extremely grateful for what he has done for us, but there's no point in him or any of his Guardian friends losing their lives in the final hours of this damned war."

Jürgen explained things to Bruno, who looked unhappy but seemed to understand. He stepped off down the trail again with Mo, Bowerman, and Jürgen following. The footpath wound into lower elevations as the afternoon wore on. The dense stands of evergreens gradually transitioned into a mixed deciduous forest dotted with pasturelands.

At last they reached a worn dirt road. Bruno halted the group, pointed to the right, and said something to Jürgen, who in turn spoke to Mo and Bowerman.

"He says this road will intersect with the main highway to the Tyrol in about three or four kilometers. It is the last usable crossroads before the highway begins to climb steeply into the Alps. He recalls there are several wooded areas near the intersection where a good ambush could be set up. He wishes us well and Godspeed."

Mo stepped forward to shake hands with Bruno who instead grasped him in a hardy bear hug and whispered in heavily accented English, "Good hunting, GI."

"Danke schöne," Mo whispered back in the only German he knew.

Bruno released Mo and looked him in the eye with a gaze that reflected both admiration and sadness. He then moved to Bowerman and Jürgen, gave each a quick hug, and disappeared into the woods without a further word.

A strange silence hung in the air following his departure. "It's almost as if he was never here," Mo said.

"Maybe he wasn't," Bowerman offered. "Maybe the Wächter der Berge is just a myth, a legend, after all."

"No," Jürgen said, "it is real. Bruno is real. There was something in his voice, his expressions, his eyes, that rang with authenticity. He is genuinely worried about us. We must be careful. Extra so."

Mo pondered the warning. "I suppose. So I guess we'd better get our asses in gear and get into position before Jagensdorf and his gangsters arrive." He reached into his shoulder holster, pulled out his Colt .45, and handed it to Jürgen. "Here, you take this and give me two of those German rifles. Keep the other two and make sure they're ready for action . . . for me or the sarge, whoever might need them."

He turned to Bowerman. "How many mags you got for the Thompson?"

"Three. Thirty rounds each. Can blow through those real fast, though."

"Well, let's hope ninety rounds will do it, then." Mo strode off down the road in the direction Bruno had indicted, Bowerman and Jürgen following.

Except for the crunch of their boots on the dirt surface, they moved in relative silence. Two or three motorized farm vehicles rattled past them, but their drivers appeared to take no interest in the trio of soldiers.

They passed several pieces of wooded land that sat adjacent to the road, and Mo again thought he saw forms moving well back in the trees.

"There it is again," he muttered, "something in the woods."

"Easy, cap'n," Bowerman said, "remember what the old coot told us. Probably a bear or a stag."

"A bear or a stag wouldn't follow us all the way down from the timber-line." Mo unslung the assault rifle he carried, flipped off the safety, and brought the weapon to the "patrol carry" position Bowerman had shown him. He hoped he'd remember the brief tutorial Jürgen had given him on using the weapon.

Bowerman unslung the Thompson from his back and moved it into a position where he could fire it quickly.

Jürgen continued to hold Mo's .45, but Mo noted he kept the safety on.

They moved past the stands of trees and paralleled a chunk of freshly tilled farmland. No bear or stag emerged from the woods into the pasture. Still, in the trees that surrounded the field, Mo continued to envision movement, but of what, he couldn't say. He guessed his mind had begun to play tricks on him, that he'd started to imagine Germans lurking behind every tree and every stump. He decided the fact he wasn't an infantry grunt wasn't helping, either.

"You don't think there's any way those Krauts could have gotten here before we did, do you?" he asked Bowerman.

"Not unless they grabbed a couple of Kübelwagens or something. Besides, why would they? I'm guessin' they think we beat feet and won't bother 'em again."

"Unless we spooked them so bad we made them paranoid. Made them realize someone really wants their asses for what went on back there at Gunskirchen. Especially that Jagensdorf asshole."

"Easy, sir. I'm not lettin' my guard down, but—with all due respect—maybe it's not Jagensdorf who's paranoid."

"Yeah, yeah, I get it, sarge."

"Deep breath, cap'n."

Mo drew two or three.

"Hold on, guys." Bowerman held up his hand and signaled for them to stop. "Up ahead, 'bout half a click, maybe more."

The main route to the Tyrol came into view. They could tell by the military traffic that continued to flow along it. It didn't appear to be a continuous stream, but Wehrmacht units straggled by every few minutes as the three men watched and waited.

"Okay, sarge," Mo said, "you're the bossman here cuz you're infantry. I'll defer to your suggestions. Whaddaya recommend?"

Bowerman chuckled. "Ya mean beyond the fact we probably shouldn't be doin' this?"

"Too late. We've crossed the Rubicon."

"Sir?"

"We're past the point of no return."

"Too true. Okay, first thing, we gotta get closer to the main road so we can see where to set up. Let's move slowly, carefully. Cap'n, you move along the right side of the road, I'll take the left. Major Voigt, if ya don't mind, sir, keep an eye on our six."

They moved forward, edging along the dirt road toward where it met the highway. As they neared the intersection, Mo could see woodlands bordering it on the south side, where the main road lifted into the Alps, and open pastures lining it to the north. Fewer and fewer German troops moved along the route.

"Hold up," Bowerman said in a loud whisper after another few minutes. The men halted.

"What?" Mo said, keeping his voice low.

"Something's wrong."

"Whaddaya mean?" Mo looked around, but spotted nothing out of the ordinary. He checked Jürgen behind him, who merely shrugged. They remained about a hundred meters from the crossroads. He shifted his gaze to Bowerman. "What's wrong, sarge?"

"Check out the intersection. Whaddaya see?"

Mo studied it for a long minute. "Nothing. Now."

"My point, cap'n. No more soldiers. Ten minutes ago there was a steady flow. Now, nothin'. I don't think the Wehrmacht suddenly ran outta Krauts headin' for the hills. Do you?"

Mo whipped his assault rifle up into a firing position.

"Hit the ditch," Bowerman hissed, and pointed at a shallow depression bordering the road next to Mo.

Mo dived into it, rolled, and came up ready to shoot. Jürgen flopped down next to him. Bowerman darted off the road on his side into a strip of land overgrown with tall grass and dotted with stumps. Just as he slid down behind an old deadfall, a volley of rifle and submachine fire ruptured the afternoon stillness. Bullets ricocheted off rocks and trees, and whined through the air like angry insects.

Bowerman got off a short burst with his Tommy gun in return. That brought only a moment of silence, then a renewed fusillade of gunfire from the trees near the intersection.

"How many?" Mo yelled.

"Maybe a half dozen," Bowerman hollered back.

"Those SS bastards?"

"Who else? Somehow they knew we wouldn't give up and they got here ahead of us."

"What do we do?"

"Keep your heads down!"

Another barrage of rifle fire ripped from the woods. The shells seemed to be honing in on where Mo and Jürgen huddled. The slugs kicked up tiny geysers of dirt and mud and clods of grass all around them. One nicked Mo in his earlobe.

"Shit."

"You hit?" Bowerman screamed.

"Not Purple Heart–worthy," he shouted back.

Bowerman set his Thompson on top of the deadfall and, without raising his head, squeezed off a blind salvo. Not effective, but at least it let the SS rats know they faced some guys who had a little firepower.

Still, Mo understood they were in deep doo-doo. They had limited ammo, only two men shooting, and were pinned down. If the German bastards decided to rush them, they could probably drop a few of them, but in the end, the bad guys would prevail.

Bowerman called out again. "Maybe we should launch a counterattack."

"Is that what the infantry would do?" Mo responded.

"No. We'd call in artillery or an air strike."

Mo turned toward Jürgen. "In the army air forces, we have a saying, 'Never run out of airspeed, altitude, and ideas all at the same time.' I think we just have."

"So," Jürgen said softly, "I think we need a blessing from Saint Horridus."

"Who?"

"Saint Horridus, the patron saint of hunters and fighter pilots. It was our victory cry in the Luftwaffe."

"I'm an American bomber pilot."

"I guess you are on your own then." Jürgen forced a smile. "But so am I." He stuck Mo's .45 into his belt and picked up one of the German assault rifles, inserted a magazine, and brought the weapon into firing position.

But two more broadsides of gunfire erupted from the trees that hid the Germans and sent both Mo and Jürgen clawing into the dirt to avoid the deadly volley. Dozens of bullets tore overhead. Mo could hear their hissing zings.

The gunfire ceased. Mo stared at Jürgen. "I thought you didn't want to shoot fellow Germans."

"I SAID I did not want to ambush them. This is different. They now make no distinction between me and you."

A German voice called out. "Luftwaffe Major, sind Sie da?"

"It is the SS commander," Jürgen said. "He wants to know if I am with you."

Mo nodded.

"Ich bin hier, ja," Jürgen yelled back.

A lengthy verbal exchange between the two Germans ensued. Neither man showed himself. After it concluded, Jürgen told Mo what it had been about.

"Jagensdorf wants us to surrender. He knows there are only three of us and that we do not have much firepower. He says if we are willing to leave our weapons with him, he will let us walk away."

"And if we don't?"

"He reminds us he has Fräulein Mayr."

"Jesus." Mo pondered their situation, but his thoughts kept recycling into the 'out of airspeed, altitude, and ideas' syndrome. He called to Bowerman and explained what was going on.

"Ya damn well know he ain't gonna let us walk, cap'n," Bowerman yelled back. "We all saw what happened back at that camp. That rat bastard ain't about to leave anyone livin' who knows where he went."

Mo turned to Jürgen, who looked back at him with an infinite sadness in his eyes and said, "The man is a Soziopath. He will not let us live."

"Not even you?"

"Especially not me. Not a fellow German who, in his view, has turned against him, against the Reich."

"Do you really think he would harm Fräulein Mayr if we don't wave a white flag?"

"What do you think? His legacy at Gunskirchen shows there are no limits to his cruelty."

"Even though he and the Fräulein were lovers?"

Jürgen stared at the sky, as though there might be answers hidden in the schooners of clouds that sailed overhead. "I do not know what goes on in the head of a Soziopath," he finally muttered.

"Ask him if he will negotiate with me."

"He knows we have nothing to negotiate with."

"Ah, but I do."

"What?"

"Bull shit. Maybe I can convince him more troops are right behind us."

Jürgen sighed. "He may just shoot you, my friend."

"But it's worth a try. Better than just dropping our weapons, raising our hands, and then being shot down like dogs."

A shout issued from Jagensdorf.

"He wants us to hurry up," Jürgen said.

"I'm sure he does. It's going to be dark soon. Ask him if he'll talk with me, face-to-face. The sergeant can translate."

Jürgen did. The reply came almost instantaneously—Nein.

"Well, that answers that."

The SS officer yelled at the trio of men again.

"He wants us to surrender, now," Jürgen said, "or he'll shoot the Fräulein."

Mo felt as if someone had punched him in the gut. He struggled to breathe, to catch his breath. Whatever decision he made in the next few seconds, someone would die. As an American soldier, he didn't want it to be Bowerman or himself, or even Jürgen, a German pilot with integrity. He had to choose.

"Call his bluff," Mo said to Jürgen.

Jürgen stared at him, his mouth working but with no words coming out.

"Call his bluff," Mo repeated, his voice steady and calm.

"Nein, keine Kapitulation," Jürgen called out.

"Narren," Jagensdorf screamed in return.

"Fools," Jürgen translated for Mo.

Jagensdorf burst from the woods holding a struggling Fräulein Mayr in front of him—a hostage, a shield. His left forearm was jammed against her neck, pulling her back against him with the force of a python. His right hand held a handgun against her temple. She squirmed and cried, her eyes wide with fear and confusion.

Only one thought streamed through Mo's mind—*how in God's name can a human being inflict such trauma, such terror, on another . . . especially one so innocent?* But he already knew the answer. Hauptsturmführer Karl Jagensdorf had devolved into something less than human.

The SS officer advanced toward where Mo, Bowerman, and Jürgen sheltered. The young woman he held firmly in front of him continued to writhe and cry. She dragged her feet and made futile attempts to kick Jagensdorf's shins.

He yelled something again.

"He says lay down our weapons and raise our hands or he shoots Fräulein Mayr," Jürgen said, his voice now quivering.

Mo, his heart beating at a machine-gun staccato rate, watched, not quite believing the depravity of the man who walked in his direction.

"Jetzt!" Jagensdorf screamed, his face crimson with fury.

"Now," Jürgen repeated for Mo.

"Nein, you bastard prick," Mo bellowed in return.

The gunshot startled him.

Fräulein Mayr sagged in Jagensdorf's grip, blood and brain matter draining from the side of her head.

"Oh, dear Jesus," Mo screamed.

Jagensdorf released his hold on the young woman and she crumpled onto the dirt road.

Mo caught a flash of movement to his side. Jürgen had risen. Bellowing something at Jagensdorf, he scrambled onto the road, broke into a sprint— a full-scale charge—at the SS officer. Holding Mo's .45 out in front of him, he squeezed off shot after shot.

Jagensdorf stood his ground, not flinching, he, too, firing round after round at Jürgen.

Both officers, still shooting, went to their knees. Five meters apart. They stopped firing only when their weapons were empty. Jürgen slumped forward. Jagensdorf canted backward, then toppled sideways.

Mo knew what would come next. He and Bowerman would be unable to stop it.

The SS guards who had accompanied Jagensdorf began their advance, moving through the woods, firing continuously.

Life's final irony, Mo thought. *I will not die in aerial combat, but on the ground, in the mud and dirt, in an infantry assault.* He fired the German automatic weapon from the prone position into the woods. He emptied the magazine in a matter of seconds. He grabbed the second rifle and continued to squeeze off short volleys.

Then. He couldn't believe it.

Deep in the trees, to the rear of the SS troops, came a different sound—an eruption of ear-splitting blasts, the thunderous reports of large-gauge shotguns. Many of them. Branches and limbs were sliced from trees as if torn asunder by violent winds. One of the Germans staggered from the forest, minus two of *his* limbs—his arms—and collapsed on the road. All of his compatriots had ceased shooting. Dead, Mo presumed. *What the hell?*

It was over in a matter of seconds. A strange, ghostly silence settled over the battleground, broken only by the incongruous twittering of songbirds. Thick, gray smoke, the residue of dozens of shotgun detonations, drifted over Mo and Bowerman—and the dead—like an airborne death shroud.

What the hell?

Mo held his gaze on the woods. He noticed Bowerman doing the same.

The quietude held. Then a soft rustle. A familiar figure stepped from the woods and raised a hand in greeting. Bruno.

Mo and Bowerman returned the gesture. Behind Bruno, they caught glimpses of other forms fading deeper into the forest, disappearing. The Wächter der Berge.

"I'll be damned," Mo muttered. "I'll be damned."

Bowerman laughed. "Yeah, we almost were."

Mo spun and darted onto the road, toward where Jürgen lay. He reached the Luftwaffe officer and found him still breathing, but just barely. Long gaps separated his inhalations and exhalations. Mo cradled Jürgen's head in his arms. The German stared glassy-eyed at Mo, and Mo wondered if Jürgen recognized him.

He'd been hit by Jagensdorf's bullets in four or five spots. Mo understood there was nothing he could do for the man except comfort him. Say a prayer. Hope. His eyes misted over.

The major mouthed something, but Mo couldn't catch it. He put his ear close to Jürgen's mouth. "What, my friend?" he whispered.

Jürgen smiled, an effort that evolved in ultraslow motion. "Rainbows," he said softly. "The rainbows are waiting for you."

UPPER AUSTRIA

24

Steyr, Austria
May 8, 1945

The war in Europe had ended.

Jim had heard that British Prime Minister Winston Churchill and US President Harry Truman had declared today VE Day—Victory in Europe. Scuttlebutt had it the German Armed Forces High Command Chief-of-Staff, General Alfred Jodl, had signed an unconditional surrender of all German forces yesterday. The formal surrender document would be signed by Field Marshal Wilhelm Keitel in Berlin just before midnight today.

Now, bathed in early morning sunshine, Jim stood in front of the Steyr Parish Church. He gazed out over a stone plaza where dozens of chairs were being arranged in neat rows. He'd been asked by his regimental commander to be the master of ceremonies for a program recognizing the end of hostilities and commemorating the sacrifices made by the 71st Infantry Division.

High-ranking officers from the division and dignitaries from the town of Steyr would be attending. Jim had accepted the request to be the emcee and understood it to be an honor but, at the same time, he found himself more than a little intimidated by it.

. . .

He began reviewing the program given him earlier by the division's Public Relations major, Cameron—"just call me Cam"—Coffman. Jim jotted a few notations by some of the names on the program to help him with the correct pronunciations.

The rattle of a Jeep jouncing across the plaza interrupted him. He looked up. The vehicle, caked in mud, scratched and dented, and sporting a broken headlight—like a black eye earned in a street brawl—groaned to a stop in front of him. The Jeep carried two men—Sergeant Bowerman in the driver's seat and Captain Nesmith in the passenger's seat.

Bowerman clambered out of the vehicle and walked to Jim. "I'm back, Loot." He saluted, but there seemed a lack of crispness to it. Exhaustion had obviously overtaken the sergeant.

Jim returned the greeting. Then a notable absence struck him. "Where's our Luftwaffe friend?"

Bowerman didn't say anything, merely shook his head, then stared at his feet.

"Oh," Jim muttered softly. "And the young lady, did you drop her off at her home?"

Again Bowerman only shook his head.

Jim felt as if a sledgehammer had been driven into his gut. "Maybe you'd better tell me about what happened," he said, struggling to get the words out. *Why now, why at the very end of this damned war did two good people have to lose their lives? Why, why, why?*

"I'd rather the cap'n did that, sir. He kinda took charge of things. I'd like to get cleaned up." He looked around the plaza. "Looks like there's some sort of a big deal gonna take place."

"The war's over. At least in Europe."

"We heard."

"I've been asked to emcee a ceremony here this afternoon," Jim said, though his thoughts remained on the Luftwaffe officer and the young Austrian woman.

"Congrats, sir. Let me see if I can scrounge up a clean uniform. I wanna make sure I get to see this."

"Go for it."

"Oh, and I'm sorry, very sorry, 'bout the Kraut flyer and the Fräulein," Bowerman said, keeping his voice low. He flashed Jim a sad look and departed.

Jim walked to the Jeep where Mo sat. His flight jacket, streaked with blood and dirt, was also crisscrossed with rips and tears. Mo himself looked exhausted, but more than that, defeated.

"What happened to your ear?" Jim asked, noting a crude bandage wrapped around it.

"Germans thought it was too big," Mo answered, without humor.

"You okay?"

Mo sighed. "Better than a lot of others."

"So . . . I gather we lost Major Voigt and the Fräulein?"

Mo nodded. "It could have worked out better for them."

"Want to talk about it?" Jim had hoped to put the killing, the loss, the depravity of war behind him forever, but he was the one who had turned a blind eye, in effect given tacit approval, to the effort to hunt down Hauptsturmführer Karl Jagensdorf.

"No. But I will. You want to take a walk? I need to stretch my legs."

"We can stroll around the plaza."

They moved around the periphery of the square. A small group of troops continued to set up chairs for the afternoon ceremony. At the edges of the plaza, a few locals offered meager supplies of early-season vegetables and fruits for sale.

Jim and Mo walked slowly as Mo, in low and sometimes choked tones, recounted for Jim the events of the previous few days. He concluded by explaining how Bruno had led them back to their Jeep and assured them the Wächter der Berge would take care of the bodies of Major Voigt and the Fräulein and make sure they received proper Christian burials. The corpses of the SS soldiers, Bruno said, would be left for the German Wehrmacht or the vultures to handle, whichever got to them first.

After Mo had finished, Jim said, "That's a remarkable story." He thought about the sacrifice the Luftwaffe officer had made. "I guess I'll never understand what drives a man like Major Voigt to do what he did."

"We can only guess, I suppose," Mo mumbled.

"Yes. And *your* guess, captain, if you have one?" Even though Jim had been in combat and seen men die, and had come close to losing his own life, he struggled to understand what drove individuals to deliberately sacrifice their lives in service to others. He wondered if it was perhaps the in extremis example of why people are placed on this earth—to serve others?

Mo stopped walking and gazed out over the plaza. He didn't say anything for a long time. An army truck lumbered into the square and stopped near the church. A couple of GIs jumped out and began unloading PA equipment—microphones, amplifiers, speakers.

"I think," Mo at last said, "Jürgen, Major Voigt—" He stopped talking and shifted his gaze to Jim, who could see the captain's eyes rimmed in red. "He became my friend, you know. We were going to go fishing in the Black Forest together after . . . after . . . after all this was over." His voice bore a sandpaper raspiness.

Jim placed a hand on the captain's shoulder. "I know, I know, I understand. It's okay."

Mo steadied himself and continued. "I think what Jürgen came to see in Jagensdorf was everything that was wrong with the Nazis, a reflection of what the Party had done to Germany. To his Germany. His home. His way life of life. The goodness he had grown up with. The integrity and decency that he had come to accept as inherent in his friends and family, even in many of those in the Luftwaffe."

"The antithesis of what the Nazis stood for," Jim interjected.

"Yes, the Nazis and their SS and Gestapo. Their concentration camps. Their death cantonments. I would guess he may have come to wonder what he had been fighting for . . . beyond his family. Or maybe when he saw that Nazi butcher blow the brains out of Frieda—that was her name, Frieda—he just snapped. Maybe he saw his twin girls, instead of Frieda, lying there with their gray matter splattered all over an Austrian road. For no reason. Innocents."

"I want away from all this," Jim said, his words soft but harsh. "Away from all this . . . madness."

"It may cling to us forever," Mo said.

"I won't let it. I want to forget it and never speak of it again. The killing, the dying, the brutality. Why, why, why?" He shook his head, as if trying to shake the memories loose.

"You got a gal to go back to?" Mo asked softly.

Jim smiled, glad to be changing the subject. "No. But I want to find one. I want to go home, go back to school, maybe build a business, find the right lady, start a family. You know, normal things, captain. And I want to put what happened here in an iron box, lock it, and bury it so deep it won't be uncovered until Christ's second coming. How about you, what do you want?"

"Right now, lieutenant, a clean uniform, a fresh bandage, and about forty hours of sleep."

THE CEREMONY RECOGNIZING the end of the war in Europe went smoothly. The 71st Infantry Division's commander, Major General Willard Wyman, made some concluding remarks, then turned the procedures back to Jim to dismiss the troops and thank the local leaders for their courtesy. "Outstanding job, Lieutenant Thayer," he whispered to Jim. "I'm impressed."

Jim stepped back to the chrome-plated Lustraphone PA microphone the comms guys had set up and, as he waited for a feedback squeal to subside, surveyed the audience. He spotted Sergeant Bowerman and Captain Nesmith seated together near the back. Both had managed to find fresh uniforms. Captain Nesmith apparently hadn't started his forty-hour sleep cycle yet.

His regimental commander gave Jim a quick smile and an almost imperceptible nod, a sign Jim took to mean "Well done." General Wyman waited patiently for Jim to conclude the ceremony. Cam, the PR major, arms folded in front of him, stood with his back resting against a concrete pillar on one side of the plaza. A few of the local VIPs had already begun rising from their seats.

The audio screech ceased and Jim inched closer to the microphone.

"If you will allow me," he said, "before we wrap things up, I'd like to add a personal note to these proceedings." General Wyman cocked his head and allowed just the hint of a scowl to wash across his face. Cam uncrossed his arms, straightened his posture, and stared at Jim. Neither officer, of course, had the slightest idea of what they were about to hear.

"I'd like to honor one of our enemies," Jim said. "Well . . . former enemies."

A palpable silence settled over the plaza.

"I wish to acknowledge the heroics of a Major Jürgen Voigt, a fighter pilot in the German Luftwaffe. Major Voigt, briefly a POW of the US Army, volunteered to assist in the pursuit of the commandant of Gunskirchen Lager, the death camp where many of us witnessed the end result of Nazi atrocities, atrocities we thought . . . well, unimaginable."

Jim paused, held his gaze straight ahead, and didn't look for a reaction from his superior officers or Mo or Sergeant Bowerman.

"Those of us who stumbled into that netherworld several days ago, and had our senses consumed by the barbarity that had been allowed to fester there, will never forget it—the sights, the sounds, the smells. In truth, if course, we'd like to forget it. But it may be a challenge. How do you bury memories of inhumanity on such a monstrous scale that even God might turn away? I have no answer.

"But Major Jürgen Voigt did. He was there with us when we entered the gates of Hades. He—a German but not a Nazi—stood beside me. I saw his shock, his revulsion, and yes, maybe even a tinge of guilt, at what surrounded us. But let me be clear here, it was not an act, not a manufactured reaction of some sort meant to gloss over a pre-awareness of that abomination. It was genuine abhorrence, something that emanated from his soul.

"Yes, he had an answer for that killing ground we had walked into."

Every face in the plaza now focused on Jim. He drew a deep breath, wished he had some water, but didn't. He pressed on.

"He paid for that answer with his life when he came face-to-face with SS Hauptsturmführer Karl Jagensdorf, the commander of Gunskirchen Lager, two days ago on a mountain road in the Alps. Major Jürgen Voigt, a German officer with a wife and two young daughters, and carrying—with permission—a US Army Colt .45, charged directly at Jagensdorf, who had just shot a young Austrian woman to death. Voigt and Jagensdorf emptied their weapons at each other. Neither survived. Jagensdorf died a beast. Voigt, a hero.

"I will take no more of your time, gentleman. I only wished to acknowledge that there are instances in which our enemies probably carry the same values we do and fight for the same things we do—country, family, fellow soldiers.

"Perhaps—" Jim tilted his head and looked toward the sky "—they are not really our enemies, only our opponents."

Flughofen Wien
Vienna, Austria
November 1992

JIM STARED AT THE MAN, Wolf Finkelman, who had just told him in emotional words, "I wouldn't be standing here today if you hadn't come when you did forty-seven years ago. I was fourteen years old then and I would have been dead within twenty-four hours."

"What do you mean?" Jim said.

Finkelman brushed a tear from his cheek. "Gunskirchen," he said quietly, "Gunskirchen Lager."

"You were there? A prisoner?"

"I remember you. The American lieutenant. I tugged on your sleeve. I hugged you. I said bless you, bless you. You brought food, water, hope. I had lost hope, my friend, all hope. It was all I had left, and even that had fled. I knew I would meet the angels of the Lord that day. I was ready. I had nothing to live for." He smiled at Jim. "Then you came. An angel in a US Army uniform."

"There were so many of you," Jim whispered, "reaching, touching, grasping."

"Yes. So many of us, and dying by the hundreds each day. You know, even after you arrived, even after we were liberated, 'saved,' many continued to die, too malnourished, too sick, too broken to live. Fifteen hundred."

Jim bowed his head, closed his eyes, and the memories came flooding back, engulfing him, sweeping him back forty-seven years to a place he'd never wanted to return to.

"Can you imagine," Finkelman said, "if you hadn't come when you did, how many more of us would have died in that Austrian hellhole? Whatever you did, Jim Thayer, to get there when you did—whether by accident, by blind luck, by divine guidance, or by your own determination and bloodshed—it was worth it. Ten times over and gilded in gold, it was worth it. I live, my family lives, and so many others do because of you. My gratitude is eternal, sir."

EPILOGUE

Jim Thayer's life changed after meeting Wolf Finkelman at the Vienna airport. Years later he would say, "What happened that day completely changed my attitude on killing people."

After meeting Finkelman, Jim was able to accept, if not the necessity of the ambush at the crossroads near Hörbach, at least the yin and yang of death and life it represented. He understood it wasn't his place to understand the metaphysical balance of it, but only to acknowledge that it did exist. That by taking the lives of some, he had saved the lives of many.

Another surprising connection to Jim and Gunskirchen Lager came to light over a decade after the Vienna airport event. In 2002, one of Jim's sons, Tommy, became the lead guitarist for the immensely popular hard rock band Kiss, led by the brash Gene Simmons. Kiss, if you are not familiar with the group, is easily identified by its musicians' theatrical "out there" face paint and flamboyant costumes, each representing different characters or personas.

Simmons, the cofounder of Kiss, was born in 1949 in Israel to Flora Klein, a survivor of the Nazi death camps. Flora had watched her mother and grandmother walk together into a concentration camp gas chamber. She survived the camps because the wife of a German officer took a liking to her, at least her skills as a hairdresser, and provided her with scraps of food. She was sixteen or seventeen years old at the time.

After poring over records at Yad Vashem in Jerusalem, Simmons learned that Flora, his mother, was in the Mauthausen concentration camp only twenty or so miles from Gunskirchen Lager at the end of the war. It's possible that without the Americans stumbling into the Mauthausen complex, which included Gunskirchen, when they did, there would be no Gene Simmons, and no iconic rock group known as Kiss.

AFTER SERVING with occupation forces in Europe, Jim returned to the United States in 1946 and completed his studies at the University of Oregon, earning a bachelor's degree in, not journalism, but economics in 1947.

In 1954, he married Patricia Cunningham, a fashion illustrator who worked for the Bon Marche department store in Seattle. The best man at their wedding was Thomas Autzen, a philanthropist and fellow UO alumnus. If you are a football fan, you may recognize the name. Autzen Stadium in Eugene is the home of the University of Oregon Ducks.

Less than a year and a half later, Jim opened an office supply store, J. Thayer Company, in Beaverton, Oregon. The business has undergone several metamorphoses over the years, but survives today in the hands of another one of Jim's sons, John, who is also a talented singer/songwriter.

Jim and Pat had two other sons, Jim Jr. and Mike, and a daughter, Anne. Jim Jr. is a real estate broker in Portland. Mike is co-owner of Pete's Mountain Vineyard and Winery in West Linn, Oregon. Anne, sadly, passed away in 2007. She was an accomplished equestrian as well as an actress and model.

At the same time he and Pat were raising a family and running a business, Jim remained active in the army reserve. He retired as a colonel in 1982. Then, from 1989 to 1994, he served as Oregon's civilian aid to the secretary of the army. He was reactivated into military service in 2000, promoted to brigadier general, and named commander of the Oregon State Defense Force (now the Oregon Civil Defense Force).

Jim earned numerous military awards and honors over the course of his career. His wartime medals include the Silver Star and Bronze Star. Later, from the Austrian government, he was presented the Grand Decoration of Honour for Services to the Republic of Austria.

Not only did Jim remain fully engaged with the military, but his civilian service proved even more extensive. As a highly influential civic leader, he served over two dozen organizations in various capacities. He sat on boards of directors and acted as a chairman, director, or president of various groups and operations.

The University of Oregon Alumni Association awarded Jim its Distinguished Alumni Award in 2005. Previous recipients included such well-known figures as Phil Knight and legendary track coach Bill Bowerman, cofounders of Nike; author and counterculture figure Ken Kesey (*One Flew Over the Cuckoo's Nest*); independent and tenacious Oregon Congresswoman (1955-1974) Edith Green; and Nobel Prize winner Walter Brattain, co-inventor of the transistor.

Jim, ever self-effacing, commented on the award the alumni association presented him, "I never had any ambition to be Mr. Big, even though I fell into things that made me look like I was Mr. Big. Not this kid—I was never that bright."

In truth, he was an exceptional man. As a lasting tribute to him, a wing in the Oregon Military Museum at Camp Withycombe in Clackamas, Oregon, is named in his honor. A life-sized bronze bust of Jim, who helped drive the funding for the facility, stands at the entrance to the museum.

At one point, late in his life, Jim noted, "At the top of my list of priorities is my church and God. Second is my family. Third is the success of my family, which has been tremendously successful. And fourth is the military." He went on to explain that while the military wasn't at the top of his list, the greatest recognition he'd received over the years was because "I was in the right place at the right time."

Gunskirchen Lager. 1945.

Brigadier General James Burdett Thayer, a true American hero, passed away at his home in Lake Oswego, Oregon, in 2018 at the age of ninety-six.

WHERE THE DAWN COMES UP LIKE THUNDER
Book 5 of When Heroes Flew

Amidst the turmoil of World War II, a daring Army Air Forces aviator is swept into an odyssey that will carry him to the far corners of the earth. Military duty and personal quest converge in this remarkable tale of grit and perseverance.

Despite suffering grave injuries in the savage terrain of Burma, Major Rod Shepherd is returned to active duty to support war efforts against Japan. But his mission extends beyond official orders: Rod is determined to locate missing Army nurse, Eve Johannsen, even as top Army brass deny her very existence.

Rod's primary mission sees him braving treacherous regions and grappling with the horrors of the Japanese regime—all while he conducts his clandestine search for answers. In the end, Rod must risk challenging the highest levels of command if he has any hope of learning the truth...and finding Eve.

In *Where the Dawn Comes Up like Thunder*, the latest installment of the When Heroes Flew series, former Air Force officer H.W. "Buzz" Bernard immerses readers in the heart-pounding aerial exploits of WWII.

Get your copy today at
severnriverbooks.com/series/when-heroes-flew

AUTHOR'S NOTE

Allow me to say up front I realize this novel was a little less about flying than my previous WWII books have been. But *Down a Dark Road* is a unique tale about a special man, and I really wanted to tell it. I did manage to squeeze in a bit about heroes flying, so I hope my avid readers of the When Heroes Flew series found that palatable . . . and a good read.

It's only natural to wonder how much of *Down a Dark Road* is fact and how much is fiction. A large portion of the book is indeed based on fact, including the scene where Jim deals with the inebriated company commander playing a piano in Richard Wagner's bombed-out house in Bayreuth, Germany.

In Austria, most of the scenes involving Jim really did occur. Jim's platoon ambushed and killed thirty-one German soldiers without itself taking any casualties. Later that same day, Jim actually did engineer the surrender of eight hundred SS troops in the town of Hörbach.

I took some liberties with the description of that event, particularly the interaction between Jim and the SS major in charge of the surrendering troops. The German officer really did have a hand grenade attached to a lanyard looped around his neck and intended to blow up both himself and Jim. But the resolution of the event wasn't nearly so dramatic as portrayed in the novel. Jim's platoon sergeant, when he realized the SS officer had the weapon, cut the cord around the Nazi's neck, grabbed the grenade, and tossed it away. It detonated, but hurt no one.

I also took liberties with the timeline (which got confusing, at least to me) of some of the events in order to make them dovetail with the well-documented date and time of the discovery of Gunskirchen Lager.

While Jim never discussed in detail what he witnessed at that death camp, there were other sobering firsthand accounts I was able to draw upon, mainly from a pamphlet published by the 71st Infantry Division shortly after the camp was liberated. The pamphlet, titled "The Seventy-First Came . . . to Gunskirchen Lager," contained not only eyewitness descriptions of the appalling conditions in the camp, but graphic photographs and drawings as well.

In the latter half of the novel there are several places where I took a little more poetic license regarding Jim. He and his patrol never came across a little sawmill in the forest and never encountered Russian soldiers probing deep into Austria in advance of the main Red Army.

While there was an event in the town square of Wels, Austria, in which liberated Gunskirchen prisoners faced, in silence, German POWs gathered across from them, Jim was not there. Jim did indeed emcee a ceremony held in Steyr, Austria, acknowledging the end of hostilities in Europe, but he did not give the ad-lib speech I allowed him to give regarding the heroics of Luftwaffe Major Jürgen Voigt, because Voigt was a fictional character.

So was Captain Mo Nesmith. But the story told to Mo by Jürgen about the employment of German jets by the Luftwaffe, and the exploits of Generalmajor Adolf Galland and Jagdverband 44, are based on fact.

Jim's platoon sergeant, Henry Bowerman, is fictional. Jim did have a platoon sergeant who spoke a little German, but I didn't have enough background information on him to flesh him out as a character in the book.

Wolf Finkelman was real, as is the interaction between him and Jim at the Vienna airport. Finkelman passed away in Houston, Texas, in 2010.

Frieda Mayr and Hauptsturmführer Karl Jagensdorf, the Gunskirchen camp commandant, are fictional. But the appalling treatment of prisoners I attributed to Jagensdorf at the Mauthausen complex is not.

(Ironically, the real commander at Gunskirchen Lager was named Karl, Karl Schulz. After the war, the Federal Republic of Germany conducted numerous proceedings against persons, including Schulz, accused of Nazi crimes at Mauthausen and its sub-camps.)

The pursuit of Hauptsturmführer Jagensdorf into the Alps by Mo, Jürgen, and Bowerman is pure fiction, of course, as is the existence of the Wächter der Berge, or Guardians of the Mountains. But not the ice caves. They are real.

The story of Jim Thayer was first brought to my attention by my wife, Barbara, who worked for Jim in his office supply store when she was a young teenager in high school. She also occasionally babysat his children. She lost touch with Jim for a number years, but then reconnected with him in his later years. It was then she realized what a remarkable life he had led and began keeping a scrapbook on him that she stuffed with newspaper and magazine articles.

Although Jim had passed away by the time Barbara and I married, she mentioned on numerous occasions she thought his WWII adventures would form the basis of a wonderful novel.

I became interested in that idea and got in touch with one of Jim's sons, John, who seemed excited about the prospects, too. He related to me some great anecdotes about his dad's exploits during the war, and provided me with a superb hour-long video, "Jim Thayer—An Oregon Soldier." The video was made in 2007 as John and Jim retraced Jim's WWII odyssey through western Europe. Jim provided first-person narratives of his wartime adventures, while John shot, edited, and produced a professional-quality video.

As usual, the internet provided a fertile field of informational sources, but I still used books to harvest details, especially when it came to gathering data on airplanes and flying. Included in my storage silo: *The Wild Blue* by Stephen E. Ambrose, *A Higher Call* by Adam Makos with Larry Alexander, *B-24 Combat Missions* by Martin W. Bowman, *Attlebridge Arsenal* by Earl Wasson and Chris Brassfield, *American Warplanes of World War* II edited by David Donald, *Warplanes of the Luftwaffe* edited by David Donald, *The World's Great Small Arms* by Craig Philip, *History of World War II* edited by Chris Bishop and Chris McNab, *Band of Brothers* by Stephen E. Ambrose, and *The Family of Brigadier General James Burdett Thayer* by Patricia Thayer Munro.

Of course, I always have to call upon others a lot smarter than I am to help me crank out something worth reading. My profound thanks to a couple of retired military gentlemen—both of whom are fine novelists in their own right—who helped me avoid stepping on my poncho when writing about infantry tactics and aviation procedures. Lee Jackson set me straight on infantry procedures, and Tom Young kept me from crashing and burning when writing about flying. Any errors you spot on either subject are mine, not theirs. And, as in the original novel in this WWII series, *When Heroes Flew*, I called upon my own experience flying in a B-24—*Witchcraft*, owned and flown by the Collings Foundation—to describe what it is like to ride in that great old bomber.

My beta readers are the best. Thanks to my long-time friend, Gary Schwartz, who's been with me from the very beginning; to my wife, Barbara, who gets the earliest peek at everything I crank out; to my brother, Rick, who keeps me pointed in the right direction; and to my newest member of the beta-stable, Galen Peterson, a novelist-to-be and a true war hero. John and Tommy Thayer reviewed the manuscript as well, and helped me better capture Jim's character.

Also, a high-five to the great crew at Severn River Publishing. That includes Andrew Watts, Founder; Amber Hudock, Publishing Director; Julia Hastings, Associate Publisher; Mo Metlen, Social Media Manager; and Chloe Moffett, editor and proofreader.

Finally, a heartfelt thank you to all my readers. Without you, a book is meaningless.

ABOUT THE AUTHOR

H. W. "Buzz" Bernard is a bestselling, award-winning novelist. A retired Air Force Colonel and Legion of Merit recipient, he also served as a senior meteorologist at The Weather Channel for thirteen years. He is a past president of the Southeastern Writers Association and member of International Thriller Writers, the Atlanta Writers Club, Military Writers Society of America, Willamette Writers, and Pacific Northwest Writers Association. Buzz and his wife live in Kennewick, Washington, along with their fuzzy, strangely docile Shih-Tzu, Stormy... probably misnamed.

Sign up for H.W. "Buzz" Bernard's reader list at
severnriverbooks.com/authors/hw-buzz-bernard

Printed in the United States
by Baker & Taylor Publisher Services